Celia Parker Woolley

Roger Hunt

Celia Parker Woolley

Roger Hunt

ISBN/EAN: 9783337000950

Printed in Europe, USA, Canada, Australia, Japan

Cover: Foto ©Andreas Hilbeck / pixelio.de

More available books at **www.hansebooks.com**

ROGER HUNT

BY

CELIA PARKER WOOLLEY

AUTHOR OF "RACHEL ARMSTRONG; OR, LOVE AND THEOLOGY,"
"A GIRL GRADUATE," ETC.

But God said,
I will have a purer gift;
There is smoke in the flame.
EMERSON

BOSTON AND NEW YORK
HOUGHTON, MIFFLIN AND COMPANY
The Riverside Press, Cambridge
1892

The Riverside Press, Cambridge, Mass., U. S. A.
Electrotyped and Printed by H. O. Houghton & Co.

To
J. H. W.

ROGER HUNT.

I.

It was at the close of a dull November day, with low-hanging skies and naked tree-branches stretched mournfully up to meet them. There was a touch of winter chill in the air. A few thin streaks of red in the west failed either to cheer or warm the scene, though bringing into stronger relief two figures, a man's and a woman's, walking down the long empty vista of M Street in the university town of Xenophon.

The man kept close to his companion's side, and talked in a low, hurried strain; while she, with downcast eyes and a strangely troubled face, listened. She was nearly as tall as he, with slender figure that had a look of fragility, heightened by the way in which she wore her shawl, wrapped closely about her and held in place with tightly-clasped hands. Her face had a refined and rather noble expression, but wore just now a pinched look of care, while the large melancholy eyes bespoke depths of feeling and mental unrest below. The manner and attitude of the two showed that intent preoccupation in themselves seen in avowed lovers.

They halted before one of the frame houses standing back from the street, but lingered at the gate. The man talked on eagerly, almost angrily, never turning his strong, clear gaze from his companion, whose face still wore a look of struggling doubt and longing.

"Oh, I dare not," she exclaimed, as he paused at last for her to speak, and with a long shuddering sigh. A dark look of disappointment swept over his face, and he compressed his lips.

"Do not be angry with me," she pleaded, laying her hand on his arm. He covered it with his own, and turned his eyes upon her with a look of tender, but sad upbraiding, before which her own wavered and fell.

"I can say no more," he said mournfully, but with a touch of impatience. "After all, it is not a thing any word of mine should decide. Only your feeling can do that."

"If it were only that!" The words were rather breathed than spoken. A flash of triumph lighted his face. "Very well, then." He clasped her hand closer. Its touch was warm and tender, but masterful. All her being thrilled to it, at the same time that her heart was clutched with a deadly chill. She could not take her eyes from his, which looked both absolute devotion to and an imploring fear of him; but if the latter touched him, it was not with pity for her.

"You talk of ' right,' " he began again, and speaking with the enforced patience we use with a child who has heard our reasons for exacting his obedience many times. "You and I believe that right is determined by inward feeling and conviction, do we not?"

She looked at him with the same eyes of worshipful pleading, while the subtle use of the words, "You and I," made her flush and tremble.

"Then we accept the responsibility of an action when we have admitted the wish to perform it. You admit the wish to serve me?" She did not answer in words, only looked at him. He knew she would die for him.

"And you know my need of you." His voice dropped here, and he released her hand. A more delicate man would have refrained from an argument like the last; but Roger Hunt, though possessing an unusually refined and sensitive nature, reaching to fastidiousness in matters of personal taste and habit, often showed a failing insight in other matters that bordered on dullness.

Roger Hunt belonged to that fanatical order of mind which is never so sure it is right as when it is standing alone. He had all a martyr's courage with nothing of the martyr's meekness; would have submitted to burn at the stake for opinion's sake, but would have made the fire-tender some trouble. The feeling of others toward him generally went to one or the other extreme of strong affection and sympathy, or downright dislike and suspicion. He was not a popular man, though capable of exciting the warm, even partisan attachment of a few. His friends praised his purity of purpose, his courage and devotion to principle, while his critics pronounced him arbitrary, unfeeling, and petty. He was better liked by the opposite sex than by his own, his virtues being such as men respected without trying to emulate, his faults of a kind only women would submit to. The woman before him recognized his faults, but blamed him for them scarcely more than she did for his defective eyesight. He suffered from what is known in technical phrase as hypermetropia, which he sometimes wore spectacles to correct. He could see a distant church steeple very well, but was continually stumbling over the nearest obstacle in his path.

Though he would have stoutly denied it himself, feeling, overlaid with a mass of argument, such as he was now employing with the woman at his side, ruled all his conduct. He was a man of keen and brilliant intellect, which he used as remorselessly at times as a physical giant does his superior muscular strength. He had a gift at dialectical discourse, which his equals often hesitated to encounter, but which rendered the one he was now addressing as helpless as a child. Roger Hunt loved Eleanor Thaxter with the intensity of a strong and impetuous nature bent on the fulfillment of its own desires, — loved her the more because of her known love for himself; for he was not the man to suffer from an unrequited attachment. The love that seeks only to give was typified in the woman who stood listening to him, there in the autumn twilight, her soul in her eyes, longing to believe wholly and only in him.

"What is it we lose?" he asked at length, with another touch of impatience. "What is it anybody loses?"

"Oh, if I could be sure of that!" she replied in trembling tones. "If there were only ourselves to think about!"

"Come now," he said, putting a restraint upon himself. "Who else is there to think about? On one side a churl of a brother," glancing towards the house she was about to enter, "who grudges the bread his sister eats." She made a deprecatory motion of the hand, but he would not heed her. "On the other, a woman at the inebriate hospital who bears my name, and, in the place I call home," with bitter emphasis, "her ill-tempered sister, who has brought up my boy to fear and distrust his father."

She trembled and turned pale at this pitiless revelation of affairs she so well understood before.

"Dearest," he went on in altered tone, bending near until his face almost touched hers, "if I meant to wrong or injure any one of them, if I did not mean to make ample provision for each and all, if I did not know my presence was as hateful to them as theirs to me — What is it any one will lose?" he repeated impetuously.

"Oh, I know, I know," she murmured. "You

are wiser than I. You have thought deeply on all these subjects; I try to understand, but "— a long tremulous sigh escaped her. "And — and how can you say no one will lose?" she began again, speaking with difficulty. "There is the child. Surely he will lose "— She ended in painful embarrassment, which her companion did not seem to share in the least, though he kept silent for a space, bending accusing eyes on her.

"No, it is you who are wise," he said in a mournful tone, ",very wise, very safe, and careful." Her thin cheek flushed.

"It is too much," he exclaimed, "too much to expect of any woman. I had begun to think there was one who understood the essential values of things, who could distinguish between the merely conventional and that which is everlastingly right and true, who had some power of just discrimination." He paused abruptly. She flushed again, and deeper, but this time with less pain at the overt reproach in his words than pride in their implied praise. No woman willingly submits to see herself lowered in the eyes of the man she cares for, either as friend or lover, even when her own judgment sustains her.

Eleanor Thaxter's acquaintance with Roger Hunt had been the supreme event in a dry and colorless existence. The knowledge that he loved her, was dependent on her for happiness, had not only brought an intoxicating delight, but had aroused the holier passion of self-sacrifice, which in such

women is part of love. Roger's words rebuked,
but also uplifted her; and though an unconvinced
judgment still lay like a stone in her breast, her
heart leaped forward in the wish to be all that he
required. She stood flushing and trembling before him.

"I shall not try to answer your question about
the child," he said, coming bluntly back to this
point. "If you think there's such a lot of precious fatherhood going to waste in me, you had better visit me in my home some time. Send me back
there if you like, if that suits your woman's notion
of things better; but I tell you, you little know the
living hell the place is to me, nor how I am growing the fitter devil to live in it every day."

This outburst frightened her a little, and she
tried to quiet him.

"A man may correct any other mistake," he
went on passionately, "may repair his unformed
judgment on every other point but this one, in
which his honor and happiness are most concerned.
A mere boy is fooled by a pretty face, and you
tell him all his hopes of happiness are to be measured by that fact. You tell me to bear things I
think it wicked cowardice to bear. I suffer the
pangs of the damned, and grovel in shame every
day anew, and you tell me I have brought it on
myself." She tried to stop him, but could not.
"Then I put my heart, torn and bleeding, into
your hands, which might make it well and whole
again; yet you can stand and hesitate, because of

a lot of human donkeys, who will forget our existence in three days. Why should we care what people will say? What is the world and its opinion to us? Less than the sound of thunder in a distant planet."

"Roger, Roger, I cannot bear it!" Her voice broke through his whirling talk like a distressed cry. "It is not of myself I think. Why should I care for myself? It is of you. Can I help you do yourself a wrong? Was my love meant for that? I would give my life to make you happy!"

"Give me yourself!" The words were at once imperious and tender. His passionate force was gaining ground. The little strength she had summoned to resist him was spending itself fast. Her face was raised to his in piteous appeal. His deep glowing eyes burned through the growing dusk. She had felt at times those eyes had power to draw her soul from her body. He bent nearer to her. "I have said they would lose nothing," he began again in a low voice. "That is true; but we — what is it we shall not gain? Think what it will be to me, you strong, sweet woman who love me so! A free life, time and the will to work; — with you, my best helper, the only being in the world who understands me, you always at my side. Misery and shame were driving me mad when I met you; I was turning into a fiend. You came, and had only looked at me once, with those dear, pitying eyes, when I knew all hope was not over, even for me. You were my good angel, sent to redeem and restore me! My heart spoke the words at once. You knew it! There was but one feel-ing between us. We understood each other as well at that moment as we do now. Do you think such things mean nothing?"

His wild impassioned words melted and fright-ened her at once. Her fears and agitation in-creased every moment, and she broke into tears, trembling and clinging to him.

"You speak of other people's rights," he went on! "Has love like ours no rights? Do you dare admit your love for me, and then leave me, tenfold more desolate and despairing than before? We love each other. Oh, my darling, think of nothing but this, of this great blessed love that has come to us! Put every other thought away! Let us leave lies and misery and the preaching of fools behind us."

She could not look into his face, it was so near, and shut her eyes in an excess of trembling fear and happiness, that might have overpowered her had he not caught and held her in his arms, safe in the descending dark. She felt his kisses on her cheek and lips, heard his passionate words of devotion, caught a whisper of advice and caution, and felt herself released. He was gone. The sound of his footsteps grew fainter in the distance, but carried a ring of victory. Dizzily, like one in a dream, she ascended the path to the house. She had given no word of promise, but she knew what she was going to do. Mind and sense were held

in the grasp of a will she had no further strength
to resist.   She could only pray, in mercy for herself, that this feeling of dumb unaccountability
might last until the irrevocable step had been
taken.

II.

Roger Hunt's home was a long distance from M Street in a fashionable quarter of the city. It was a large and handsome residence, but for the past two years had worn the forbidding look a house has when closed to visitors, and only partially used.

He was late. Admitting himself with a night-key, he stepped into the dimly-lighted hall, venting an exclamation of impatience over the darkness, and turned the gas jet, held by a bronze naiad perched in airy attire on the newel post, to full head ; then passed on into the dining-room, where his sister-in-law and boy sat at table.

The two looked at him without a word as he took his place, and until the servant in waiting had placed the soup before him and retired, when his sister-in-law spoke : —

"We waited an hour," she said, regarding him gloomily from behind the tea-urn. "Children ought not to eat so late."

"I have told you never to wait for me," was the reply. Another silence, broken only by an occasional word between the boy and his aunt, followed and lasted throughout the meal, Roger taking the evening paper from his pocket and reading from it between courses.　When he had finished, the three arose, and his sister-in-law spoke again.

"Are you going out this evening?" she asked, in the same constrained manner as before.

"I am not."

"Then I should like to attend the evening meeting.　Children ought not to be left with servants." Miss Watson never missed a chance of formulating her principles.

"You can go," said Roger, cutting her short; and turning away he passed from the room into the library on the other side of the hall.

The boy followed his aunt upstairs, watching her with a listless air as she put on her bonnet and cloak, heavily trimmed with crape for a father who had been dead seven years.　He accompanied her down again, to the outer door, where he received her parting instructions about bed-time.　When the door closed behind her, he went back into the dining-room, the only lighted room in the house, except the library.

His aunt had not kissed him good-night, but he had learned long since to dispense with attentions of this kind.　He knew she loved him, and though she was very strict with him, in his strange, unchild-like fashion, he loved her.　Towards his father the boy's feeling was one of mingled curiosity and indifference.　He knew him as a man of abstracted looks and ways, and of independent habits that often set the entire household awry; who seemed to remember his child's existence only at intervals, at which times he gave him a good deal of pocket-money, and even sometimes tried to romp and play with him; but he did this in an awkward way that made the boy uncomfortable, so that he liked better to be forgotten and unnoticed.

Roger Hunt was not wholly to blame that he had so little power to win his child's confidence. There was as little mental as physical likeness between them, the boy bearing a marked resemblance to his mother's family, so that it always pained and often displeased his father merely to look at him. Roger had not the nature which enters readily into the needs of others. He cared little for children, any way, though he would have been both shocked and offended at the thought that such a feeling could extend to his own son. The circumstances of his marriage have already been partly described in the words he let fall to Eleanor Thaxter.

While still in college he had fallen under the spell of one of those youthful infatuations which pass for love. Annie Watson was the youngest child of a stern Puritanic household, but who inherited none of the pious and orderly instincts of the family. Her unruly disposition began to assert itself from the first, and she was regarded as a moral alien almost from babyhood. At the boarding-school in Xenophon, where Roger first met her, she was a participant in every piece of mischief going on, holding in open ridicule the stiff, old-fashioned discipline on which the school prided itself. To Roger's callow fancy, himself no easy subject of rule, this lawlessness, covered with girlish charm and grace, looked like moral independence; and nothing could have persuaded him then that he had not found his true spiritual mate. They were married against the advice of all of his friends and the direct command of her father. A month had scarcely passed when Roger discovered his terrible mistake. Life, that looked so fair and promising, lay like a shattered vase at his feet. He found himself bound for life to a vain and conscienceless creature who had married him partly through a spirit of mischievous defiance, partly through flattered self-love at being sought by one so manifestly her superior, but chiefly for the reputed fortune he was to inherit from a bachelor uncle. This fortune came into their possession two years after their marriage, and was the means of completing Roger's domestic ruin. Had he followed his own wish, he would have continued to live in the same quiet fashion as before; but his wife would submit to no such tame disposition of affairs, and to please her he fitted out a fashionable establishment on one of the avenues. The young wife plunged into social life, the husband shut himself in his library, a moody and bitterly-disappointed man.

Annie Hunt, however, had neither the talent nor force of character to become a leader in the gay world whose honors she coveted. Craving always some fresh excitement, intent only on the moment's gratification, her easy nature yielded readily to temptation, and soon she was floating rapidly down the current of social folly and excess. One form of this dissipation began to excite the whispered comment of their friends long before it became known to Roger, immersed in his books, and living only in formal union with his wife. When he discovered it, his horror and shame knew no bounds. He pleaded, he threatened, he stormed. There were tears and promised amendment on the frightened wife's side, followed by weak attempts at reform; but month by month the disgusting evil grew, until it became an open scandal, and he was forced to send her away from home. A hypothetical cure was effected, which on a return to the old scenes soon ended in a relapse, followed by another banishment; while Roger Hunt, as he had said to Eleanor, groveled in shame and could hardly look his fellow-creatures in the face. Since then, poor, wrecked Annie Hunt, a creature all instinct and weak desire, had spent her time alternately in the Asylum and at her home, having now been an inmate of the Asylum eight months, with her name on the list of incurables. It was a subject of wondering comment among his friends that Roger had sought no legal redress for his sufferings, some censuring his conduct in this respect, others praising it; but to a nature like his, open defiance expresses the highest courage. Since it was law that held him in bondage, he would not condescend to appeal to it for aid; he would rather resist and defeat it. He asked nothing at the hands of that glittering abstraction, called Society, which had so injured him, as he conceived; he repudiated it instead.

Some degree of self-extinction is involved in all forms of compromise, and Roger Hunt did not mean to be extinguished. On the contrary, he was in the mood to assert himself more distinctly than before. He had long since ceased to think of his wife as a responsible creature, yet he felt no sentiment of pity save for himself, the victim of an egregious and mortifying blunder. His love for her dead, he was led by an insidious kind of reasoning to persuade himself that all feeling of responsibility in that direction was annulled, save that of her material support, which was easy to extend. She was his and a part of him no longer, he proudly declared; and he put her as far away as possible in his thoughts. His soul rebelled at the thought that his entire future must be regulated by this heedless mistake of the past. He was not yet thirty, with life spread before him like a bounteous feast, tempting sense, imagination, and the intellect alike, yet must consent to repress all feeling, deny himself all exercise of a man's natural instincts and desires, pass his days like an anchorite in a desert, supported neither by the anchorite's faith or conviction of duty. The thought was monstrous.

Sympathy for Roger Hunt's position could not but be felt even by those who liked him least, and was heightened in his friends' minds by their knowledge of the additional vexations — of a small gnat-like order, but the more unbearable to one of his disposition — he suffered in the presence of a woman like Sarah Watson in his house, his complete moral antipode.

Miss Watson had given up a life of useful independence to assume her present position. She could perform a difficult duty if need be, but without cheerfulness or grace. She had many excellent traits, but they were combined with a temperament that made all her virtues appear exasperating faults. She had few overt faults, however, unless mental narrowness and a certain fierce pride of character be counted such. She was one of those whom contact with wrong - doing always hardens more than it enlightens. She did not try to understand the wicked behavior of people, only feared and condemned it. The thought of her sister, of whom she had always disapproved, aroused scarcely any other feeling than one of self-injury.

In this she was like Roger, yet the likeness proved no bond of union between them. The intense, exacting nature of each took an instant, yet deep-rooted dislike of the other. The two had lived together under one roof in forced mutual tolerance for three years, bound together only by their common deep misfortune. Days often passed with scarcely the exchange of a word, but it was impossible that natures so hostile should not sometimes clash in a downright quarrel, whose immediate cause was generally the most trivial. The boy

Roger had more than once been a witness of these scenes, more curious than disturbed, and leaning usually to his aunt's side.

Had the thought ever presented itself to Roger Hunt that any one's sacrifice except his own was involved in his present domestic arrangements, he would have brushed it impatiently aside. It seemed to him he paid the debt of his sister-in-law's services to the full in his forced submission to her presence. Everything she did and said irritated him; the tones of her voice, the straight folds of her bombazine dress, the set propriety of all her ways offended him like a direct assault. Her entrance into the room where he was filled him with resentment, yet so thoroughly had her presence impregnated the atmosphere of the house that he felt hardly more relieved of it in her absence. The truth was, as he had said to Eleanor, Roger Hunt was growing to hate his home. It shut down on him like a tomb every time he entered it. The resolve he was about to execute, to leave it forever, filled him, to-night, with nervous exaltation.

Seating himself at his desk in the library he wrote several letters, then arose and began selecting a few books to pack in a valise that lay carelessly disclosed on the floor. While thus engaged he caught sight of his son standing in the open door, and paused abruptly.

"I think I will go to bed now," said the boy with the undue gravity that marked his manner.

"Very well," his father replied, and stood looking at him helplessly. "Shall I go upstairs with you?"

"It will not be necessary. Good-night."

"Good-night," Roger repeated mechanically, and stood listening while the little feet slowly climbed the stairs. He went back to his work, but it seemed as if each of those small ascending footsteps had fallen on his heart. The room was stifling and he threw open a window, but the draught chilled him and he closed it again. His heart beat with excitement, and for a moment he could see nothing clearly in the room. He went back to his work, then stood still to listen. His fancy caught an unusual sound, and he rushed from the room and halfway up the carpeted stairway. He stopped and listened again. All was quiet. He had fancied he heard the boy crying softly to himself in the dark. After a moment he spoke: "Did you call, Roger?"

"No," was the reply sleepily uttered from muffling bedclothes. He lingered still.

"Do you want anything?" he asked again.

"You might bring me a drink of water," the inevitable request of childhood gone to bed, from young Astyanax downward.

His father carried a glass of water to the bedside. The room was unlighted save from the hall below, and his hand shook.

"You 've spilled it," said the boy in a peevish tone. Roger tried in a man's clumsy fashion to repair the mishap, while the boy lay drowsily back on his pillow.

"Good-night," said his father, again.

"Good-night." Roger hesitated, then bent over the bed.

"Don't you want to kiss me?" He could feel the surprise in his child's eyes, looking up at him through the dark. A kiss was exchanged between them.

"I am going away," Roger said, as if in explanation of such a request.

"To-night?"

"No, not to-night."

"Then we could have said good-by to-morrow."

Roger smiled bitterly and turned away, but was still reluctant to leave the room. At the door he stopped and spoke again.

"Don't you want to go with me?" The question was even more of a surprise to him than to the boy. Suddenly the thought had darted into his mind, — Why not take the child? Eleanor would be better pleased; it would serve to pacify her conscience.

"Where to?" was the question from the bed.

"Oh, to a good many places; across the ocean, perhaps."

"Will aunt Sarah go, too?"

"No." The boy deliberated a moment.

"Then I had better stay here. I might get sick, and there would be no one to mend my clothes."

Roger went out of the room and downstairs. The impulse that had so suddenly seized him had as quickly died. The utterly prosaic way in which his suggestion had been received, the absence of all childlike interest or enthusiasm, struck his own feeling cold.

"He cares nothing for me," he said to himself, with more anger than sorrow. "He never will. He will be better off without me. I am as useless here as I am miserable;" and with resolve newly strengthened, and knit brow and compressed lips, he resumed his preparations.

Half an hour later Miss Watson returned and, passing the library door, paused a moment on the threshold. Her eyes fell on the open valise with some surprise, but she would ask no questions. Her brother-in-law, she supposed, was about to take another of those sudden, unexplained journeys from home, which formed part of the ill-regulated behavior she so strongly disapproved of. Roger felt all his old antipathies arise when he saw her. He returned her look with a full clear gaze.

"I am going away," he said at last.

She made no reply, only stood regarding him with her usual expression of gloomy disapproval.

"It is likely to be a longer journey than usual," he went on with a peculiar look she recalled afterwards.

"If anything should happen," he spoke with slow distinctness here, "you know my business adviser, Mr. Somers. He will give you necessary instructions."

He took a strange satisfaction which experimental natures always feel, in this daring half-reve-

lation of his plans, picturing the retroactive indignation with which his words would cover him in
her mind. She listened to his further directions
without speaking, and when he had finished, she
proffered but one request.

"If you are likely to be away until after
Thanksgiving, I should like to take Roger with me
to Milton." This was the name of the town in
which the old homestead stood, rightly selected,
Roger thought ironically, for its pious appellation
and Arctic climate. He smiled a little as he gave
the required permission, thinking how useless all
commands and wishes of his would have become
by that time. Miss Watson had a word to say on
another subject.

"I saw Dr. Manford to-night." A frown crossed
her listener's face. Dr. Manford was one of the
consulting staff in the institution that sheltered
Annie Hunt.

"Well?"

"She has had another attack. She escaped
from her room last Monday, and before they could
find her she had broken into the medicine closet
and " —

"That will do," said Roger with a motion of
displeasure. "We are familiar with that story."
She turned and left him.

Under the impulse of this latest news he wheeled
suddenly about and faced a portrait that hung
above the mantel, which until now he had avoided
looking at. It was life-size, a two-thirds figure of

a young woman dressed in ball-room attire, with uncovered neck and arms, and a face that combined some remaining childlikeness with an insolent grace and abandon. Roger knew not why he kept it there, unless to justify the dislike he had always had of it. The gaze of the bright, shallow eyes fell on him mockingly.

"Heartless and brainless!" he exclaimed in his thoughts. "A doll! A butterfly! Why do such creatures exist to tempt and murder honest manhood? What harm can I do to her equal to that she has done me? The man that will bear such shame as mine deserves to! I thank heaven I am a free man at last!"

The eyes in the portrait — eyes he had once praised with all a lover's terms of fond endearment — fell on him with the same mocking smile, while his flashed back eternal defiance.

Turning away, another object caught his look; an open letter lying among the loose papers on the table, directed in a woman's hand. It was from Eleanor; he seized and covered it with kisses. Sinking down into a large, leather-covered chair, he leaned back with closed eyes and deliberately let the image of this other woman fill his soul. Judgment and will were soon in a blissful trance, and imagination had full sway. A troop of tempting thoughts and fancies bore him far away into a dream world of his own, where two figures moved at will, holding sweet converse together; where daring impulse ruled in place of law, and where feeling was the measure not of happiness alone, but of duty.

There are men of more sturdy ethical consciousness than this one, if not so aspiring and self-determined, who recognize the true nature of experiences of this kind; who know that the self-indulgence thus practiced is as demoralizing as any act of physical greed or passion. Roger Hunt indulged his emotions as other men do appetites. He did not know that the vain, ignorant woman, whose portrait he had turned his back upon, who had formed the habit of resorting to the wine-cup to ward off a headache, to steady failing nerves, or arouse a dejected spirit, was less culpable than the man who deliberately yields himself up to the narcotizing influence of his unhallowed dreams and longings. His mind was carefully trained, and stored with wisdom from many sources, but it was not open to comparisons of this kind. His spirit sped on its enamored flight. Conscious that he was impelled by no vulgar or sordid aims, his methods seemed, therefore, above reproach. It was nothing to him that men would abuse and misjudge him. There was not a person living whose opinion he valued on a subject of this kind as much as his own. "Every man is the arbiter of his own destiny," he was fond of saying. He was not afraid of the thing he was about to do.

III.

ROGER HUNT and Eleanor were on their way
across the Atlantic when the news of their secret
flight from home reached the public, through the
large-lettered head-lines of a morning newspaper.
It gave a severe shock to the community in which
Hunt had lived so long in high esteem, though
personally known to but few. Investigation into
the affair revealed the whole dark history of his
home life, and public opinion wavered a little, trying to strike a balance between the sufferings and
faults of one whose career now seemed closed.
Roger Hunt's friends had always been more or less
his apologists, and now felt themselves more severely taxed than ever before for this relationship.
Some of them tried, in makeshift fashion, to explain his conduct on the ground of the near kin-
ship a man of his talent and attainments bears to
genius, with its known eccentricities. A few of
these friends had come together, through a mixture
of chance and intention, at the house of his most
intimate one, George Somers, who was also his
lawyer.

It was here that Roger first saw Eleanor Thaxter, in attendance on a small literary gathering that
met weekly under the superintendence of Mrs.

Somers, for the study of Plato. Mrs. Somers knew Roger before her husband did; she had been acquainted with him since his college days, and was entirely familiar with his history, understanding his faults and virtues better than any other acquaintance. She had a sisterly fondness for and pride in him, aided by a generous feeling that the knowledge of his general unpopularity aroused. The other members of the little company were Henry Hamilton and his wife, and Mortimer Gray, a young journalist and Mrs. Somers's chief assistant in the Plato class. Mr. Hamilton was a man of shy, retiring manners, who gained a substantial living for himself and family in wholesale hardware, but who had always cherished a secret passion for literature, which expressed itself in one form in a worshipful admiration for Roger Hunt. Mrs. Hamilton was a woman of upright stature and opinions, prominent in church work and the city charities, whose conservative instincts led her to look askance at the Plato class. She had always disliked Roger Hunt as much as her husband liked him.

"It does n't surprise me so much, now that I 've recovered from the first shock," said George Somers, in the judicial tone that suited his professional standing and growing physical bulk. His wife laughed sarcastically, and with a suspicion of hysteria.

"It is just the sort of thing a man like Hunt, situated as he was and with his peculiar notions, could easily persuade himself to do."

"What were his ' peculiar notions'?" Gray asked. He did not know Hunt very well, had never been able to approach him, but he had fallen into the habit of noticing Miss Thaxter of late.

"Oh, the sort your incipient revolutionist always carries concealed about him. He had a fierce belief in liberty, for one thing" —

"Liberty! " exclaimed Gray, in a puzzled tone. "Is there any one nowadays who does n't believe in liberty?".

"Ah, but you see how Hunt defines it. Then he had a moral courage that was sublime, though it was apt to mistake its object."

"Yes, I 've often noticed that," Hamilton put in eagerly, leaning forward with a slight flush on his delicate skin. "There was a singular combination of purity and daring in him. It — it reminded me of Shelley."

"I should think so," his wife replied, and Mr. Hamilton's spirits drooped a little, while the rest of the company looked abashed.

"He seems to have been a rather queer mixture of the hero and the crank," said Gray, to fill in the pause.

"Well, most of your heroes have their cranky side, you know," Mr. Somers replied, leaning back in his great chair.

"I never saw much of the hero in him," said Mrs. Hamilton.

"He had many fine traits, though," her husband said, plucking up his courage. "It won't do to judge a man like Hunt as you would a common adventurer. The public will condemn him without reserve, but we should discriminate. We should think of the motive that lay behind. Hunt is not the man to act from a low motive."

His wife regarded him pityingly. "Mr. Hamilton always overrates his friends," she said in apology for his weakness.

"I think that is a very good fault," said Mrs. Somers, looking at him encouragingly. "I should like to be counted among his friends."

"You wouldn't have to ask me twice," put in the young journalist, coming to the other's relief. He had the modesty of his years — and sex — and felt uncomfortable, thinking perhaps he ought to make his excuses and go, but yielding to the wish to stay. Mrs. Somers smiled weakly.

"Mr. Hunt thought a great deal of Mr. Hamilton," she said, in continued kindness to the latter.

"That was because Mr. Hamilton is such a good listener," his wife answered, mercilessly. Her husband flushed, but rallied again.

"Mr. Hunt was worth listening to," he said. "He was one of the finest conversationalists I ever met."

"I don't know, I'm sure," his tormentor replied. "I never heard Mr. Hunt converse. I've heard him talk. He was perfect at monologue. Your good conversationalist knows how to listen as well as talk; but Mr. Hunt never listened, at least he never listened to me."

Mrs. Somers looked as if she knew why. "His manner was rather fitful," she said apologetically, "but to those who understood him he seemed not only a brave but a generous man. I have known him to do the kindest things "—

"And I have known him to do the rudest, and the most selfish," the other quickly interrupted.

"I am sure Roger Hunt was never intentionally selfish," said Mrs. Somers warmly.

"Oh, 'intentionally'!" her listener repeated, scornfully.

"He would make any sacrifice for a friend "—

"'For a friend'! Very likely. How much sacrifice and kindness has that woman experienced who has taken charge of his house for three years?"

"The testimony seems a little conflicting," said Gray, turning to the master of the house.

"Not at all," was the reply. "Both ladies are right. They are looking at different sides of the shield, that is all. Hunt is a man whose manners are determined by his feelings, and his feelings are always strong."

"It's perfectly scandalous," said Mrs. Hamilton, coming back to the main issue. "It makes one feel as if the very foundations were giving way. I don't know what you can expect of the lower orders "—

"Yes, it's a dead give-away to the lower orders," said Mr. Somers. His visitor looked at him in stony incomprehension.

"I must say, George, I don't think this is a subject for weak-minded jesting," said his wife in marital reproof. "I don't care anything about the lower orders," she went on, in some excitement. "I beg your pardon, Mrs. Hamilton, but I don't. But I do care for my friends," catching her breath.

"I thought Miss Thaxter was only a recent acquaintance," said the other woman.

"I 'm not speaking of Miss Thaxter."

"You see there was an old attachment between Hunt and my wife," Mr. Somers explained, with husbandly freedom, "but she happened to be engaged to me " —

"George, you know that is n't true," his victim broke in, with heightened color and visible annoyance.

"Not true that you were engaged to me? And so they 've kept up a kind of Platonic friendship ever since."

The injured wife sank helplessly back in her chair, and the guests looked sympathetic discomfort, while the speaker laughed and took another tone.

"Oh, well, Hunt was n't altogether a bad fellow. I admit I had a sneaking fondness for him myself. But I 've always known a dynamite bomb was about as safe a piece of furniture in the house as he was. He has made a nice mess of it now, but the consequences will fall on his own head."

"Not so severely as they will on hers; they never do," said Mrs. Hamilton severely.

Young Gray looked newly disturbed and interested here, but listened attentively.

"I 'm afraid that 's so.   I suppose it will prove in this case, as in others, that the woman will come in for the severest blame, especially from her affectionate sex."

"No, Mr. Somers, not from me.   Of course I blame Miss Thaxter, but it is easy to see she was like wax in his hands.   There was always something uncanny about the man to me.   I declare, if I did n't know it was nonsense, I should say he had gained some queer kind of influence over her. Did you ever notice his eyes?" turning to her hostess.   The latter looked a little conscious and said she did n't know.

"I don't believe in such things, of course," Mrs. Hamilton went on, "but I distrusted him the moment I saw him."   Young Gray rose from his chair.   He shook hands with Mrs. Hamilton and thanked her — she could not conceive why — then bowed his adieux to the gentlemen.   Mrs. Somers followed him in sisterly fashion to the door.

"If it had n't been for the presence of the ladies I could have characterized that fellow's conduct without half this trouble," he said, as he took her hand at parting.

"Roger Hunt is n't a 'fellow;' but never mind the ladies.   Say what you wish."

"Very well, then, I say he is a damned scoundrel."   He spoke without heat, but with a gravity that gave his words a religious sound.   She smiled sadly, and shook her head.

"It 's all right if it makes you feel any better,

but it is n't a bit philosophical. Of course I feel sorry for her too," she added in some afterthought. The young man reddened a little.

"I think I shall forego philosophy," he said, and opening the door passed out.

"It is n't necessary to resort to the supernatural to explain Hunt," Mrs. Somers heard her husband say as she returned to the parlor. "Call him an egotist. Most men admit they should pay some regard to the laws of the social universe, but occasionally a man arises who feels it his mission to present the world with a new pattern. Now everybody admits the need of new patterns. You should hear the way Hunt reasons it out in the letter he wrote me the night before he went away."

"Yes," said Mrs. Somers, leaning forward from the chair in which she had seated herself. "His letter is really quite remarkable. And it is only fair to look at it from his side. Of course his reasoning is as wrong and ridiculous as can be," in deferential aside to Mrs. Hamilton, "but it is only just to remember how he looks at it. He believes his to be an exceptional case; we know there are exceptional cases. Shelley thought his was," turning this time to Mr. Hamilton, "but I never cared much about Shelley."

"Which proves it was n't, I suppose," her husband put in.

"Then there was George Eliot. We all admit that hers was an exceptional case."

"I beg your pardon, Mrs. Somers, not all of

us," and Mrs. Hamilton straightened her figure to
a more upright position than before.

"I 'm very narrow-minded," she went on with a
chilly smile. "I 'm not an agnostic; I leave speculation to Mr. Hamilton. There are a few things
I feel I 've gained pretty complete knowledge of.
One is that a man's responsibility is measured by
his intelligence."

"What do you mean by ' intelligence ' ?" Mr.
Somers asked. "Hunt had a fair degree of book-
ish knowledge; he was well up in the classics and
mediæval art, but in some other respects he was a
perfect ignoramus. I often used to say the same
thing to him," he added defensively. None of
them seemed to notice they were speaking in the
past tense.

"I suppose he was like most specialists," said
Mr. Hamilton. "His range of information was
high rather than broad. I am in sympathy with
Mrs. Somers. Her generous defense " —

"Oh, I 'm not defending him," Mrs. Somers
broke in, in some alarm. "I only think we should
look at a subject on all sides."

Her husband laughed, in irritating fashion.

"Kitty prides herself on her ability to think as
every one else does. She has n't led the class in
Plato two years for nothing. But there 's no danger her practice will run ahead of other people's.
It 's all summed up in the word I 've selected,"
he went on, showing he liked to theorize as well
as his wife. "Hunt is a born egotist. Nothing

would offend him more than to think gravitation
had anything to do with his power to stand upright.   He likes to think it's all due to his own
will and intention.   Did you ever notice that trick
he has of standing very straight at times, so that
he tips a little backward?" to Mr. Hamilton.
"That expresses very well his notion of moral independence."

"Well, he has tipped backward a good ways this
time," said Mrs. Hamilton rising from her chair.

"Yes, that's true," her host assented, as he
rose also, but with somewhat greater effort.

"But he did everything that was honorable about
it," Mrs. Somers put in anxiously.   "He provided
for his child very handsomely, — the larger half
of all he had, did n't you say?" turning to her
husband.

"I don't know as I said the larger half; one
half is as large as the other in all the arithmetic I
ever studied."

"That is nothing," replied Mrs. Hamilton.
"What is money when coupled with a disgraced
name?"

Mrs. Somers tried to murmur something polite
and conciliatory, but the uncompromising plain-
ness of her guest's words offended her.   It was with
great relief she saw the two depart.   Her disturbed
feelings found a natural vent in the first words
addressed to her husband when they were alone.

"Well, George, I don't know how you can call
yourself Roger Hunt's friend, and talk about him
as you have to-night!"

"I don't know as I'm anxious to prove that relationship, just now. I would sacrifice as much for a friend as most people, but not my gift for psychological analysis. No one would in this age."

He drew out his watch and pronounced it bedtime, then went below to attend to the furnace. Their income was modest, and they lived simply with a single servant, who took most of her evenings "out."

Mrs. Somers climbed the stairs to their room above, marveling with some irritation over those self-sustained qualities in the masculine mind which enable it to stand upright, on its two feet, so to speak, under circumstances that reduce the feminine consciousness to meaningless pulp. It was ridiculous, she knew, but it did seem the sign of a hardened nature that in the midst of trouble like this, and with that uneasy sense of complicity which their long intimacy with Roger Hunt aroused, George should remember to fill the furnace. For herself, she had wandered in and out of the house all day in a maze of gloomy absent-mindedness, committing all the mistakes within reach. She had dusted the library with the hearth-brush, watered the geraniums in the dining-room window with the remaining contents of the milk-jug, and given the grocer's order to the postman. She was standing before the dressing-bureau, removing her hairpins when her husband joined her.

"That girl left the back door unbolted again," he said.

"Did she?" she replied, indifferently. She shook her loosened hair over her shoulders, then began brushing it.

"I can't help it," she exclaimed, after the braiding process had begun. "I did like him," catching her breath a little. "I can't bear to give him up like this. I don't see what he was thinking of! And Eleanor Thaxter! Mark my words, George, she will be perfectly miserable!"

"No, she will be imperfectly miserable; but that's worse."

"Oh, I wish you would n't try to talk like one of Henry James's novels," she exclaimed pettishly. He attempted no answer to this, winding his watch and placing it under his pillow.

"How long have you seen this thing 'going on?'" he asked her, when he had taken off his coat and hung it over a chair. She wheeled about and looked at him.

"Do you mean to say you've seen it 'going on?'" she asked him sharply. He smiled and looked a little foolish.

"I saw him kiss her once."

"George!" she gasped.

"With his eyes, I mean."

She seemed still more displeased with this, and turned back to the mirror.

"Your way of talking about this will put us all in the wrong," she replied a moment after. "I wish you would be more careful. I know you've set Mrs. Hamilton thinking. She's the most exasperating woman I know! " flinging the finished braid over her shoulder. "The trouble with such people is they have n't a particle of imagination! "

"Then they 'll help preserve the balance against Hunt. He has n't anything else."

"Oh, don't speak of it," she groaned. "When I think of the questions that will be asked us! It will ruin the Plato class! "

"Yes; you see what such things come to.'"

She made no reply. Seated on a low ottoman, forgetful of her surroundings, she fell into a perplexed and dreamful reverie, in which her old sympathetic understanding of the friend, thus lost, came back to her, with sorrow for the disappointments he had suffered, and blame of fate that had imposed them. She thought of his wrecked career, then of the real use, source of deserved joy and happiness, this new love might have been, had it been honestly obtained. Pity for their great mistake, the suffering that must have been theirs in any case, softened harsher thoughts for a moment.

"I feel so sorry for them both," she sighed. "Any one can see they are just made for each other."

"Well, Kitty, you 've sunk pretty low."

"Oh, I know it," springing to her feet. "I feel as if there was n't a single moral fibre left in me."

"You 'd better get into bed and go to sleep."

"Sleep! " she exclaimed scornfully; but she went on with her preparations. Soon she paused again to give expression to another remembrance that darted across her mind.

"George, it's as I thought. Mortimer Gray was beginning to care about her."

"He ought not to find it hard to stop now. I wouldn't worry about Mortimer Gray."

"It's awful!" she moaned, "perfectly awful! If we only knew how it would end!"

"What do you want to know that for? For my part, when a thing begins as bad as this, I am content to have my knowledge stop there."

"Yes, yes; you are right," she replied quickly. "I shudder to think of it."

"Well, I've got through thinking about it, at least for to-night. I'm tired of both of them. I'm going to sleep."

He got into bed and pulled the clothes up over his ears. She sighed and knew he would be as good as his word. Slipping into her place by his side, his regular and not very gentle breathing soon told her that for him the day's cares and vexations were forgotten. She listened with envy, mixed with a slight feeling of umbrage. For herself, she knew she should lie awake half the night, fretting about other people's troubles she was not expected to help.

IV.

THERE was a reason why Mrs. Somers should
feel more disturbed over this affair than her husband did. Roger Hunt had called to see her the
day of his flight from home. The ostensible purpose of this visit she now saw covered another, half
revealed, impossible for her to conjecture at the
time, and which she reflected on indignantly. He
meant, she believed, or at least wished, to make
her his confidant, but had not quite dared to; being
deterred also by a failing sympathy in her own
manner he had then complained of. She asked
herself with some displeasure what reason she had
ever given him to think she had any sympathy to
bestow in such a cause? The remembrance of the
interview was so unpleasant that she could not in-
crease its discomfort by speaking of it to any one,
not even to her husband.

Roger called in the forenoon, and found her in
the library, which was also the living-room. The
pretended object of his visit was to fetch her a set
of engravings illustrating the Acropolis, which he
had come across the evening before; remembering
to have heard her express a wish for something of
the kind, he at once resolved to take them to her,
glad of an excuse to see her again, and hoping for
other results.

She received the gift with delight, thanking him, running through the pages, and exclaiming over each in her animated fashion; while he, seated opposite her, watched and listened to her with half-pleased, half-moody expression.

Roger Hunt had a singular feeling towards Kitty Somers! There had been times when he almost fancied he was in love with her. They had known each other since his entrance into the university, when he made his home with herself and widowed father, the university chaplain.

Hunt was no more popular among his college associates than those of after-life, and from the first Kitty Platt, as she was then known, and a favorite with all the college folk, found herself in a position of defense towards the new-comer. Roger never knew how many slights and impish tricks he escaped through the watchful intervention of this friend. Compelled thus to try to understand him, she soon came to feel a sincere admiration and affection for him. She was one of those women who know how to form friendships with men, without letting the relation degenerate into that weak imitation of a stronger passion, disguised under the name "Platonic," a word she disliked, and had justly resented her husband's use of. She and Roger Hunt soon became excellent friends. His more ardent temperament, the way he had, and still kept, of entering into every fresh relation as if it were the newly-discovered end of existence, led many to predict a still nearer bond of union between them, which, for all that the present biographer knows of the potentialities in such matters, might have been fulfilled, had not a sudden move in the human chess-board taken place, which altered everything.

Roger Hunt had no sooner met Annie Watson than that current of wild, swift passion was set flowing, in which the quiet stream of a noble, uplifting friendship was engulfed and lost sight of. Kitty Platt was made the confidant of this fresh experience as of every other, and could not forbear signs of her dismayed surprise. She unwisely attempted to remonstrate, and was rewarded with a month's coldness and withdrawal of favor for her pains. She then learned what Roger Hunt's professions of friendship were worth, the real measure of regard in which she, his nearest and most trusted counselor, so he had often told her, was to be held, now that her opinion had run counter to his on a matter of vital concern to himself.

A woman is never in a fair position to reason her friend of the other sex out of a mistake of this kind; and it takes a very modest man to refrain from putting his own construction on the interference he encounters in such matters from such a source. Roger Hunt was not a modest man, and had ever since cherished certain illusions respecting this particular episode in his life, which even the circumstance of his friend's marriage to another had not seriously disturbed. Though he made a companion of George Somers and had come to

depend on him a good deal in practical affairs, to
himself he never pretended to regard Kitty Platt's
marriage with any other feelings than mingled pity
and contempt. The two men were but slightly attracted at first, and had it not been for the restrained nature of the one, and the fact that a woman stood between them, their acquaintance would
probably never have passed the most formal limits.

George Somers appeared on the scene about the
same time as Annie Watson. He was one of the
"specials," and regarded with the usual feeling of
patronage that class arouses in university life; so
here, too, the generous instincts in Kitty Platt's
nature, always active, found an object. In her
fresh vexation over Roger's folly it is probable that
the contrast appeared more plainly between her
gifted but erratic friend and this newer acquaintance, the quiet, muscular young man, with his
steady eyes and plain sensible talk, and a mental
balance always preserved. Roger's headlong woo-
ing had quickly culminated in the marriage which
was so soon to lead to ruin and misery on both
sides, while the courtship of these two was still
slowly progressing. When their marriage followed,
it was but the public sanction of a relation that·
had been given two years to ripen in and had long
passed the stage of quivering nerves and thrill-
ing pulses. That was why it seemed so prosaic an
affair to Roger, who by this time was something of
a scoffer at marriage. He was soon on an intimate
footing in the new household, though his restored

relations with the mistress were based on no admission of a mistake on his part. He admitted a mistake, but had his own way of explaining it, which made it rather redound to his credit than otherwise; and he still nourished a little feeling against Kitty Somers. On the other hand, pity for his misfortunes, and knowledge of those peculiarities other people blamed so unsparingly, combined to soften judgment with these friends, who felt they had something to spare out of their own married content to one so severely used as Roger Hunt.

It was Roger's misfortune, more than his fault, perhaps, that he was so seldom able to emulate another's generous estimate of himself. Opinion rarely went beyond its first preconception with him, unless personal interest became strongly engaged. He still held to his first view of Kitty Platt's marriage, but it was not a subject of much concern to him, and he found it less difficult therefore to conceal his feeling. The spirit of frank *camaraderie* which existed between husband and wife, the spirit of badinage which entered into most of their talk, the absence of demonstration in their manner, were the signs, to Roger's romantic fancy, of indifference and mental disparity. He knew they sometimes differed seriously, exchanging opinions with entire candor and some warmth — quarreled; an impossible circumstance in true marriage, he argued, which to be tolerated at all must be perfect, its success and happiness being measured by the first transported feeling leading to it.

Had Mrs. Somers known the kind of speculation she was made the subject of in her unhappy friend's mind, she would have been, first, indignant, then amused. She had learned to indulge and bear with much she disapproved of in this direction. Intellectually she honored and looked up to Roger Hunt as to no other friend; and because she knew his faults so well she understood other traits few would take the pains to understand. She had a judicial head, though essentially feminine, with her blonde hair and slender figure. The habit she cultivated of looking on all sides of a question, and, as her husband said, of trying to think as every one else did, discredited her in many minds with the usual degree of womanly sensibility; in Roger's also, sometimes. She herself, however, was often conscious of a mental perspective blurred by feeling. Could she always stop liking people when obliged to disapprove of them, or like only those she approved, human analysis would be easier. As it was, pity melted her on one side, while reason upbraided her on the other; and the strain was never more severe than when trying to reach some fresh conclusion about Roger Hunt.

As they sat together on the occasion of his last visit, and she thanked him again for his friendly remembrance of her, he called her attention to the inscription on the inside of the cover, holding the prints in place; her name, with the date and his own initials.

"I wrote it in pencil, so that you can erase it whenever you wish."

She looked at him questioningly, but smiling also.

"Why should I wish to erase it?" she asked, laying the volume aside and taking up a piece of crochet work near by.

"You may — some time." There was something in his tone that made her glance at him again. He sat sideways on his chair, his arm resting on the back, his head leaning dejectedly on his hand.

She saw he was out of sorts, but experience had taught her that certain moods of his deserved less attention than neglect. She was beginning to dread the responsibility of her position, and was in daily fear lest Roger should seek her advice about procuring a divorce. She had not as strong prejudices on this subject as many New Englanders, her general theory being that people who are too weak to bear their marital troubles and spare the world the sorry exhibition of them, may be excused for seeking a formal remedy; but she did not like to class her friends with these.

"Are you coming to the Plato class Friday evening?" she asked, turning the talk to a safe topic.

"No."

She looked at him in a little surprise.

"I shall not be in town," he added.

She, too, was accustomed to his habit of frequent journeyings from home, and asked nothing more on this point just then, her mind being occupied with something else.

"Then I am glad you came in. I want some

advice. I have written a letter to Miss Thaxter, asking her to take a topic next month. Do you think she will consent?"

As she spoke she took the letter from the table near by, sealed and directed, then dropped it back again, resuming her work. She was not looking at her visitor, and did not see the burning flush that swept over his face.

"I have been thinking about her a good deal," she went on. "She interests me. She is intelligent. You can tell that by the way she listens; but she is very shy. She needs drawing out."

Roger covered his eyes with his hand to hide the intelligence which seemed to blaze from them. His heart beat rapidly.

"Then you like her," he said at last.

"I said I was interested in her. I don't permit myself to like people any more until I am sure of them," with an experienced air. "I feel sorry for her. George says he does n't see the use of being sorry for people until we 're asked, but I can't help it. She seems so alone, some way. She has one of those faces that stay by you. Don't you think so?"

It was impossible to answer such a question, and he drew his hand several times over his own face, to compose the expression tumultuous feelings within seemed to have placed there.

"I don't believe she is very happily situated with her brother "—

"He is a brute!"

She looked up at him in surprise.

"Do you know him?"

He made some indirect reply.

"Well, I don't know as it will do any good, but I 've asked her to give us something on the Phædo. I hope I shan't frighten her."

"Give me the letter," said Roger, extending his hand; "I will post it for you." She murmured something about not troubling him, but he leaned forward and took the letter, placing it in his inside pocket. She viewed this disappearance with feminine distrust, born of unlucky experience.

"I 'm afraid you 'll forget it;" but he assured her he would not.

"I am glad you like her," he added with a hesitancy unusual in him. "Two such women as you ought to be friends."

"Oh, I don't know. I fancy we are not much alike; Miss Thaxter is one of the timid, dependent kind."

"That should make you like her all the better," with some warmth.

"Yes, if I were a man. Where are you going?" coming back to the subject they had left. He waited a moment before replying.

"To New York." He paused, then added, "From there across the water."

"Across the water! Again? You went abroad last year!"

" 'Abroad' is the only place for a man like me. I can breathe over there. I suffocate here." She knew what this meant, but chose to disregard it.

"Happy man!" she exclaimed enviously, "who talks of a trip to Europe as I would of a visit to Boston! When will George and I go, I wonder. Will you take little Roger with you?"

He frowned.

"I think you ought, Roger," speaking more seriously. "Such a boy needs his father." His face darkened still more.

"He has his precious aunt, and does n't care for his father. We are better off apart. I offered to take him with me, but he declined," satirically.

"Nonsense! What does a child like that know of such matters? You should keep him with you; he would do you good. And why do you dislike Miss Watson so much? She is not very agreeable, I know;" and she shrugged her shoulders in memory of the single visit she had paid Roger's sister-in-law, from which she came away feeling, as she told her husband, as if she had been lunching on an iceberg. "But what would you have done without her?"

"Hanged myself, perhaps, and so escaped worse misery."

"I see you are in one of your black moods."

"No; on the contrary I am in one of my best. I never felt stronger or happier than I do to-day." She looked at him attentively. His eyes met hers with an unfaltering, yet unfathomable gaze she long remembered. He leaned suddenly towards her.

"I wish I dared tell you something," he said impetuously.

"If you dare not it must be either because you do not trust me " —

"I trust you always — up to a certain point."

She smiled, rather enjoying a home thrust of this kind.

"Or because it is something that had better not be told."

This was not so encouraging, and he fell back in his chair with a vexed look on his face.

"You disappoint me terribly sometimes," he said. "I don't suppose you realize what an unfeeling remark that was."

"A wise one, though. There are many things that had better remain untold."

"A man seeks sympathy in a woman, not wisdom."

"And usually gets too much sympathy. I consider myself born to counteract the general tendency," holding up her work to measure its length, then letting it fall into her lap again. "I give my friends what I think they need, not what they want. If my judgment fails " —

"It is your heart that fails."

"It is time men learned to value women for something besides what they call 'heart.' But let us come back to our muttons. What are you going to Europe for?"

"That is part of the 'thing that had better not be told,' " ironically. She looked at him now with some anxiety.

"Roger, what are you going to do?"

"Something you will mightily disapprove of."

"Is — is it about Annie?"

"I wish I might never hear her name again."

"Roger, that is wicked, and perfectly senseless besides. Why are you so rebellious? It is so unworthy of you. I don't say you have not suffered, have not been wronged even, but you make everything harder for yourself. You think only of how you can escape things. We are not put here to escape but to bear things."

"You may talk that kind of pious cant to those who believe it. As for her " — his face darkening again.

"Roger, hush! You loved her once. Think what a child she was! She was not wicked, only weak. Such things are a disease. Oh, I have blamed myself a thousand times that I did not go to her at once and help her. No one tried to help her. I am not blaming you," in reply to some word of angry interruption from him.

"I loved her, as you say," with a proud look, "and she killed my love."

"Yes, yes, I know," feeling it useless to argue this point.

"And when love is dead, marriage is dead."

She shook her head. "There is where you make a fatal mistake, Roger. Love is the only reason for entering marriage, but is only one for continuing in it."

"You are growing very subtle."

"I only believe that in marriage as in everything

else we must be willing to abide the consequences of our own actions. We cannot take people into our lives, and then thrust them out, because they are not everything our first fancy pictured.''

"I was deceived.'' She regarded him with a mournful smile.

"Don't think I do not feel for you too,'' she replied, "but, Roger, don't you see, it is those who are weak and go wrong who need our help most, not those who only suffer from others' wrong-doing. You think you are the chief sufferer, that your life has been wrecked, but it is only the sense of blame in ourselves brings real suffering. It is her life that is wrecked.''

"I was mistaken in saying you had no sympathy,'' he said coldly. "You have, but not for me.''

"It is for both, but you are the stronger; you need less than she does. Think how many resources of happiness are still left you.''

"You think the man who falls into a pit deserves less compassion than the one who dug it for him?''

"One has physical hurts to heal, the other moral,'' she said softly.

"That's all very fine, but what man has deeper moral hurts than mine?''

"I speak of the moral hurts caused by our own mistakes, but I see I have offended you.''

"No; only disappointed.''

"It's the same thing, I fear,'' with a rueful smile.

"No," after a pause. "I choose not to be offended. I want to part friends," rising and extending his hand.

"Part? Oh, yes; but you have not told me why you are going."

"Why?" He bent a pair of large reproachful eyes on her in which a gleam of defiance flashed out.

"Say it is because I think the guilty alone should bear the penalty of their misdeeds; that the man who has fallen into the pit need not go forever maimed and disfigured in consequence" —

"What do you mean?"

"Say it is because life is too rich and sweet for a man not to profit by all his chances of happiness, and because Roger Hunt means to let no human creature or circumstance debar him from his natural rights. Now your disapproval of me is heightened tenfold, I suppose."

"My bewilderment certainly is. Roger," with that anxious note again in her voice, "are — are you going to get a divorce?"

He laughed scornfully. "What do I want with a divorce? If you knew in what contempt I hold all man-made regulations on some things" —

"There, there! no more wild talk," breathing more freely.

"I think you are not feeling very well," she went on, dropping back to the commonplace, "and I hope the sea voyage will do you good."

"Thank you; those words are very suitable; but

when a starving man comes to your door, you should give him something more than a clean napkin and a silver teaspoon.''

"I will give you more when I find out what it is you want.''

"What I want I shall take.''

"That is what the house burglar does.''

"I am not afraid of your comparisons,'' and he looked, she afterward remembered, as if he were afraid of nothing. "The house burglar has not my motive.''

"I don't know, I am sure,'' shaking her head wearily. "He wants what does n't belong to him.''

"Precisely! And I want what does belong to me, what nature and reason say I have a right to, what no one but a coward would hesitate to take. I puzzle you more than ever, I see. But I free all my friends from responsibility. Remember,'' with a glance at his gift lying on the table, "you have my permission to rub out the name whenever you like.''

"You deserve I should do so now.'' She followed him to the outer door.

"Good-by,'' he said, turning and taking her hand again.

"It is a real 'good-by,' then?'' she asked with an incredulous smile. He deliberated a moment.

"That is for you to say. What will you say, I wonder,'' bending that same inscrutable look on her. "You are the most courageous woman I know, but, after all, that is not saying much.''

"No, not much."

"And so, I fear it is a real 'good-by,' but it is for you to say — for you to say," and he released her hand and passed through the door.

Afterward, when she looked back on this visit, she said to herself, after her first indignation over its presumption had passed, that it was like Roger Hunt to talk and act in this way, he who was always playing with fire, and was bent on developing all the dramatic possibilities of every situation in which he was placed. She went back to the library more weary than excited over the discussion that had just ended. It could not be anything very bad that he was going to do, if he did not mean to get a divorce. It was only fair, she thought, he should praise her courage. It required some to be the friend of such a man.

V.

When Sarah Watson learned what had happened, she felt that the sum of her undeserved wrongs was now complete. A bitter moral wrath possessed her. She resented all attempts at condolence or assistance from others, encasing herself in a cold inflexibility of manner that aroused a feeling of sympathy for Hunt. Calling the boy to her in her room, she placed him before her and fixed her stern eyes upon him, not to frighten him, only to compel attention. She began, after the order of the Catechism, by asking him his name. He was used to her manner and looked at her thoughtfully, with eyes much like her own.

"My name is Roger Hunt. 'Roger Hunt, Junior,' I write it at school."

"You will write it 'Roger Hunt, Junior' no more."

He looked at her with a puzzled frown. "Why not?"

"Because there is a Roger Hunt, Senior," was the brief reply. He gathered her meaning more from her manner than her words.

"My father has done something that displeases you," he said at length, with the unchildish gravity that marked him.

"You have no father. He has disgraced us all !
He is a false, bad man ! Men have been imprisoned and locked behind iron bars for doing what
he has done! " The boy turned pale and trembled.
The speaker was shaking with anger, and the look
in her face frightened him.

"Do you mean you will have my father imprisoned?"

"No. He has nothing to fear from me. Let
him go his way. Your father has given you to
me." She placed her hands on his shoulders and
looked at him with burning eyes. "Hereafter your
name is not Roger Hunt, but Charles Watson."

"That was my grandfather's name," the boy replied, his mind unable to take in all that had been
said, and fastening itself on the last words. As
he spoke, he lifted his eyes to a portrait that hung
above the mantel, done in dark-colored oils, that
shadowed forth the figure of an old, stern-faced
man.

"And your grandfather was a good man. He
would have scorned to do what your father has
done. He had right opinions about everything.
Men respected and feared him."

"What is it my father has done?" the boy asked
more composedly. His first alarm was passing
away, this reference to his father's opinions reas-
suring him a little. The latter had made some unpleasant remarks about the missionary society, perhaps, or did not approve of hot cakes for supper.
When his aunt explained what had happened, not

all the details, but sufficiently, he grew more serious.

"Shall we be poor?" he asked, "and have to work for a living? Is that the reason we are going away from this house? Am I not to have the new pony I was promised?" The meaning of the new state of things began to dawn on him, and he looked ready to cry.

. "You shall have the pony," the other replied, with a shade less of hardness in her tones, "but we shall go far away from this place."

"To Milton?"

"No," a spasm of pain contracting her face. "Much farther — to some place where nobody knows us."

The boy showed no signs either of grief or pleasure at the thought of leaving his home, which was to him a place with four walls, like any other.

Miss Watson and her young charge went away quietly a few days later, and when their departure was discovered, no one knew in what direction they had gone, not even Mr. Somers, with whom she had been in business relations. The latter could explain nothing to his wife save the fact of her legal adoption of the boy, and his change of name.

"She had no right to do that," said Mrs. Somers warmly.

"She had a perfect right to do it."

"Oh, legal right, perhaps," tossing her head in feminine scorn for this literality, "but she had no moral right. The boy is his father's child, whatever happens."

"I'm afraid that is true, but you can't blame her for wanting to cover up the fact as much as possible."

"One would think you sympathized wholly with her.   She is a dreadful woman, I think."

. Mrs. Somers had been among those who had gone to Miss Watson's assistance and been coldly repelled.   The latter felt she must be reduced, indeed, to accept help from any of her brother-in-law's friends.   There was a more practical question in the wife's mind.

"Did she leave her business in your hands ?"

"No," with a humiliated flush.   "She has withdrawn it.   I'm sure we can't blame her.   No wonder she wants to cut loose from all of Hunt's friends."

"Friends!   Does she think we are his friends, that we uphold him in a thing like this?"

"I don't know what she thinks.   I know I feel as if I had committed a dozen crimes myself, and was still at large preying on society.   If those two suffer half the remorse I do in this business, they'll be sufficiently punished.   But I've washed my hands of the affair.   I've written Hunt and told him to put his business in some one else's hands."

"You have!" in a startled tone.   Then after reflecting a moment, "I don't know whether I approve of that or not."

"Of course you don't.   I knew you wouldn't, and that you'd want a week at least to find out. That's the reason I posted the letter on my way home." She scarcely heard this sarcasm, her mind darting quickly to take in another feature of the case.

"It will make a difference, won't it?"

"A difference?" Then, as her meaning dawned on him, "Yes, it will make a difference." She was thinking of their income.

"And Roger Hunt talks of consequences falling on the guilty alone," she thought. Aloud, —

"Then of course you did right to give it up."

With all her strong-mindedness, Kitty Somers had the usual feminine appetite for self-immolation.

"Well, that is n't just the way I got at it, but it makes no difference, so we are agreed."

"Those two," as George Somers had characterized them, were sitting at that moment on the deck of a Liverpool steamer within twenty-four hours of land.

They had met at the place agreed on, traveling thence to New York together. From the first Roger had been in his most joyous and confident mood, so that Eleanor, full of palpitating fears, looked at him with increasing wonder. He was, however, under as intense excitement as she, which in him demanded an active outlet, keeping him restlessly busy, and watchful of the smallest event and circumstance connected with their journey. As the trip by rail drew to its end, her first anxiety began to abate, and she fell into a lethargic state in which all thought was for a time deadened. An atmosphere of constant protecting kindness surrounded her, of delicate attention and care, that charmed the imagination almost as much as it warmed the heart.

Her life had been bare and lonely, bereft of almost all graceful and kindly service from others, and little attentions which other women would have received without notice touched her inexpressibly. Before this she had lived only in the background of other people's affairs, been a silent spectator at the feast of life which nobody had expected her to share. Here in this new world she had so daringly entered, she found herself in the place of both centre and circumference. Roger was more marvelously kind, thoughtful, and loving than even she had dreamed he could be. Somewhat of her feelings shone in the warm, grateful look she gave him as he left her for a few moments' rest towards nightfall, after arranging her shawl and pillow with a woman's skill.

"How good he is," she murmured to herself, and kept repeating the thought in her mind, clinging to and supporting herself with it. In some way she could not fathom, this goodness must stand for rightness, she thought; at least, if there was a difference, she had not yet learned it.

"He is good to everybody," she added in dreamful reverie, recalling an incident of their day's journey together.

Among their fellow-passengers was a woman with a sick child, whose fretful crying disturbed every one in the car, and had nearly worn out the mother. Roger and Eleanor watched her sympathetically for some time. At last Roger sprang to his feet.

"I 'm going to help that woman," he said, and stepped towards her. Reaching her side he held out his arms to the little one. "Let me take her," he said kindly. "You are tired." .

The woman looked up at him gratefully. "If she will go to you."

Children would by no means always go to him, nor was he profuse in invitations of this kind; but in this case the child looked at him gravely a minute, then reached up its arms confidingly. The mother sighed the relief she felt, and Roger took his charge to another seat and held it quietly in his arms until it fell asleep. Had Mrs. Somers witnessed this scene she would have shown no surprise, her familiarity with others of a similar nature having prompted the remark to Mrs. Hamilton that Roger Hunt was one of the kindest men she knew. To Eleanor, who was watching him, this act seemed one of heavenly goodness.

Roger carried the sleeping child back to its mother and laid it gently down on the opposite seat, politely waived the woman's thanks, then went back to his place at Eleanor's side.

"That was very good in you," she said looking at him affectionately. "I feel as if I had a new proof of you. They say children are always correct judges of character."

"That is a pretty superstition," he replied

lightly. "Children's judgments are as whimsical as grown people's," he added, with a smile. "I don't know as you could say anything worse of them. But I care very little about people's opinions of me. What I value is their feeling for me, — especially somebody's," he added, in a lower tone, and with an expressive glance that brought the color to her cheek.

"Then if my opinion changes some day, you will not complain?" she answered with a faint smile.

"Think what you please about me, only continue to love me."

She looked as if that would be easy, yet a little doubtful, too.

"Does not love spring from the sense of worth in its object?"

"Not necessarily. Love is its own excuse for being, like beauty. Love is better understood without analysis, or rather it is not necessary to understand love at all, only to admit its power and reap its rewards."

"That sounds very daring."

"Those who love must be willing to dare many things."

This brought them back to the knowledge of where they were and what they were doing. The old fluttering anxiety came over her.

"Have they found out about it yet?" she asked in a whisper.

"No, it will not be known for two days yet. By that time we shall have been twelve hours out to sea." He looked at her wtih strong, confident eyes. "Are you afraid?"

Her eyes fell and a tremulous sigh escaped her. She slipped her hand, which was cold, into his. "I am yours."

"Think no more of it," he said, reassuringly. "The thing is done."

"Yes, it is done. I—I do not regret. I only want to make you happy. I can do that better when we are—by ourselves."

The last words betrayed the nervous apprehension, mingled with a sickening sense of shame, from which she suffered, and which she should be free from, she thought, when beyond the possible chance of meeting any one who might recognize them. Roger could not fail to share the first feeling, to some extent, though he did not let her see it.

On board the steamer he hastily scanned the passenger list, and returned to her with a triumphant air.

"We are as much alone as if we were the only ones on board. The rest are Western people, with a lot of theatrical folks."

She heard him with relief, but the sense of shame had not departed; the hour of complete content was still delayed. Though the eyes that met hers were those of entire strangers, they disturbed her in a new way; their careless talk fell discordantly on her ear. She was glad she did not escape the affliction of seasickness which kept her in her stateroom during most of the voyage.　Once across the water, half the globe's distance between them and their former home, alone with Roger, with only him to think about, she should be happy, these strange, undefined alarms would disappear.

Roger was perfectly well.　He was an experienced traveler, and the free life on board ship suited him perfectly.　The broad expanse of sea and sky matched his boundless thoughts.　The independent solitariness of these days in mid-ocean had for him an inexpressible charm.　It was a disappointment to him, aside from his concern for her, that Eleanor did not bear the voyage better. He went into the stateroom at frequent intervals to look after her, busied himself with loving cares and devices to relieve her suffering, but something in her looks, as she lay white and wan on her pillow, baffled him.　He tried to persuade her to rise and go out with him on deck, but she put him off day after day, and gently resisted him.　He was a more patient man with those he loved than with others, but he could poorly brook opposition even here; and, convinced that she was pursuing exactly the wrong course, felt obliged at last to express his disapproval, not harshly but plainly.

"Oh, I know I am disappointing you," she cried out, after one of these attempts of his, making an ineffectual effort to rise, and sinking weakly back, the tears rolling down her cheeks.　"I am nothing but a care to you, I never shall be."

He took her in his arms, quieting and comforting

her. His touch and presence gave her new strength always, and she would not let him leave her. Anxious to please him she made another effort, and rising let him lead her into the open air. He found a sheltered place for her, covered her with rugs, and placed himself at her side.

"Now, is n't this glorious!" he exclaimed in exultant tones, his face aglow with boyish delight in the scene. It was a faultless day, though the season was late, one that retained a hint of Indian summer softness even in mid-ocean; with a clear sky, brilliant sunshine, and sparkling foam-crests on every side. She looked at him with a smile, happy in his enjoyment.

"You like the sea?"

"More than anything else. I ought to have been a sailor."

"Those I have seen have not pleased me very much. I like you better as you are."

"Oh, not a sailor of to-day, with its palatial steamboats and gentlemanly captains; but one of Drake's or Captain Kidd's times. I should have made a splendid pirate."

"Like Byron's Corsair?" she asked with the same shadowy smile, trying to enter into his mood.

"Yes, with Medora in her island tower," was the quick response, leaning fondly towards her. She flushed a little.

"Medora's fate was not a happy one."

"A fig for Byron as a reader of human destiny; a man with only the impulse, not the will, to execute any of his purposes; a poor, whining misanthrope, at best."

She reflected on this a moment.

"What a worshiper you are of the human will," she said at last.

"Why not? It is the one thing that allies man to the gods, the foundation of all character."

"What becomes, then, of the Christian virtues of resignation and submission?" she asked with a little anxiety.

"They are left for the Christians to practice. I never was one, you know." He flashed one of his bright, daring smiles at her as he said this. She was accustomed to hear sentiments of this bold nature drop from his lips, and seemed in no way startled, though not quite satisfied.

"Surely it is necessary for all of us to practice them to some extent."

"Oh, in the arrangement of details, very likely; but there is only one condition of happiness, and that is liberty." He bent his deep, brilliant eyes on her.

It had often seemed to her, as she looked into those luminous depths, that a beautiful spirit looked out in turn, incarnated for a time in flesh, but owning no law save its own free impulse, which moral innocence rendered safe. For it was part of the strange dominion Roger Hunt had over those who believed in him, that this effect of innocence remained even during his most lawless behavior. This was seen in the efforts of friends like Mrs.

Somers to excuse and defend him, and was doubtless due to the absence of anything like grossness
in his nature. Whatever his sins, diseased appetite
did not form their motive. He was a man to whom
all forms of mere physical indulgence were abhor-
rent, one whose good taste would often keep him
safe where his principles failed.

"It is too large and daring a thought for me,"
Eleanor replied to his last words. "I feel as if I
were riding a whirlwind when I try to master it.
It tires me. I am not so strong as you. You will
have to be strong enough for us both."

What lover is insensible to an appeal like this?
This clinging dependence seemed adorable to Roger
in the first flush of the strong manful wish to shield
and direct it. He bent over her with words of rapturous tenderness.

Some of the passengers noticed them, and opinion was confirmed that this was a newly wedded
pair, or an unusually attached one, traveling, it
seemed plain, for the invalid wife's health. Their
wish to keep by themselves had been too manifest
not to be respected, the two winning much sympathetic admiration meanwhile, Eleanor for her delicate beauty and physical weakness, and Roger for
his devotion to her.

Roger had, however, been drawn into slight acquaintance, during Eleanor's confinement to her
berth, with two of his fellow-passengers, a young
married couple from Denver; the woman a bright,
animated young creature full of the novelty and

excitement of her first trip across the ocean, the man, her masculine appendage, big, slow-witted and bashful.

Mr. and Mrs. Frank Devine, Roger gave their names to Eleanor, as the two passed them in their daily promenade on deck, the lady bowing to him with a smile, and turning her eyes with kindly interest on Eleanor, while the two men touched their hats.

"She is coming to speak with you," Roger said.

"No, no," exclaimed Eleanor. "Take me below, Roger. I can't see them."

"Hush," he said, for they were drawing near. At the same time, however, he removed the rugs and assisted Eleanor to rise, drawing her hand through his arm, and steadying her a moment on her feet. The motion of the vessel and the dread of speaking with strangers made her deadly pale.

"Ah, Mr. Hunt, this is a magnificent day, is it not?" a fresh and musical voice spoke in his ear the next instant, while its owner bent another look of friendly interest on his companion and waited to be presented, her husband standing near and looking ill at ease.

Roger made some suitable reply, meantime bestowing a warning pressure on Eleanor's hand, and looking at her steadily a moment as if further to prepare her, before he spoke the words which gave the first public sanction to their stolen relation. He did not use the phrase "my wife." It was not necessary to stretch conscience in the tell-

ing of a falsehood so severely as that, and Roger
had persuaded himself such words contained no
special meaning or merit for either of them. He
contented himself with the formal mention of
names; but when Eleanor heard herself called
"Mrs. Hunt," a vivid flush overspread her face,
and retreating, left it almost ghastly. It was as
if some one had suddenly hissed "Liar! Cheat!"
into her ears. A sick and dizzy feeling nearly
overcame her, and Roger, hurriedly making excuses for her, led her below. If he guessed the
emotions which were really disturbing her he ig-
nored them, assigning only physical causes to this
new attack of weakness, and assisting her back to
her berth. Shame and dread kept her own lips
sealed, and they spoke, when at all, on indifferent
themes.

"Who are they?" she asked after some mention
of their new acquaintances, and lying quietly on
her pillow.

Roger told her the little that he knew. "It is
easy enough to read the story of that marriage," he
added.

She asked him why.

"He married a pretty face, and she, money,"
was the reply. "They have n't an idea in common.
He thinks of nothing but stocks, and already feels
himself in the way when in his wife's presence.
She is trying to cover up her disappointment by
cultivating the arts."

"Where are they going?"

"'Where is she going?' you mean. To Germany, to study music."

"And what will he do?"

"See her comfortably settled, then go back home to make more money for her to spend in ways he cannot share. And there are people who profess to respect such a union as that, who call it holy, who would think it a crime if any one laid hands on it; while ours," he bent over and half raised her in his arms, "ours they would call wicked and impure. Fools! let them say what they like. We know it is false. If love like ours," bending and kissing her with all a lover's warmth, "if love like ours be not its own justification. as true as heaven and as right, then the whole of life is a lie." He spoke with that passionate fervor which always thrilled and convinced her.

"Yes, yes," she murmured, "it is the true life we are trying to lead. Love must be the true guide."

"Spoken like my own brave Eleanor," and he folded her more closely in his arms, sealing his praise with another kiss; then, laying her gently back on the pillow, left her.

"God will forgive us when he knows," her thoughts ran on, prayer-like, when she was alone. "He knows how Roger has suffered, how much he needs me. Oh, help me to be true to him, to be strong for his sake, to make him happy."

Does it strike any one strangely that one so far astray should clothe her thoughts in the form of religious aspiration, still dare raise her petition for divine aid? Devoutness of purpose is not to be measured by an erring judgment, and a soul may retain all its innate purity even when committing so grave a fault as Eleanor's.

VI.

Eleanor Thaxter knew but little of the world.
From childhood she had been unhappily situated,
first in a home provided by an uncongenial step-
father, afterwards in her brother's family, where
poor health obliged her to remain, though she
knew her presence was accounted a burden. She
was not a gifted woman, and but indifferently ed-
ucated, according to present standards, but her
lonely life and a brooding disposition had led her
to think deeply if not clearly on many things. She
had the rare gift of sympathy.

Up to the time of her introduction to the Plato
class, her life in Xenophon had been dull and solitary, making her acquaintance with Roger Hunt
run along with a newly awakened mental life; and
it was with that mixture of pride and humility with
which women acknowledge debts of this kind, she
looked up to this new friend. There had been a
strong mutual attraction between the two from the
first which neither had greatly tried to resist, and
which in natures like theirs comes to acquire a
superstitious quality, compelling reverence where
utmost caution should be used, and making
strength of feeling its guide and sanction as well.

Roger was holding forth in his usual energetic

fashion on some passage in the Symposium, at one of these weekly gatherings, with an earnestness that offended some of his listeners and amused others, and grew more dogmatic as he proceeded, when he caught Eleanor's eyes fastened on him, wistful, admiring, sympathetic. Piqued by the opposition he had met in other quarters, the look at once warmed his heart and fired his imagination. Before this he had taken but passing notice of the new member, but after the formal exercises of the evening were over he drew near and entered into conversation with her. The first words exchanged between them help to explain what followed.

"You did not disagree with me?" he said, fixing her with that large, direct gaze, that always held her like a magnet.

"I? Oh, I am too ignorant. I know almost nothing of the subject," she replied, flushing.

"Still, you did not disagree with me?"

"No, I did not disagree," she replied after a slight pause, with lowered eyes.

"Then I don't care whether the others agreed or not."

She threw a startled glance at him, and drew a little away from him.

"Does my plain speaking offend you? If it does I will go away. I came over here to talk with you, because something told me you were different from the rest; you would understand" —

"Are you trying to convert Miss Thaxter to

your dangerous theories?" Mrs. Somers asked, in a lively tone, stopping near them a moment on her way across the room.

"Miss Thaxter needs no conversion," was the prompt reply, and again they exchanged a deep look, which Eleanor could not long sustain. Mrs. Somers passed on. The company began to break up, and Roger, ascertaining that his companion was without an escort, accompanied her home.

How the acquaintance progressed after that, no one knew. To the two most concerned it seemed at once to have reached the height of a blissful, if unconfessed, understanding. It was of a kind whose outward signs of growth are of little consequence. Sharp as Roger Hunt's experience had been, it had profited him little in some things. He could no more think temperately about his feeling for a woman, hold it at arm's length, while he seriously examined and judged it, than he could refrain from lifting a cup of cold water to his lips when thirsty. And he was always thirsty. His acquaintance with Eleanor was not a week old before he had pronounced her, in his heart, the one woman Nature meant for his own; while she, after a few ineffectual struggles, yielded herself wholly to the thought of him. The absent conventionality of their intercourse was to him the sign of its truth and honesty. The suddenness of this new feeling that had taken possession of them both, was, he argued to Eleanor, proof of its miraculous quality, its heaven-sent nature and mission. He panegyrized it in all the exalted terms he could command, while she listened, borne on the current of his swift, impassioned discourse, as on a resistless river. It could be no accident, he told her, that had thus brought them together. The stars in their courses were not more true to their appointed destiny than he and she in yielding unreservedly to this new power that had seized them so mysteriously. To question or resist it was to violate the holiest injunction of nature. Thus, curiously enough, with a phraseology borrowed from religion, though himself a believer in none of its forms, he compelled her to listen to him. Never was an erring cause defended in loftier discourse, clothed with purer sentiment, or upheld by graver argument than that of this strangely united pair.

To the majority of his acquaintance Roger Hunt was a cold and passionless man, and their surprise at this last action of his was therefore the greater. They did not reflect that a course like his may be inspired less by rebellious blood than an arrogant will.

Like most unpopular men, Roger repaid society in its own coin, holding its average judgments and standards in open scorn. His was a solitary nature, capable of living quite alone if need be, yet sufficiently human to attach itself hungrily to another, whose sympathy and answering regard he was sure of. His acquaintance with Eleanor was no sooner begun than he began to show a dependence on her in a hundred little ways, — ways which

at once thrill and uplift a woman's heart, proud in
the knowledge of her power to serve the man she
loves.   This knowledge in a nature like hers could
but become the basis of an appeal in her own mind
for her lover's rightful claim on her.   His love
was the dearest possession life had ever bestowed.
She was living in a new world.   Gratitude began
to bear down the scales.   It could not be wrong,
she reasoned, to strive to be all she could to one
who was everything to her, whom fate had so un-
kindly treated, whom she could help as no one else
could.

Their voyage at an end, completely separated at
last from all the scenes and associations of the past,
alone together in a foreign clime, living a life of
constant dear dependence on each other, Eleanor
realized in some measure her dream of happiness.
For a time they lived, the world forgetting, and by
the world forgot.   Eleanor's very ignorance and
inexperience stood her in good stead here; making
her dependence on Roger more apparent to both
every day, the source of even more grateful happiness to her than to him, while the strange sights
and events incident to constant travel contributed
to throw a romantic illusion over everything.
From time to time there were moments of startled
recollection and half-wakened memory, such as we
note in sleep, when the knowledge that we are
dreaming pierces through the dream itself, delaying
or abruptly destroying its sweet delusions.   It was
indeed a dreamlike existence she led in these days,

the more easily proved such that she prayed continually never to waken.

Roger seemed thoroughly happy, and this fact did much to stay and comfort Eleanor. His had been the greater sacrifice, she argued; if they had done wrong, the consequences, so far as others were concerned, were far more serious on his side than on hers; yet Roger was content, and therein lay all needed proof that no wrong had been done. He spoke freely and carelessly of the past, like one who had nothing to conceal, while she longed to forget everything but the, passing moment. Had Roger suspected this state of mind in her, he would have taken more pains to spare her feelings on some points; as it was, he often hurt and weakened her in ways he knew nothing of. Yet since his thoughtlessness generally took the form of some new belief in her, or claim upon her love for himself, it never aroused any sense of injury in her.

For example, a more sensitive lover, one, that is, more sensitive in her behalf, would have thought twice before letting her see the letter from Mrs. Somers; but Roger thought only of the surprise it would be to her and the diversion it might afford them both. Eleanor had been a secret and rather passionate admirer of Mrs. Somers, having that feeling towards her which a woman of shy, but aspiring nature often has for another more resolute and self-sustained. If she had had some of Mrs. Somers's self-reliance and courage, she had often told herself, her life would not have been so sorry a failure. That was before she knew Roger. When she mentioned some such feeling to him, he had both chidden and encouraged it.

"Mrs. Somers is a talented woman," he said. "A man could hardly help admiring her, and feeling a certain degree of companionship with her, but he could not love her. Such women neither know how to love nor how to inspire love. A woman's greatest gift," he went on, looking at Eleanor affectionately, "is appreciation. Look through history and show me the man who ever did anything great and fine in the world, and I will show you some loving woman by his side, who believed in him when the world did not, who lived only for him. Can you fancy such a woman in Kitty Somers? She thinks too much of herself."

In a way, Eleanor felt there might be truth in this, still some of the old admiration remained. It touched her deeply to know that this woman she had thought so much of, and made a kind of picture of in imagination, had been kindly disposed towards her, had thought so well of her, indeed, that she wished to make her a sharer in her own pursuits, had stood ready to treat her as a friend and an equal at the very moment when — She could not think of it.

"Why did you show me the letter?" she asked. She spoke with an energy quite new to her. Tears were in her eyes, her voice choked. Roger looked at her in perplexed surprise.

"I thought it would amuse you," he said.

"It does not amuse me to know that people despise me," she said with a little resentment.

"Does the letter say that? I thought it said something quite opposite."

"She despises me now, of course."

"If she does, it is a proof of her ignorance and prejudice. So why should you care?"

"I do care."

"I am sorry." He seemed hurt, and she drew nearer to him with a look of contrition.

"Forgive me, dear, but it — it is so different with a woman. And she was your friend. You liked her, I know. You used to like to talk to her. You valued her good opinion. I have heard you say so many times."

He was silent, partly because he was still a little displeased with this power of the past to rise like a disturbing ghost between them, partly because his own thoughts were busy with the days that were gone.

"Will she despise us?" she urged, looking at him anxiously.

"No; Kitty Somers is a sensible woman."

"Do you mean she will approve of what we have done?" eagerly.

"I did not say that; probably she will deem it her duty to try to think as others do."

By "others" Roger meant her husband, whose letter he had received some time before. Its polite but rather curt tone rankled in him still. He had

had a foolish hope that Kitty Somers would write to him, if only to reproach and repudiate him; but in this he had been disappointed. Everything was over with this pair of friends, he felt, and with more regret than he admitted any other result of his action, but he felt prepared to support the loss.

They remained abroad nearly three years, following the usual round of the tourists, but making long stops at points of principal interest, forming almost no acquaintances and living by themselves. The first few months were given up solely to sight-seeing, and that absorbed attention to each other which in an honester kind of union is called the honeymoon. Then Roger began to long to get back to his literary work. Setting up a study wherever they happened to be, he spent his mornings in writing, meaning to finish a work begun before he left home, a brief monograph on some art topic, and offer it to an English publisher. Eleanor missed him, but rejoiced in a change which placed their lives on a more natural footing. She, too, began to study, working at the languages, and following a course of reading Roger had marked out for her on mediæval history. He rallied her on these self-imposed tasks, declaring she was getting as learned as Vittoria Colonna.

Eleanor was indeed doing her best to saturate herself with the spirit of a foreign age and clime. A careful observer would have noticed a fitfulness in these attempts at mental occupation, and the look of painful self-absorption that rested on her face from time to time. Roger Hunt was not a careful observer, even of the woman he loved, whose changing moods he soon began to notice, but only in relation to himself. Eleanor continued to meet him with a smile, and the old love-light in her eyes, which, for him, hid any deeper expression of suffering or doubt. At times, though, the strained spirit gave way and he was made witness to some strange outburst of pent-up feeling by which he discovered, by degrees, the mixed and struggling nature with which he had to deal.

Man-like, Roger Hunt had done the thing he wished and was careless of what followed. He had burned his ships. Regret that could neither correct nor undo anything involved a waste of time and emotion, and he did not wish to undo anything.

Eleanor, too, had burned her ships, but only to sit disconsolately in the ashes of the ruin she had wrought. There were times when she seemed as helplessly bound to this single deed as a felon to his chain and ball, when the feeling of bondage was so strong that the effort to repress it was maddening, and she could have shrieked aloud. Afraid to think any longer, she would throw herself feverishly into some new task or occupation, copying Roger's manuscripts, and entering eagerly into all his plans; stifling conscience with the remembrance of the irregular careers of most men of genius Roger was so fond of referring to, and supporting herself with the thought that what Leonora was to Tasso and Du Deffand to Hume, she was to the as yet unrecognized man of genius by her side. A certain kind of inspiration, not unlike moral enthusiasm, would sometimes spring from thoughts like these, and for days she would seem to walk on air, to be living what Roger called the life of the spirit. Then would follow the inevitable reaction, a recurring period of doubt and remorse. Thus two years passed and found them at the beginning of the third winter in Naples, where they had been since October.

Here they lived quietly in apartments in one of the dingy but spacious structures belonging to a decayed nobility, and presided over by a Scotch landlady, whose British antecedents forbid the use of any foreign nomenclature in her description. Roger kept up his usual habit of morning study. He had finished his book and realized his dream of an English publisher. It had brought him no money, but had won him some favorable recognition among scholars in his line of work; this, he told Eleanor, proudly, was all he wanted. Both rested content in the thought that if the book had been of a poorer quality it would probably have been more successful. The stay in Naples was prolonged through Roger's interest in some Pompeiian excavations that were going on, his present studies lying in that direction.

One afternoon they paid a visit to a bric-a-brac shop on the Strada San Lucia to examine again some vases of curious workmanship which had attracted Roger's attention. Eleanor, who had but a vicarious interest in matters of this kind, wandered aimlessly about the crowded little room, coming at length on a portfolio of old engravings. Their artistic merit was not much, as even a tyro like herself could see, but the subjects interested her; there was one illustrating a passage in Dante she did not understand, but which attracted her more than the others. Her unsystematic habits of study had left her strangely ignorant on some points, and she put it to one side to consult Roger about it when he should be at liberty. He and the shopkeeper were engaged in a discourse of a character at once learned and bargaining. When it was broken off, to the latter's disappointment, without a purchase, Roger came over to Eleanor's side. She at once asked him to explain the picture. It represented two floating figures, clasped in each other's arms, a strange expression of exalted joy and despair on their faces, the whole scene shrouded in a dim and murky atmosphere. Roger recognized it at once, and frowned slightly. Briefly, and with attempted carelessness, he sketched the story of Francesca da Rimini.

Eleanor then vaguely recalled the legend, bending her eyes with new and painful interest on the faded print.

"They were lovers?" she said in a low tone.

"Yes. Shall we go now?" He had no objections to discussing the subject in all its bearings so far as he himself was concerned, but he dreaded its effect on her.

"Like Lancelot and Guinevere?" she whispered again.

"Like all the noblest loves of all the ages," was the quick reply; "like that of Gemma Donati's husband for his wonderful Beatrice, for that matter," shrugging his shoulders. "Dante need not be so hard on the rest."

"Was he hard on them?" lifting her face anxiously to his. "Did you say this was in the Inferno? Then they are being punished. How does he punish them?"

Roger, who had given a scant account of the story before, now gave her the poet's interpretation.

"'Blown about by furious winds!'" she repeated wonderingly. "'Doomed never to separate!' What a strange punishment!"

"No punishment at all," laughed Roger. "Sour old Dante defeats himself there. They are together, and forever," letting his voice fall. "What do they care for anything else? What are the terrors of hell to them? They carry heaven in their hearts." He seized the hand hanging at her side and pressed it warmly.

She looked at him, and tried to smile, but her eyes were full of vague, troubled appeal.

"It's all the world for love, and the world well lost," he added pressing her hand again. "Love is enough, is it not? I am sure those two thought so."

"Yes, yes, of course," she murmured, pressing closer to him as if for support.

"Now let us leave this musty old shop," he said, tossing the print aside. "It is time for our sunset sail." She followed him reluctantly, looking back at the picture. She wanted to take it with her, but dreaded to speak her wish to him.

They spent the next hour on the water. A blaze of gold and crimson light covered the bay, and made the surrounding heights look like the jeweled setting to a priceless gem, imparting to the entire scene an effect as illusive as it was beautiful. Eleanor sat in the stern of the boat, watching the skies and Roger's skillful handling of the ropes. How ready and accomplished he was about everything, she reflected, and what a helpless creature she was, beside him! He had taught her how to steer, but she did it awkwardly, so that generally he preferred to handle both rudder and sails; an arrangement that pleased her quite as well, for she liked to lie back on the cushions, dreamily noting all that was going on about them, and feeling herself wholly in her lover's hands.

The next morning she paid an early visit, alone, to the little shop, and purchased the print. Taking it home with her, she found a copy of Dante and shut herself in her room. Before long she had mastered both poet's and artist's meaning, and sat lost in troubled thought. So absorbed was she that she did not hear Roger enter the room. He drew near and placed a hand on her shoulder. She started and colored deeply when she saw him, rising from her chair.

He looked displeased when he saw the print again.

"What did you buy that thing for?" he asked rather sharply.

"It—it interested me," she replied, falteringly. "And I thought it might be a help when I came to read Dante."

"It's a poor print," turning the talk to an unimportant phase of the subject. "Did that knavish shopkeeper tell you it was a proof?"

"Oh, no, no. I only paid two florins for it."

"Humph! I don't understand why you want to spend your time poring over such a dismal subject. You had better let Dante alone; Petrarch and Boccaccio will help you much better. Dante's theory of punishment is perfectly fantastic from beginning to end. · The poem is as useless reading as the Arabian Nights, and not half as entertaining."

"Don't you consider Dante a great poet, then?" she asked in surprise.

"I suppose you can call him great," in a grudging tone; "but he belongs as exclusively to his own age as the monks that burned Savonarola. He'll do you no good. You're morbid enough already."

"Am I morbid?" a sensitive flush rising to her face.

"You are the sweetest woman in the world," clasping her in his arms and kissing her. In his heart he was ready to add that she needed looking after like a child, but with a feeling of tender excuse, for he was still at that stage when the protection of her weakness was a dear task. Like most resolute natures, however, he disliked irresolution in others. Not even the knowledge of his own strength, and that chivalric compassion her weakness aroused, could prevent him from growing weary at times of moods he could neither caress nor reason away. He took the print from her and locked it in a drawer, retaining the key, while she looked on with a shamefaced smile. He then tried to gain possession of the book, but here she resisted him.

"I promise it shall not hurt me," she said; then, ashamed of this excess of feeling, "You say it does not teach the truth, yet you are afraid of its effect on me. You must think me very weak-minded."

"Well, yes, sometimes."

"Why do you call his theory of punishment 'fantastic'? It seems to me the symbolism he employs is very real, the leaden hoods for the hypocrites, and the river of blood for the violent."

"It's the most childish literalism!" he exclaimed impatiently. "That notion of arbitrary punishment was exploded long ago."

"But the punishment that is the natural consequence of sin?" she suggested.

"Sin! My dear Eleanor, you talk like the elder of a Presbyterian meeting-house."

"I don't mean sin in the theological sense, but surely we must all admit there is a great deal of evil in the world."

"There is a great deal of ignorance."

"Moral ignorance, you mean?"

"That is only another sign of intellectual deficiency."

"Well," after meditating on this a moment, "it makes no difference. If evil comes only from ignorance, it is all the more pitiful. It should teach us greater charity." She did not ask herself whether it had in his case.

"You won't find much charity in Dante," he said.

"No, he is terrible," with a shudder. "He is merciless, yet he is so true; I mean in some ways. He shows how a wrong action always stays by you. You can never get rid of it!"

"Why should you want to?" Roger asked calmly. "The healthy mind accepts its mistakes along with the rest of experience. Remorse is often the most useless thing in the world, and only another form of self-indulgence."

"Surely we should admit our mistakes?"

"We may admit them, but need not torture ourselves with red-hot irons over them. One mistake is in essence much like another. If I had not made a misstep in my mountain climbing last summer, I should not have been laid up a fortnight with a sprained ankle. But there was no moral guilt in the affair."

"It was dark, and you could not see," she said, excusingly.

"In other words, I was ignorant. It would

have taken your saintly Beatrice a long time to reach so rational a conclusion."

"Don't you like Beatrice, either?" in fresh surprise.

"How can I like a woman who has no blood in her veins! who is made up of pious self-complacency capped with an aureole! Heaven defend me from superior creatures like that!"

"If it's the superiority you object to," she said with a faint smile, "you certainly have reason to be satisfied now. It was not the woman Dante loved, but the redeemed spirit."

"Perhaps so; I don't know much about spirits, 'redeemed' or otherwise. I am content to love the woman," with a look warm but reproachful.

"Yes, dear, I know. You are only too good to me, always. But a woman should stand for the highest and the best to the man who loves her. That is what Beatrice was to Dante. And — and it kills me," her voice breaking, "to think I have not been that — that it was I who helped you to do wrong, that" — She was past speaking now, even had he not quickly checked her.

"Not a word more of that," he said, and with an effort she controlled herself.

"You help me to do wrong!" he repeated. "There was no wrong about it! It was you who made it possible for me to live!"

"Oh, is it true, dear? That is what I want to believe! There is nothing in the world I want to believe so much as that!"

" ' Want to believe !' What a singular expression! Why will you give way to these childish
fancies, Eleanor?   Do you love me?" raising his
head proudly.

"Do I love you?"

"Then I don't understand this talk about believing and wanting to believe.   Love makes its
own beliefs, as it does its own laws.   When it can
no longer do this, it has ceased to be love."

This was the point which their discussions always
reached, beyond which Eleanor dared not press her
thoughts, where to question was to differ.   She
could only stammer some words of lame excuse,
admitting her weakness and promising amendment.

"If you love me, you should trust me," Roger
continued, in reply to some new protestation from
her.

"So I do," reproachfully.   "Who else is there
for me to trust?   I have no one in the wide world
but you."

He took her in his arms.   "Yet you have moments of being sorry you have me.   Your courage
fails you, and you repent " —

"I repent of nothing," she said hurriedly.

"How do you suppose a man feels when he asks
a woman to do what you have done, and discovers
that instead of making her happiness he has killed
it?"

"You have not killed my happiness!   I never
dreamed of the possibility of happiness until I saw
you.   I am the most ungrateful woman in the

world.   Do forgive me," and she pressed nearer to him.

"It is only because I get so tired," she said, with a sigh, after she had grown quieter and the kiss of peace had been exchanged.   "I can't think things out."

"Stop trying.   You torture yourself worse than any anchorite of the Middle Ages, and about problems that are as useless."   He smiled as he spoke, relieving the words of their harshness.

"I promise, I promise.   Here, take the book and put it away," picking up the volume from the table and thrusting it on him.   "I never want to see it again.   After this I will think only of you, and how to make you happy."   He looked pleased at this, and kissed her again.

"If you wish me to be happy, you have only to be so yourself."   The condition sounded very simple.

"Now, bathe your eyes and come down to lunch. Flora McDonald," Roger's pet name for their Scotch landlady, "has concocted a new dish for us, a villainous mess of greens, which must have exhausted their evil intent in their looks, so I think we can eat them with impunity.   This afternoon we will go and take a look at old San Martino."

VII.

On their way to the old monastery, which is now owned by the government and put to secular uses as a museum, Roger and Eleanor passed through the great market square, the Piazza del Marcato, which, as it happened to be market-day, presented a lively scene, one the passing tourist is glad to catch sight of. The square was lined with gayly adorned booths; the lemonade merchant's stall, garlanded with yellow fruit, standing next to the inevitable macaroni stand, with strings of drying paste that looked at a distance like dirty colored yarn. Groups of half-naked lazzaroni lay in sunny spots, stretching out dirty hands for alms, for this was before their banishment to the region of the Malo Grande on the coast, though still at that point in their career which Dumas describes as one of decadence, marked by the obligation to wear a single garment.

The scene was a familiar one, and they would gladly have avoided it had they remembered the day, though once within it they found much to interest and amuse them. Passing by one of the fountains which decorate the open space, the Fontana di Masaniello, Roger repeated the story told in the guide-books of young Tommaso of Amalfi, dating from the middle of the seventeenth century, who, in rage over the fine of one hundred ducats imposed against his wife for smuggling a small package of flour into the city during one of the numerous sieges of war, roused his oppressed countrymen to revolt; the uprising, after a brief period of success, ending in the young leader's death. The legend was of the kind that always aroused the narrator's enthusiasm. Soon after they paused to watch a young girl dancing the tarentella. She had all the traditional beauty of her race, dusky skin, through which the red blood glowed, dark, melting eyes and supple limbs. Eleanor looked on with a sense of discomfort, but Roger was a true cosmopolite, and watched the dancer's agile and sinuous motions with delight. Catching sight of him, she flung out her limbs in a few wild contortions as a finale, and eagerly pushing her way through the crowd, dropped on one knee at his feet, extending her tambourine for the performance's payment, an expression of cunning greed sharpening the face that had looked so joyous and innocent before. Roger was displeased, the illusion was destroyed. He dropped a coin into the tambourine and drew Eleanor away.

"These Neapolitans are the most avaricious people under the sun; they do everything for money, nowadays."

They passed out of the square through a small gate near the church of San Eligio, commemorating the patron saint of the workers in metals.

"I did n't know they ever canonized any one except for some religious deed," said Eleanor.

"Sometimes they make a slip in another direction. The church's progress, such as she has attained, is marked by her mistakes."

The little gate was surmounted with two heads, recording the judgment of Isabella of Aragon, back in the early part of the sixteenth century, against a dissolute member of the Caraccioli family, compelling him to marry the girl he had ruined, and then beheading him in his bride's presence; a verdict Roger warmly commended, discussing the subject with the same impersonal interest he would the dome of St. Peter's.

They were obliged to pass through one of the poorer back streets to reach the point from which they wished to ascend to the upper part of the city. The pavement swarmed with children, who looked up at the passers-by with cherubic faces and Raphael's heavenly eyes. In the door-ways sat the mothers, engaged in some household task and gossiping with each other.

"How beautiful these Italian children are!" said Eleanor. "Yet how quickly they change, and grow coarse and common, especially the girls."

"That is because they have no minds," Roger replied.

"Yes, it must be so." She had never thought of it before, but the answer pleased her beyond its literal meaning. Most men, she reflected, do not care whether a woman has a mind or not, but it was not so with Roger; this was to her another sign of that goodness she wanted most of all to believe in, that ideality of purpose which, in spite of appearances, she knew ruled all his actions.

They were near the end of the close, ill-smelling street, when they saw a large, swarthy-skinned woman sitting in front of one of the houses, mending a fishing-net, a group of children playing at her feet.

"Here is Donna Maria," said Roger, in a low tone, half amused, half vexed. "Now for some theatricals."

At the same moment the woman looked up and recognized them, springing to her feet and coming to meet them, calling the children in delighted tones. She greeted them with the national effusion, and continued to pour a stream of voluble talk on them, her large figure, with the children clinging to her skirts, quite blocking their progress. In a few minutes Roger was in possession of the entire family history since their last meeting, interlarded with repeated fervent thanks for some past benefit, and ending in a shower of blessings for himself and the sweet lady.

Roger's relation to Donna Maria was one that did him credit. Soon after their arrival in Naples he had started on a foot excursion to San Martino alone, passing through this same street. Drawing near Donna Maria's house, he heard the sound of violent blows within, and a child's piercing shrieks. Without thought of consequences he rushed inside,

and saw a sickening sight, which at the same time
made his blood boil.   A big brute of a man was
beating a child of about four years with a large
stick, while the latter lay writhing and screaming
on the floor.   In a corner, huddled together, their
faces blanched with fear, and guarded by a young
girl of sixteen, stood the other children of the
household, crying and covering their eyes from
the scene.   Near the infuriated man stood his wife,
imploring and berating him in turn, careless of
the bloody cuts she had herself received on neck
and face.   In physical stature Roger looked like a
boy beside this giant, whose face was swelled and
purple with rage, and whose brawny arm was
raised for another blow.   He sprang forward and
wrested the stick from the man's hands, and with
it pointed the master of the house to his own door.
With blazing eyes and fixed countenance, he looked
the impersonation of a strength dependent on no
material aid, as fearless as it was just.   The man
swore a little and threatened, but Roger's look
cowed him, and he slowly shuffled outside; while
the mother hastily gathered the crying child in her
arms.   From her Roger learned the history of the
affair, no unusual tale, so far as the incidents already revealed, in the lives of poverty and brutal-
ity abounding in this quarter; but containing one
more shameful feature still, which Roger learned
of by degrees.

Lisa, the oldest daughter, sixteen only, but
woman grown in this clime, was betrothed to one

Antonio, a young boatman on the bay below. All was going well, when a young English traveler, old in the practice of the criminal passions that ruled him, let a pair of wanton eyes fall on the girl as she stood in the market square; waylaying her shortly after, he made an insulting proposal to her. Frightened and indignant, she sought her parents' protection, but into her father's face as he listened, crept an evil look. He boldly sought out the English visitor, and came to terms with him. It was the revolt caused by the news of this bargain, made known to mother and daughter, their tears, entreaties, and threats of exposure, which led to the scene Roger had disturbed.

His rage was now at white heat, and he took the case into his own hands. He took Lisa home with him, and placed her in Eleanor's care. Then he sought out the young Englishman. St. Michael, armed with invincible power, did not more swiftly descend upon the dragon than Roger swooped down on his unsuspecting victim. Judge, witness, and advocate, in one, he stood before him with blazing eyes and lashing tongue; and as he had ordered Donna Maria's husband from his own house, so he ordered the young reprobate to leave Naples within twelve hours.

The righteousness of his cause was proved by the prompt obedience he received in both cases. Not content with this, Roger sought out the town authorities, and even consulted with the American consul, for it was necessary to spend his newly gathered energies in some direction. The consul talked pacifically of climatic influences in the formation of national types, and invited Roger to dinner. The girl Lisa stayed with her new protectors until her marriage, which was soon after arranged. About the same time her father was impressed into the king's service, and Roger became, in a sense, the family guardian.

Donna Maria wept copiously at parting with her lord, and tried to persuade Roger to procure his release, but he told her she was well rid of him, and that he deserved to be shot in his first battle. She detained him now to tell the last news of him, praising and complaining of him in a breath. The children hung about, raising seraphic eyes to Eleanor and shyly stretching out their little hands to touch her dress. Breaking away at last, they pursued their journey. Eleanor had not felt so happy in a long time, as in this renewed testimony of Roger's courage and generosity. Her face glowed with grateful light, and she hung fondly on his arm.

"That woman will never forget you. She grows more grateful every day, I think."

"Consul Foster would tell you it was only the climate," Roger laughed in reply, "and I begin to think myself, that the Donna's gratitude is of the kind some one has described as 'a lively sense of benefits to come.' She keeps begging me to get her husband home."

"Do you suppose she loves him still?" Eleanor asked.

"Oh, these people love as they eat; like the animals they are."

"Yes. She seems to have no conception of the outrage he meant to practice on his daughter."

"No, you couldn't expect that."

"What was it she said of Lisa?" Eleanor's Italian was not as good as Roger's.

"She and Antonio have gone to work on a vineyard near Sorrento. Perhaps Antonio thinks life on the water too uncertain for a married man. They are expecting a boy, and wishing they knew how to Italianize the name of Hunt." An inscrutable expression swept over Eleanor's face, and she made no reply. She was tired, and when they reached the place where they were to begin the ascent, Roger called one of the boys who stood waiting with a donkey, and placed her on it. He himself was a famous walker and tramped on by her side.

They did not go inside the monastery, but were content to-day to admire its noble proportions from a distance, seating themselves on the greensward to rest. Roger stretched himself at full length, drew his hat over his eyes to shield them from the descending sun, and fell asleep. Eleanor sat beside him, looking out over the crowded roofs of the town to the blue distances of the bay beyond. Vesuvius's pillar of smoke rose slowly on their left. As she sat there, unobserved, the bright look her face had worn when they left Donna Maria slowly faded, and the old expression of care returned.

It seems a wretched fatality that natures most prone to suffering should be continually finding new cause for it; yet science could explain this, as she does the readiness of water to run down hill, on the principle of least resistance. Eleanor's powers of resistance had never been great, and lately threatened to desert her entirely. Before her discovery of the picture, her doubts had been of a remote intangible order, depressing the heart, but taking no definite shape in thought; now they began to present themselves in concrete questions she could neither answer nor set aside. Worse than this, it was not her own weak, untaught power of reasoning that had failed her, alone, but Roger's too began to appear inconclusive on some points. Eleanor was in that pitiable state which hero-worshipers must all reach sooner or later. She had chosen a judgment as mortal as her own for her final court of appeal, pinned her faith to one as human as herself. No lover however generous and tender, no friend however wise and strong, can bear the test it was Eleanor's necessity to impose on Roger. Had their relation been of a more natural order, the need to believe him perfect would not have been so great.

As her thoughts went back to the banished picture and the story of the doomed lovers, she said to herself that Roger was wrong. It would be a punishment to be bound to each other like that, never to loosen those clinging arms, supporting each other in a mad whirl of passionate impulse and desire, to read in love's glance no innocent joy or safety, only the shame of its own misdoing.

Eleanor had been taught by Roger to glorify feeling, to exalt it above every other motive of conduct; but here in a half dozen lines an old dead poet had shown her how the right to feel may be as dishonestly indulged as the right to eat and drink, how feeling has as much power to enslave and degrade as to purify and liberate. Roger talked of the sweets of liberty with an eloquent tongue, but Dante showed how there is a liberty that leads to moral bondage worse than death.

From loving each other in that wild sweet way, it was easy to see how this helpless pair might come to hate and spurn each other, or at least loathe the love that can only weaken and destroy, long for hate's reviving power. Yet their dark deed binds them together, and forever. That is what Dante meant, said Eleanor to herself. "Eternity" is the dread word written on every page of the Inferno. That was what she meant when she said to Roger that he showed how a bad action always stays by you. Obedience is the first great law of the universe. Obedience to what? Eleanor did not know ; but she was beginning to know the loss and desolation disobedience brings. She sat in darkness, though the landscape was bathed in golden sunlight. The day was warm, but she shivered. A numb despair crept over her ; yet she remained intensely quiet. A passer-by would only have seen a woman sitting on the ground, her hands clasped over one knee; wondering a little, perhaps, at the intent, strained look in the eyes fixed on the distant horizon. By her side Roger slept quietly.

VIII.

WE are creatures of moods, the most self-consistent of us. Our mental maladies, like our physical, have their seasons of ebb and flow, their fluctuations, periods of climax, and slow return to more normal conditions. The spirit, as well as the body, can bear only its degree of suffering, then it breaks; or, more often, reaction takes place, and it bounds back, through some impulsive energy of its own, into the realm of hope and happy activity again.

Even as she sat there on the wooded slope overlooking Italy's fairest landscape, lost in despairing thoughts, Eleanor felt something within give way, as if a strained nerve had snapped, only the sensation that followed was one of strange, merciful relief. Pain was glutted and had released his hold. Remorse was weary and ceased to importune her.

Physically she herself was more weary than before, and wakened Roger to tell him so and ask him to take her home; but the sudden cessation of pain within seemed like a new and positive strength gained, and she felt almost light-hearted again. She talked in a cheerful strain to Roger as he led her down the path, though she leaned heavily on his arm.

Once more, warned by this experience, she threw herself into the tasks that would keep her near him. She strove heroically to banish all intruding memories, to throttle certain thoughts and fancies at their birth, to think of nothing but the present hour. Roger had told her that to make him happy she had only to be happy herself. ⸲ The condition was one a loving woman ought to be able easily to satisfy, she told herself. Roger, she knew, thought so. She was beginning to be a little afraid of Roger, for as she studied him she saw how, not his happiness alone, but his love was dependent on the condition named. She saw how these variable moods of hers wearied him; and as her power to suffer grew, she felt her hold on him loosen.

Roger Hunt had suffered some deep disappointments in the personal relations of life, which, aside from the question of his own accountability, had left a permanent impress on his character, imparting a distrust of his kind that even Eleanor must to a degree suffer from. He bore these disappointments with melancholy pride. If Eleanor, he reasoned, should fail him, prove unequal to the thing she had undertakn, to his high demand of her, as he phrased it, show herself a creature of small womanish fears like the rest of her sex, it would not be strange, perhaps; he would try not to blame her; but he declined in advance to hold himself responsible for the consequences. Thoughts like these she was beginning to read, in things of small but significant import; his own changeable manner, with a tendency to irritability, mysterious words dropped now and then, long periods of silence, the waning freshness and spontaneity of the entire relation between them.

They had reached that period which married people, secure in the naturalness of the tie that unites them, dare call by its right name, the "settling-down" period; but which, in a connection of this kind, is full of danger. With shame, that reached at times moral abasement, and with quickened fears on all sides, Eleanor began to recognize how frail was the bond between Roger and herself. She was not afraid of any open act of injustice, but every day showed her more clearly how this stolen Eden of theirs must be guarded at every point. They had purchased their coveted liberty, but at the cost of every moment's natural ease and security. They talked of living the true life, guided only by their own sense of right, scorning lower and more commonplace standards, but the event was proving that their life was no simpler and truer than those they looked down on among people who obeyed the laws and lived as their neighbors did. Appearances must be kept up here as elsewhere. Eleanor was given to understand she must be happy.

The winter months passed, and they lived on, quietly still, but not so entirely by themselves as before, Roger having made a few acquaintances among scholars, native and foreign, engaged in lines of work similar to his own, and suffering himself to be introduced to a small circle of literary and artistic people presided over by Lady Mandel, a resident English woman of middle age, intellectual tastes, and checkered history.

Roger's willingness to avail himself of social privileges of this sort was one of the most marked signs of change in him, of lessening dependence on her, which Eleanor observed with apprehension, but with a degree of relief also. Once or twice she had accompanied him to Lady Mandel's fortnightly reunions, but the effort to enter into occasions of this kind was most difficult. Her nature was very shy, under the kindest circumstances, and here, where she felt herself so falsely placed, her embarrassment increased, and reached the point of dullness. Added to this was the displeasure she could not but feel in the free speech and manner of her cigarette-loving hostess, nearly all of whose guests were men, and a hurt, puzzled surprise that Roger should care to be one of them.

Strangers were always coming and going at Lady Mandel's, where generous hospitality reigned, and one was always certain to meet some people of "more or less importance in their day," as well as curious visitors and idle hangers-on. On the evening of Eleanor's last attendance, at a rather late hour, the little circle was pleasantly agitated by the entrance of a young American pair, just arrived in Naples, and making the regulation tour of the peninsula. Eleanor recognized them at once, with quickened pulse and a strong wish to escape;

their steamer acquaintances, Mr. and Mrs. Frank Devine of Denver. Roger, absorbed in an erudite discussion with a German professor on the nature of Tyrian purple, did not notice them until he heard his name spoken in accents of pleased surprise by the lady. She greeted him in the demonstrative fashion of her age and country, exclaiming anew her surprise, asking innumerable questions, and congratulating herself on her good fortune; for now Professor Hunt would tell them all about Naples, what to see and how to set about it. They could only stay three days! The speaker used the title instinctively, and let the one with whom she favored it see that she regarded him as a most fortunate find. Eleanor could see that Roger, too, was pleased. He professed himself happy to be Mrs. Devine's escort wherever she liked.

"And you are going to 'do' Naples in three days?" he said, with a teasing smile.

"That is all we can spare. Is n't it enough?" she asked anxiously; then, pouting a little at his look of amusement, "I don't see how we can give Naples more than three days, when we only gave Florence a week."

"No, of course not," said Roger, sympathetically. "You must n't upset the ethics of the traveling public like that. The author of Murray would have to rewrite his guide-book."

"Now you are making fun of me;" but he assured her he regarded her coming as a great boon. There were many points in Naples he had not yet

visited himself. He made an engagement to accompany her to Virgil's tomb, and the grotto of
Posilippo.   Then there was the drive to St. Elmo,
the Pompeiian collection in the Museo Borbonica,
sail across the bay to Capri, etc., etc.   There was
a little ironic laughter in Roger's eyes as he enu-
merated these well-known points, which the conventional tourist never misses.   Mr. Devine was
presumably included in these engagements, though
he neither spoke nor was spoken to.   Roger ended
by telling her that she must not ask him to take
her to the cave of the Cumæan sibyl.

"Why not?" she asked.

"No man has ventured to accompany a woman
there since Æneas met his fate."

She laughed at this, but feebly, not in the least
understanding him, then frankly admitted her ignorance, and asked him to explain.   He told her
the legend of the sibyl who practiced her wily arts
on the hero, leading him to his untimely end, and
sacrificing him to the infernal gods.   She laughed
again, understandingly.

"But you do not believe in the gods," she said.

"How do you know that?" he asked, raising his
eyebrows.

"Oh, I remember some of our talks on the
steamer."

Here she turned and included Eleanor in her
glance.   "Professor Hunt fairly overwhelmed me
with his knowledge, on all manner of subjects.
He made me quite afraid of him."

"You do not appear so now," said Roger. "I suspect I have some reason to be afraid of you."

"You have, indeed; has n't he, Frank?" turning to her husband, who still stood in an attitude of patient attendance at her side. "Poor Mr. Devine!" she added to Roger in pretended aside. "He is tired to death of traveling. He came after me last spring, and we 've been going about ever since. He hates Europe, and I know never means to let me come over again. That is the reason I must improve my time now."

Her husband made no response to this, looking stolidly before him. Roger cast a careless glance at him, then brought his eyes back to the one addressing him. Eleanor felt sorry for the young man, and making an effort, addressed a few words to him; but conversation proved difficult, and soon the two were again listening to the lively dialogue of their more brilliant mates. Eleanor overheard Roger making an engagement to meet Mrs. Devine and her husband at the chapel of San Gennaro. He ended with an invitation to them to return home with him for dinner, glancing casually but meaningly at Eleanor. Mrs. Devine was profuse in her thanks, but looked to Eleanor to confirm this invitation. The latter flushed and hesitated, then stammeringly said that she should be very happy. Her embarrassment was too manifest not to be noticed, and was punished with a cold response from the younger woman, whose manner had a touch of additional brightness and warmth

when she turned again towards Roger. She repeated that she wanted to see everything, and feli-
citated herself anew on the valuable assistance she
was to receive from him, again addressing him as
"Professor."

Roger felt he had borne this pleasant infliction
long enough.

"I am not a professor," he corrected her.

"You are not?" with flattering surprise. "But
I am sure you ought to be."

"Thank you. I might consent to receive the
title at your hands." Eleanor looked at him in
some surprise. She had not seen him in such good
spirits for a long time. Mrs. Devine laughed and
said she would wait until he had proved how much
he knew about Naples. "I supposed every one
here was professor," she said, glancing about her.
"Tell me," she added, moving a step nearer to
Roger, and speaking in a lowered tone, "did we
do right to come here? I heard about Lady Mandel in Vienna. My music-teacher gave me a letter, but Mr. Devine does n't like him, and did n't
want to bring me. He will feel differently about
it now, though, since we have found you here."

Even Roger was not proof against a fleeting embarrassment here. He smiled queerly and glanced
at Eleanor. She had overheard, and a vivid flush
dyed her face. Mr. Devine had moved a little to
one side, relieving himself from a conversation in
which he could find no share, by pretending to examine some engravings on a small table near by.

"Don't ask me," Roger replied, recovering himself. "I know nothing about any of your conventionalities, and care less."

"You literary people are so independent," the lady sighed.

Eleanor could bear the situation no longer and rose nervously to her feet, stepping forward and asking Roger, rather abruptly, to take her home. He looked surprised and a little displeased, but consented. She turned to Mrs. Devine with a few words of apology, but the latter was still a little hurt and distrustful, and took leave of her coldly.

"So *la belle Américaine* is a friend of yours?" Roger's hostess said to him, as they stood together a moment, while Eleanor was putting on her wrap. "How do you manage to grow so many handsome girls over there?"

"Is she handsome?" he asked, in some distaste. "I had not noticed."

"You had not noticed! Humph! Then if you have no eye for a pretty woman when you see her, it 's to be hoped you have none, either, for an ugly one. Some of us can get a little comfort out of that."

Roger made no reply, not telling her whether this reasoning applied or not. He found Lady Mandel undeniably coarse and offensive at times.

"Your compatriot is not only beautiful but talented. Herr Rosenthal writes me she might make her mark as a pianiste if she chose, but," shrugging her shoulders, "what can you expect? She has a husband, and he is rich. It is money spoils all of you Americans. You are worshipers of the Golden Calf, — not you, perhaps," she added, with a contemplative gaze. "You are a dreamer. You live in the clouds."

"The clouds are of a rather earthly manufacture, just now," he replied glancing through the smoke-filled rooms.

"They will do you no harm if they are," she retorted. "You are the first man I ever knew, of brains, I mean, who objected to tobacco smoke."

"Thank you; the cause progresses slowly, I admit."

"And as for a lady's smoking," waving her piece of cigarette, nearly extinguished, "I suppose such a conception never entered your mind until you came here."

He felt like asking her what reason there was to suppose it entered his mind then, but forbore, and, seeing Eleanor waiting, bade her good evening.

When they reached home he was about to leave her for an hour's reading in his study, when she detained him.

"Roger, I want to speak with you a moment."

He had taken a lamp in his hand, and stood holding it, with his face partly turned towards her, waiting.

"Roger," speaking with difficulty, "that lady — Mrs. Devine — must not come here. We must not let her."

"Indeed! Why?" he asked coldly.

"It would make her husband very angry; he would have a right to be angry."

"What do I care for her husband?"

"She would be angry, too. She would never forgive us. We must not take advantage of any one, Roger. It would not be right."

"You and I have different notions of right, sometimes."

"Roger, I beg you to grant my wish. Do not compel me to receive her. You know she would not come — if she knew. No woman would" — Her voice broke.

"If she knew what?" he demanded. "If you think there is anything in my past life I am ashamed of" —

"It is not that. But," rising and going towards him and laying a hand on his arm, "we must not do any one a wrong, even though we feel it to be a fancied wrong only. I never knew you to want to deceive any one, Roger."

The last words had their effect, but he would not admit it to her. For a moment he stood with his eyes bent frowningly on the floor, then turned abruptly and left her, without a word. She heard him close the study door, and went wearily to her room, too much oppressed with weightier matters to feel hurt at his manner, and relieved to be by herself.

The next day Roger kept his appointment, but took his new friends to a popular café to dine, excusing the non-fulfillment of the first arrangement on the convenient pretext of Eleanor's poor health. Mrs. Devine received his apologies with apparent good nature, but the acquaintance had received a perceptible check, and the next time they met her manner was more formal, arousing a little resentment on Roger's side, who was glad when the travelers had finished Naples and gone on their way. He continued, however, to cherish a slight grudge against Eleanor. He could not persuade her to accompany him again to Lady Mandel's.

"What is it you are afraid of?" he asked her once, while arguing the case with her.

"I did not say I was afraid. But I can't go, Roger; I can't meet those peeople. Don't ask me, dear. Don't think I don't want you to go; I am so glad you can have a little society. But I — I don't need it. I have you," smiling bravely up at him, through unshed tears.

"You forget that I have to answer all sorts of questions about you."

"Questions?" she repeated in some alarm. "Do you mean that people are talking about us, that they suspect" — She could not go on, and turned a little away from him.

"Suspects! Who cares what anybody suspects? My dear Eleanor, can't you put a little more breadth into some of your ideas? We are not living in a New England village, nor expected to carry a copy of the decalogue into a social drawing-room. For that matter, there are reasons why Lady Mandel need not be very scrupulous in such matters. There are some not very nice stories afloat about her."

He had overreached himself here. Quickly the retort rose to her lips: "Is that the reason you think her a fit companion for me?" but she suppressed it. She remained gently obstinate to all his arguments and entreaties, however, and he soon formed the habit of going without her. She was glad to have him go, though often lonely in his absence. She had all a loving wife's power of self-abnegation, and though she had once been first in all his thoughts, submitted now to be made second in many ways. She had learned that no two people, however dear, are wholly sufficient to each other's needs; that the hunger for human companionship is manifold, and must feed on many lesser loves as well as on one that is supreme. There were times when to feel herself restored to simple natural relations with the world, she could have foregone the most rapturous bliss she had ever tasted in this unhallowed relation. She was like one who has fed on sweets, until the palate longs for a taste of homelier fare, which it cannot gratify because the chance of its honest earning is lost.

Eleanor was feeling, with relief, that the question of her social duties was settled, when Roger came home one day and told her, with a pleased look, he had met an old friend, one of his former townsmen, Henry Hamilton. Eleanor tried to place the name, but could not.

"Don't you remember Hamilton, that little shy man we used to meet at Mrs. Somers's?"

Yes, she remembered now, but indistinctly still.

"He was immensely glad to see me. He always liked me. There's a lot of sense and good feeling in the little fellow. Usually it's a bore running across old acquaintances in that way, but I declare, I believe I was rather glad to see Hamilton."

Eleanor listened with a sympathetic face.

"Is he married?" she asked after a while, an inevitable question with her, sooner or later.

"He's married, with a vengeance."

"Was Mrs. Hamilton a member of the Plato class?"

"She! She would as soon join a burlesque opera troupe. A most unbearable woman!"

"Is she with her husband?" Eleanor asked, gathering some other meaning in his words than lay on the surface.

"Of course. You don't suppose she'd let him come to Europe without her. She gave me the cut direct." He tried to speak with airy indifference.

"Did n't she speak to you?" Eleanor asked in a concerned tone.

"What do I care if she did n't? Such a woman makes virtue detestable. She has n't an idea that is n't a prejudice, nor a conviction that is n't founded on some kind of antipathy! I pity Hamilton from the bottom of my heart."

"I am afraid she thinks there is reason for some prejudice in this case."

"She may think what she pleases." Eleanor knew he was as indifferent as he seemed. She looked at him wonderingly, envying, as she had many times before, that strength of purpose, that having once asserted itself, can stand upright, without one backward look. To his dying day Roger would feel about this act of theirs as he did the hour it was resolved on.

"I suppose most of our acquaintances would have behaved as she did," she said thoughtfully.

"Very likely."

"Mr. Hamilton did not?"

"No! He is a gentleman. He is not one of the self-appointed guardians of the universe, like his wife; he knows how to keep his opinions until they 're asked for. That 's all I ask of any man. I invited him to dine with us to-morrow."

"Roger!"

"Well?"

"Without his wife?"

"You don't suppose I asked him with his wife?"

"I — I can't receive him, Roger."

"May I ask why?" in the voice and manner she had learned to dread.

"I can't act as hostess to your gentlemen friends."

"This is very mysterious. You could not receive Mrs. Devine because she was a woman."

"Surely you must see, dear, that if I cannot receive women, I ought not to receive men."

"These refinements are beyond me."

Voice, words, and manner hurt her deeply; but evidently his failure to understand was perfectly honest. He would not, she believed, draw her into any situation that would convey a slighting opinion on his part. He surrounded her with every possible care and attention in other respects, but failed entirely to comprehend matters of this kind. It was because he himself was so strong and fearless, she tried to think, that all signs of weakness in others irritated him.

"It — it hurts me, Roger, that you do not see how I feel about some things; but I know you do not mean it. I will receive your friend, since you wish it."

"I wish you to do nothing," he replied coldly; "you have not the courage to stand by afterward. We have had enough of that. When two people undertake what you and I have undertaken, the least they can do is to try to live up to it."

"'Live up to it!'" she exclaimed, the last barriers of restraint and caution giving way. "You ask me to live down to it, I think."

She broke away from him abruptly and left the room, locking herself in her chamber, where she cried herself into a blinding headache, which kept her in bed the next day, and furnished the excuse for her non-appearance when the expected guest came.

Roger was more deeply displeased with her than ever before, and treated her for days with marked coldness. Gradually, however, the affair seemed to pass. Each kept a shamed remembrance of it, and felt the discouragement it offered to the future, but they were growing dulled to these experiences. Eleanor exerted herself with fresh and contrite energy to uphold their tottering happiness, to please Roger in ways it was easy to please; but the strained expression of her face, the eager restlessness of all her movements, the bright spot of color that came and went in the thin cheeks, all spoke of a strength upheld by failing sources within. Still, she tried.

Some time before this incident they had planned a series of short excursions to neighboring points, one of which was to be a three days' visit to the ruins of Pæstum, which Roger wished to examine. Eleanor was in more cheerful spirits than she had been for a long time, as she completed the preparations for their departure. The clouds were lifting a little, she thought. Roger had been more kind to her for the past few days, and she had been able to banish distracting thoughts, and devote herself wholly to him. She had spent the morning copying for him, and he had teased her, as he used to do, about her long, slanting hand. He was a better penman than she, and it was but a feigned service she rendered him in this way, one of the pretty deceptions of their earlier days, but that only proved Roger's goodness the more. She went to bed early that she might get the full rest she needed, and fell into a sound sleep that lasted until morning.

Some malign spirit must have watched beside her, for she awoke unrefreshed, with a dull headache, and the feeling, she knew so well, of sick depression at the heart. It was as if she found herself suddenly prostrated with some old malady. She rose and dressed, but the depressed feeling still clung to her like cold mist. All the old motives, her desire to please Roger, the fear of losing his love, had faded and were naught. She had neither will nor desire for anything. She listened to Roger's talk at the breakfast-table with dull ears, and followed his preparations to depart with slow indecision.

At last, when he was ready, with hat in hand, and valise strapped over his shoulder, she paused in the act of putting on her bonnet, and laid it down.

"Could n't you go without me?"

He looked at her in surprise.

"I — I don't feel very well," she added in a little confusion.

"Then we will both stay at home, and take another day." The tone was kind, but he showed some natural disappointment.

"No, no. There is no reason why you should not go." She spoke with the faintest touch of irritation. She now saw that what she really wanted was to be alone.

"I don't think I care much about ruins, anyway," she added, trying to smile.

"Your feeling has changed since last night; but

of course, if you are not well" — He swung the valise from his shoulder.

"No, no," she urged him again. "You must not stay. There is no need. I want you to go." The last words were spoken in an insistent tone she seldom used, and he looked at her attentively.

"I mean I don't want you to be disappointed." He set the valise on the floor.

"Very well, then," with a little petulance, " if you are so determined, I will go," and she took up her bonnet with an aggrieved air.

"I must say I don't understand this," said Roger. "If you mean that you want to get rid of me " —

She made no reply, feeling displeased in a new direction. He did not often speak so coarsely.

"You need n't go," he added sarcastically, as she began tying her bonnet strings, "for I shall."

He lifted the valise and flung it over his shoulder again. She dropped her hands, and looked at him helplessly.

"You know I did n't mean that; I only meant I ought not to spoil your pleasure. I don't see why I should go if I don't want to."

"You need n't."

"I mean, I don't see why you should care whether I go or not."

"Very well. I won't care." He adjusted the strap more securely on his shoulder. She looked at him tremblingly, then sinking into a chair, broke into tears. He would not look at her at first, and was strongly tempted to leave the room; but half maddened by her sobs and the uselessness of the entire scene, he drew near and looked down on her with a face of mingled bewilderment and blame. Her tears flowed faster.

"Eleanor, what is the matter?"

"Nothing," hiding her face convulsively in her handkerchief. Lifting it again she looked at him wildly. "Everything," she broke out impetuously, waving him away. "Everything."

He bit his lip, and turned sharply from her. Again the impulse seized him to leave her and go on his way, but he dared not, and came reluctantly back to her side. She grew a little quieter.

"Oh, go without me," she said, looking up at him, tears still running down her cheeks. "I deserve you should. I deserve you should never care for me again."

He schooled himself to patience, and sat down near her. Soon she checked her tears, and looked at him penitently.

"I will bathe my eyes and then we will go," and she started to rise. He placed his hand on her arm.

"You cannot go now."

"It is not too late," she urged, looking ashamed.

"You are in no condition to go. It will give you a headache."

She had that already, but did not say so.

"I can't bear to disappoint you so," she murmured.

"You need n't disappoint me. I 'll do what I can to help you not to," with a melancholy smile. "I will go without you."

She looked up at him quickly. This self-restraint disturbed her more than his anger did.

"Good-by." He rose, and bending above her, gravely kissed her. Her lips trembled and she looked at him timidly.

"I have treated you shamefully."

"Never mind that now," he said hastily.

"You are obliged to see the ruins any way, are n't you?" she asked penitently. "You are going to write about them; it was n't to be merely a pleasure trip?"

"That 's all right."

She followed him to the door.

"I don't know whether I 'm doing right or not," she said with a sigh, as they paused a moment in the narrow arched entrance. "I don't believe I could go now, any way," pressing her hands to her throbbing temples.

"You had better lie down." His face still wore a look of restrained quiet, and his eyes failed to meet hers, as he kissed her again and bade her good-by. Her own were full of tearful entreaty. She clung to him and a little sob broke from her, but he put her away and left her.

She cried a little when she was alone, but it was only a gentle after-shower, that had a restoring effect. When she grew calmer she said it was better for both that Roger had gone without her. Few married people, she reflected, lived in such constant companionship as they did. Remorse growing fainter, she felt an undeniable sense of relief at being alone. She smiled mournfully at the thought of growing tired of Roger, but it was true each would experience a new kind of happiness in the reunion to follow this first parting. It would be all the sweeter for their quarrel.

But Eleanor did not want any more quarrels. They were harmless enough, perhaps, with married people, whom habit and the external bond that holds them suffer to behave as naturally as they like; but they were full of unseen dangers here. She blamed herself wholly for this one, and resolved more strongly than before to control these variable moods, to bring this habit of useless self-questioning to an end. Her duty was to Roger alone, not to the world they had turned their backs upon.

Roger remained away three days. At the end of that time Eleanor had experienced all the pain and loss of loneliness, along with its benefits, and looked eagerly for his return. She decked the rooms with flowers, and, with Flora McDonald's aid, prepared a little fête, putting on Roger's favorite dress and awaiting him with girlish expectancy.

At the first glance she saw he was still displeased with her. She had half expected this, and tried not to notice, but her heart sank. She deserved to be punished, and Roger, she had learned, despite his theories, knew how to punish, almost as well as Dante.

Lying in the shade of a mass of ruined marbles the day before, Roger had reviewed his situation and decided he had reached another turning-point. His life was already liberally strewn with these moral milestones, periods of culminating thought and feeling on certain subjects, that pointed another start in a new direction. An early quarrel with his widowed mother, just before he went to college, gave rise to the first; several minor differences with his classmates, his first threatened rupture with Kitty Somers, and the abandonment of his home, worked the others. It was now time to erect one more. He went over the past and mapped out the future. He had a gift for theorizing, and a pitiless way of laying out lines of conduct for himself and others, employing a dramatist's skill in invention.

He began by making the first distinct acknowledgment of his disappointment in Eleanor. This is a momentous point for any lover to reach, especially one of Hunt's intense and brooding nature. Wiser men than he, if not so bold, choose not to drag disappointments of this kind into full consciousness. Honest confession may be good for the soul, but often for its slighter ailments only. Roger Hunt, however, had long since formed the habit of baring all his mental processes to the full daylight. He called this honesty.

Where once Eleanor had been his chief inspiration and joy, she was now an admitted care. Instead of promoting his happiness, she thwarted it. He saw himself in the light of a man likely to be hindered and seriously disturbed in his general plan of life. It behooved him, therefore, to prevent this if he could.

Oddly enough, perhaps, Roger never once thought of putting Eleanor away from him. He had tried that sort of experiment once, and great minds, we are told, do not repeat themselves. Let him have the credit of holding himself more strictly bound here, because in men's eyes he was bound not at all. Affection and sympathy might give way, but a certain old-time chivalry had always been strong in him, though sometimes waywardly exercised. He was not the man to desert a woman in Eleanor's position.

But, lying there in the shadow of a broken column, unconscious symbol of the human life dreaming and speculating at its feet, he took the firm and formal resolve that she should stand in his way no longer. As he had taken this journey without her, so he would go on through life, free and unhindered. He, too, had been sensible of the benefits of solitude the past three days. He could live alone, if need be; if the need were imposed, that is, in another's failing trust or understanding of him.

For most of Roger Hunt's resolutions took the form of accusations against some one else. Eleanor, he said to himself, had failed him. She no longer truly loved him. If her love were what it should be, it would obliterate all other feeling, every motive and desire that checked or opposed it. He recalled the bitter words she had let fall in their late talks together, letting displeased memory crystallize them into hard and unforgivable shape. Whatever Eleanor did or suffered by reason of her own nature, the claims of her peculiar personality, he had never even remotely considered. Like many a man besides, he knew and estimated the woman of his choice solely in her relation to himself.

Pursuing his thoughts, he arranged his future course on grounds at once purely abstract and wholly personal to himself. He wished to lead a tranquil life. A scholar needs mental quiet above everything else, which must not be disturbed by recurring periods of emotional excitement. Such was his power of self-delusion that he did not dream he was at this very time laboring under intense excitement, the greater that it was able to shape itself to such cold and deadly purposes.

He repeated that a scholar must be surrounded with harmonious conditions; if they do not arise naturally, they must be arranged for. He would do nothing harsh or unjust, but he would live his life. He believed a brilliant intellectual career awaited him,.which the social cloud under which he lived could no more dim than the deer-stealing did Shakespeare's. A man of mind makes his own way in the world, he had told Eleanor many times. A woman of mind may do the same, he had added, and cited examples; but her spirit had failed to meet his on this point. She was only a loving woman, misled in a false direction.

Roger's present behavior did not make things easier for her. Days passed and still he kept up the manner that marked his return. He was polite and attentive, never unkind, more equable in manner than she had ever known him before, but she felt herself kept at arm's length in everything. She was patient and uncomplaining at first, but after a while the feeling of hurt surprise sharpened into resentment, and she grew cold and reserved in turn, keeping herself apart from him; but if he noticed the change he made no sign.

By degrees she woke to the knowledge that her empire was over.

Then followed a few hours of wild despair, and terrified visions of the future, to end which, and to know the worst, Eleanor resolved to speak to Roger. One day, as he was rising from the table, she spoke his name entreatingly, and with a slight accent of fear.

"I — I wish to speak to you," she said, rising, and going towards him. The strain 'of the last ten days had told on her terribly. She was very pale, and large blue rings under her eyes told the number of sleepless nights she had passed. She was five years younger than Roger, but looked as many years older. She trembled as she stood before him, while her thin hands clasped and unclasped each other nervously. Any other man would have been moved, just to look at her; but Roger had resolved not to be moved. He waited for her to proceed, not looking at her.

"Roger, what does it all mean? I can't live in this way."

The muscles in her throat worked painfully, and she put up her hand to relieve the pressure. Roger lowered his eyes, then raised them again. Their coldness chilled her to the heart.

"Roger, don't look at me like that. What have I done? I know I was wrong that day. I am always wrong, but," struggling to smile a little, "have n't I been punished enough?"

"I have no desire to punish you." This was not true, but perhaps he thought it was. "On the contrary, I should like to make you happy, but I seem to have lost the power."

"Roger!" reproachfully. "Who could make me happy if not you? It is not your fault if I am not happy, nor — nor mine."

"Yet there is a reason for it, I suppose, since you admit the fact."

"I do not admit the fact. The reason, if there were any, could be but one, — my love for you," her voice sinking.

"I should like a better proof of that love."

She looked at him with wide, reproachful eyes. "Proof!" she repeated wonderingly. "Proof!" with a bitter accent. "Have I not given proof? When a woman gives her soul for a man " —

She stopped, aghast at her own words. Some malicious spirit must have been waiting to catch and trip her. She meant them not at all.

"Roger, I did not mean that," stepping towards him. But his face had hardened into iron; lightning gleams flashed from his eyes.

"If that is the way you look at it, what must you think of me?" he cried. "Thank Heaven, I am not yet sunk so low in my own mind. You talk of love, yet can desecrate it with a thought like that! You can think of me as a vulgar adventurer! "

"Roger, Roger, I do not! "

"You no longer believe in me! You are sorry for what you have done! "

"No, Roger, no," faltering beneath his look.

"You would not do it again?" His voice rang out like a challenge. His stern gaze held her like a magnet; then she cowered and shrunk before it. With a low moan she sank down on a chair, burying her face in her outstretched arms on the table before her.

"I would die for you, Roger; I wish I could."

"You are not required to die." The words stung her.

"Oh, I know, dying is too easy," she broke out, and, rising, rushed away and made her escape from him.

She knew now that a permanent change had come over Roger's feeling for her. She had been witness more than once to the sudden revulsions of feeling that he was apt to experience towards people he had once liked; now it was she, herself, who was to be the object of this altered regard, this fixed estrangement.

The next day Roger left her on another exploring tour in aid of his studies, this time with no mention of desire for company; and henceforth she was given to understand, not in words, but in countless little ways that speak so much more, that he meant to pursue his way without her. She knew he felt himself deeply wronged at her hands. Outwardly he treated her with nearly the same consideration as before; was attentive to all her wants, fetching her shawl, accompanying her on her walks, and guarding her against imprudences; but holding himself aloof from her day after day. For herself, she struggled against this state of things, and submitted to it by turns, nourished hope and then despair, was tearfully patient one day, stolidly resigned the next. Under this severe inward strain her frail physical health threatened to give way. She grew weaker, and told herself with despairing hopefulness that she should not live long. Roger would be free from her soon.

Several weeks passed in this way, when something happened that marked another turning-point, hurting her as nothing had yet done, yet, in a way, confirming belief in Roger anew.

He entered the house one day with an American newspaper in his hand, his manner betraying a little excitement. Calling her into the study, he pointed out a short paragraph, marked with a blue pencil. It was the notice of the death of Annie Hunt, in the asylum in which her husband had left her. The blood pulsed wildly through Eleanor's veins, as she read the few printed lines, and she turned an anxious and questioning gaze on Roger. The paper was a month old.

"We can be married now," he said, after a moment's silence. Her heart beat faster still. "We will go to Florence, and have the ceremony performed there. I will write the consul to-night."

She looked at him with large, startled eyes. His own were bent on the paper. If there had been a ray of light in his face, a sign of gladness for the poor relief such an act might bring to her, his words would have melted her at once, stirring generous admiration beyond the need to profit by them, perhaps.

"You would really marry me, Roger, now?" she questioned him mournfully.

"Now?" he repeated uncomprehendingly.

"When you no longer love me?"

If he had really ceased to love her, that might be a reason the more, with many high-minded men, for offering her every other means of protection and grace in his power; and Roger Hunt had as true instincts in some matters as his less erring fellow-creatures; but this was hardly a line of argument to satisfy a woman placed as Eleanor was. He recognized the double appeal in her words, and answered indirectly.

"I cannot pretend the matter is important to me. You know my feeling on such points. It is your doubts and scruples I wish to satisfy. I would satisfy my own if I had any. I seek your happiness." He really believed this. "Events seem to prove that I wronged you once. I now offer you such reparation as lies in my power."

"Reparation!" she repeated reproachfully. "I never said you wronged me. I never had such a thought. I alone am to blame for what I did."

"Precisely," he replied quickly, "'to blame.' That is the way I know you regard it."

"Roger, why do you torture me so?" she cried, in an anguished tone, "turning and twisting my poor words."

"Do you mean you have no sense of blame?"

She was silent. He smiled bitterly.

"No woman can have a sense of blame in a case like ours, without reflecting gross dishonor on the man" —

"That is not true," she interrupted warmly.

"We will not discuss the point. We should have learned by this time the uselessness of discussion. Will you go with me to Florence?"

"No." It required an effort to speak the word, but she mastered it. Pride and affection had received a crushing blow at once. Life never seemed so poor a failure as now; the pain and humiliation of this moment could never be equaled. Roger looked at her with new perplexity mingled with the old displeasure. What new freak was this?

"What good will it do now?" she said in reply to this look.

"Most women would think, a good deal."

"That is what you have always disliked in me, my thinking as other women do. I do not wish to be married," she added, after a moment's pause, and in another tone. "I do not wish" — she checked herself.

The vision of that other woman, cold in her loveless coffin, had risen before her. How could she profit by a thing like that? It was like murder. The thought of Roger and herself standing before the altar, seeking the sanction of rights they had stolen, sickened her. No; she would let her deed stand.

"You had better reconsider the matter," he said coldly. "I shall return home now, and" —

"Going home?" That did, indeed, put the matter in a new light; but when she looked into his face, rayless as a piece of black velvet, her pride came to the rescue of her fears, and she repeated her decision, with a touch of haughtiness.

"As you please," he said, and understanding the audience was terminated, she left him.

A few days later she entered the study unannounced, and hurriedly requested to speak with him. She was strangely agitated, in a way he had never seen before. Her face wore a look newly shamed and startled, yet had an uplifted expression, too. He rose to place a chair for her, but she stopped him.

"I — I have changed my mind, Roger. I think differently about it now."

He did not understand, and looked at her in puzzled surprise.

"I will go with you to Florence."

Then he understood, and laid down his pen.

"Not for any good it can bring me," she went on, with increasing agitation. "Not for ourselves at all. — Oh, Roger, Roger, you must love me a little now. Take me back, Roger, take me back," and she threw herself, weeping, on his breast, where he was constrained to hold and quiet her. It was by degrees he learned the truth. Not for herself, but for the sake of the unborn life, fluttering beneath her heart, she would go with him.

X.

ROGER and Eleanor returned home early in the following spring. They sailed directly for New York, where they remained several weeks. A lucky accident threw a piece of literary work into Roger's hands, the examination of some ancient Indian remains on the western banks of the Mississippi, in a locality famed for its fine air and commercial enterprise. He took Eleanor with him, meaning to make but a temporary stay, but as the climate proved beneficial to her, and his interest in his studies grew, they remained longer. Both felt the advantages of this distant separation from earlier scenes and associations. It was like living in a new world; and shortly after Eleanor's child was born, Roger decided to make Garrison his future home, where they lived fifteen years.

As often happens, Eleanor gained a new lease of life with that of her child, and though always delicate seemed nearly restored to health for several years. As often happens, also, the younger life paid the penalty. Estella was a puny and sickly baby, requiring much care. She was a peculiar child, and had not escaped the infection of the strangely-mingled natures that formed her own. Physically and mentally also to a degree, she resembled her father. Dark, expressive eyes, with a sensitive mouth and intelligent brow, showed a nature at once passionate and susceptible, which a reserved disposition, that bordered on the distrustful, held in check.

It was natural that during her early years, when she was ill and needing care, the child should seem to cling to the mother and avoid the father; but as time progressed, and she grew stronger, able to run about and play like other children, what had once been a necessity seemed to have grown a habit. At least this was the way Eleanor tried to reason about it, watching the two with much solicitude. The little Estella seemed at the same time to shrink from and be intensely curious about her father. She would sit watching him, with big thoughtful eyes, an hour at a time, apparently neither unhappy in his presence nor afraid of him, only deeply puzzled and reflective. If he spoke to her she answered him with a gravity that was almost comic, repelling him as his first child had done when he tried to play with her; his awkwardness here demonstrating his insincerity to her acute, childish intelligence. She would submit to be instructed by him, not amused. For companionship, she sought her mother, whom she at once idolized and overruled, loved and obeyed or disobeyed as the whim seized her.

Roger was both piqued and flattered by his daughter's behavior towards him. Her likeness to himself pleased him and awakened expectation;

and as she grew older and began to study under his direction, her marked precocity in certain ways gratified him still more. When he noticed her failing tenderness at all, it was to attribute it to the mother's influence, who was herself the object of much daughterly petting and caressing; but he fancied he missed these marks of attention much more than he did.

Eleanor had hoped much from the birth of her child in the restored relations between herself and Roger, but she was disappointed. She had never won back her lover, who had been less a lover still since he became a husband, though scrupulously attentive to all her needs. They lived under the same roof, but solitary and apart, Roger devoting himself more and more to his books, Eleanor trying to live in her child.

A child compensates for nearly everything else to most women, the maternal sentiment easily supplying the place of the conjugal, but it was not so with Eleanor. The supreme love of her life was that which ached and quivered in her heart still every time she thought of Roger. Though the hope of reconciliation grew fainter year after year, she fed on it still in her dreams. Of late the hope had mingled with another, which is also the final dread. When she was dead, Roger would think kindly of her again, and restore her to the old place in his heart.

The change in Roger was complete, and had now been so long established that it had become fixed habit, yet Eleanor had never outgrown the surprise of it. Every day she marveled anew. Was this the old Roger, this man of the grave unsmiling countenance, who paid formal visits to her room and then withdrew into himself, who seldom spoke with her except on some business or household topic; this the impassioned lover who had sacrificed everything for her? Was it a sacrifice? she asked herself, and was it for her? How little women know men before they have displeased them!

Roger himself, as she knew, believed he was behaving most commendably. The wisdom of his conduct was proved in his own mind by its deliberateness. A single purpose ruled him; but there were times when this singleness of purpose seemed to Eleanor almost demoniac. It was as relentless as hate. Only God, whose righteous motive is always assured, had a right to such an unbending will as Roger's. Human strength must bear some proportion to human weakness, else it becomes devil's strength. Such were some of the thoughts Eleanor evolved out of her loneliness.

Yet Roger's strength was strength, she told herself, in more self-accusing moods. She was the embodiment of weakness, physical and moral. Roger was the most consistent man she knew. What he undertook he accomplished; when he failed, it was circumstances that were to blame, not he. If an editor declined an article, he talked of literary favoritism, and the intellectual degeneracy of the age; if he took cold, he blamed the weather. No wonder he grew tired of such a bundle of nerves and self-contradiction as she was, Eleanor thought. Yet she suffered — suffered acutely, both from loss of love and of love's ideal. But that deepest loss of all, loss of the power to love, she had escaped. This power to love showed chiefly now as power to suffer, which was the reason Roger could not understand it; yet since such love shows a moral sensibility which shall redeem and save at last, its owner is to be accounted fortunate.

Though for a few years Eleanor's health improved, the seeds of disease were deeply planted, and as Estella grew to girlhood the mother's condition began to fail again, then halted in that long period of slow decay which belongs to old-fashioned consumption. Thus Estella's image of her mother was associated almost entirely with the sick-room, which was also to her the living-room of the house. Here she brought her dolls and games, here she had learned to sew, and here, in late years, she brought her books to learn the lessons recited in the library. Flowers bloomed in the window, the room was sunny and large; but it was the young girl's figure flitting in and out, lithe and slender like her father's, that brought real light and warmth into it.

Estella's love for her mother grew with the latter's dependence on her, and was of much the same worshipful and tyrannical order she had shown when a child. She petted and scolded her, according to her needs, confided all her young troubles and perplexities to her, and protected her against intrusion. A competent nurse had charge of the sick-room, between whom and Eleanor, after four years' association, the bond of a warm personal affection had grown. The cook ruled in the kitchen, and Roger kept for the most part in his study; Estella alone seemed to have the run of the house.

The home of the Hunts was one of the most tasteful residences in Garrison, a stone cottage, with dormer windows and a jutting balcony or two, which had caught Roger's eyes, whose skill in such matters had made the most of these and similar features. In the town's early history it had been the officers' quarters connected with the garrison sent out by the government to protect the river at this point. It rested at the foot of the bluff, on the summit of which stood the large and showy mansion of the chief magnate of the place, Thomas Clarke, a successful real-estate dealer, whose rapid fortunes were inseparably connected with those of the town.

No one had seen the possibilities of the neglected cottage until Roger took it in hand. Then expressions of admiration and envy were heard on all sides. It was a distinct contrast to the prevailing "modern" architecture in which Garrison reveled, and no one spoke more unqualified praise of it than Mrs. Clarke, who had liked her own house with its climbing turrets and spreading porches very well until she saw this.

Not that the social aspirations of one in her position could have been easily compressed to this smaller scale, but she felt her taste corrected on many points. It was chiefly in the inside appointments of her new neighbor's abode, she felt regret strongest. Here also it had been Roger's taste that ruled. Low ceilings, neutral-tinted walls, rugs in the place of carpets, cushioned window-seats, furniture for use, not adornment, and mementos of travel and cultured leisure scattered about in idle profusion, — these were features of housekeeping which Garrison, big, thriving, and ambitious, but "crude," as Mrs. Clarke said, now attained its first knowledge of. She went back to her gilt-papered walls and plush upholstery with a new feeling of distaste that she knew would never leave her. She felt that "Professor" Hunt, as she at once distinguished him, was an acquisition of an unusual order to Garrison society, and congratulated herself on having one of his manifest attainments for a neighbor.

Nina Clarke was two years older than Estella. Like her, she was an only child, and had been brought up in the same exclusive fashion, imposed in the one case by the sense of wealth and social prominence, and in the other by rigid ideas. Neither was allowed to attend the public schools, and Estella used to watch the children enviously as they went to and fro to the schoolhouse farther down the street. Her father was fitting her to enter the university at Monroe in a neighboring

State. She had no companions near her own age save Nina. The two girls liked each other well enough, but without enthusiasm, and each lived by herself a good deal. Their intimacy had increased somewhat during the last year, and since Roger had consented to receive Nina as a pupil. Though Estella's senior in years, she was no farther advanced in her studies, and not being quick to learn, as her classmate was, was in danger of falling behind.

Thomas Clarke was of a physical type that bespoke his social importance, big, florid, loud-mouthed and flashily attired, yet not innately coarse or vulgar. His wife, Lucy Gray, was a school-teacher in a small Connecticut village when he met her; though his mental and social superior, she had cheerfully joined her fortunes to his, seeing in his native pluck and sagacity the promise of all the success he had since won.

Mrs. Clarke was as ambitious as her husband, but to finer issues. He was content with the material prosperity he had won; she wished to make it the basis for higher and more difficult acquirements. For recreation he kept a stock farm, and a trained gardener who took charge of the large conservatory on his place in town. Mrs. Clarke was proud of her husband's success and of him for securing it, but she disliked the *parvenu* element that abounds in new, unformed communities like Garrison, and was always on the lookout for something different with which to grace her table and enrich hospitality. A man like Roger Hunt was to her a godsend. To a degree, Garrison shared her pride in him. Unless two or three editors of the municipal press and the school-superintendent were to be counted such, he was the only literary character the town could boast. The occasional appearance of his name in the current reviews and magazines, his known authorship of two or three books, his secluded and scholarly habits, all these helped the popular imagination to idealize him, and set him apart from the common horde of money-getters. Roger fell into his new position with entire ease and a sense of fitness. He could say, honestly, he had not sought the distinction that had befallen him, for he took no more pains to win people's good opinion now than he had ever done.

He refused all social invitations, and thereby won, without intending it, the reputation of being a devoted husband. He cultivated but few acquaintances, and had no intimate friends, though he was on a rather familiar footing with his nearest neighbors, the Clarkes.

The two men, each believing strongly in his own right of predominance, were mutually hostile from the first, but Thomas Clarke was too good-natured to quarrel with any one. Mrs. Clarke understood his feeling, and to a degree sympathized with it, but it constituted no reason in her mind, nor for that matter in her husband's, why she should abandon an acquaintance that promised so many advantages. Mr. Clarke had as little wish as he had power to control his wife in such matters. The two lived together in a harmony born of general sympathy with each other's aims, and large tolerance for minor points of difference.

Mrs. Clarke was the type of woman, busy, self-complacent, ambitious, which Roger usually held in hearty dislike; but her adroitness had overcome some of his first prejudices. Their relation was of the nature of a prolonged truce. In conversation they fenced and flattered, made bold demands for benefits on both sides, and when alone preserved the sense of sincerity by criticising each other freely.

Roger liked the freedom of this relation when nothing else in it tempted him, while the knowledge of influence possessed was as pleasant as ever. Though he found much to displease his taste, and excite ridicule, he was sensible also of the manifest advantages the acquaintance entailed. Mrs. Clarke also understood the compensatory value of things. The bargaining instinct was as fully developed in her as in her husband, only her trade was not in corner-lots and quarter-sections. When the thing she wanted was not offered, she knew how to ask for it. Thus, one day she brought the conversation round to her daughter Nina, her deficient education, and the impoverished means in Garrison to improve it. She ended by boldly asking him to become her instructor, and he, though disliking it, felt obliged to consent.

Nina was seventeen at this time, awkward, over-

grown, and distressingly bashful. She had inherited the assurance of neither of her parents, and
seemed born for self-effacement. Any daughter,
however self-confident, would have been kept in
the background by Mrs. Clarke, who though as
ambitious for Nina as for herself, did not belong to
that order of mothers who live only to extinguish
themselves in their children. The shyness of her
general manner developed into absolute terror
when Nina was in the presence of Roger Hunt.
She knew her mother's feeling about him, and
looked up to him with mingled fascination and
fear, as a being of another order, in a way that
would have flattered him keenly had he suspected it.

Nina and Estella were to begin Vigil, and geom-
etry together. The new pupil proved even more
dull than Roger expected. He could not know
how far expectation had produced this result, nor
how his own manner operated to kill all mental
effort in her. Nina toiled like a slave, but with
continually failing results. She would sit up half
the night to learn a lesson by rote, only to find
memory and courage fail her completely when
again in her teacher's presence. Many a night
she cried herself to sleep. Yet she never thought
of seeking release for herself or uttering any complaint. She blamed her own dullness for everything, and looked with envy upon Estella, who
learned her lessons so easily, and who, more wonderful still, did not seem in the least afraid of her
father. There was nothing Nina came to desire

so much as a word of praise or encouragement from this quarter. Had she shown a degree more of assertion, manifested the least resentment, she might have won what she craved; for Roger, to do him justice, did not know he was either unkind or unreasonable; he only knew he was intensely bored. As it was, Nina longed and labored in vain; yet some element of stolid resistance in the girl kept her at work. Estella watched her with mingled pity and curiosity, sharpened at times by a feeling like contempt.

One day she proved almost as slow as Nina in the construction of a passage in their Latin exercise, and her father let his irritation and sarcasm fall on both alike.

"I suppose I am stupid," Estella replied to one of his remarks, "but it won't cure me to tell me of it. Why don't you explain it to us?"

Nina looked at her in frightened astonishment. If a ferule had made its appearance from some concealed place, and Estella been asked to hold out her hand, she would not have been surprised.

"I expect you to recite the lesson. It is my part to listen," her father retorted.

"I know; but if neither of us can recite it," swinging her foot idly.

"That's a sweet·confession to make. How long would you remember it if I did explain?"

"I don't know," was the reply, in the same undisturbed tone, "but I suppose somebody must do something, if we are to get on." Roger apparently thought so too, for he took the book and began a clear though sharp exposition of the dark passage. His words were luminous and to the point, and soon both pupils were in entire mastery of former difficulties, one of them feeling more than usually abased over her dullness.

"Thank you, papa," said Estella, in her pleasantest tone, as the two gathered up their books to leave the room; "you've made it as clear as daylight, hasn't he, Nina?"

"Humph! Let us hope the daylight will last, at least twenty-four hours."

"Oh, but it never does, you know, papa," Estella laughed, casting a saucy look backwards, as the two passed through the door together.

"I shall never please your father," said Nina, when they were by themselves.

"Nobody pleases papa who tries very hard," was the reply. "I mean," Estella went on in answer to Nina's look of surprise, "you shouldn't think so much about pleasing him; you should think about the lesson."

"How can I help it? He makes me so nervous, and I know I am dreadfully dull."

"He used to make me nervous, too," said Estella, with an experienced air, "but I made up my mind not to let him. What is the use? It only bothers and hinders you. If you do the best you can, what more can people expect? I think papa is very unreasonable sometimes."

Estella had a way of saying such things that did

not seem disrespectful, making candor look like
impartiality.

"It must be a great trial to a man so gifted as
your father to teach a girl like me," Nina went on
after a moment's pause.

Estella made no reply to this. She was proud
of the reputation her father had gained, but it added
little warmth of feeling. "Gifted" people are apt
to suffer some diminution of glory in the minds of
those standing nearest them.

The lessons continued until the late spring, when
Nina accompanied her mother on a visit to New
York, spending the summer at the seashore, and
not returning until the middle of autumn. Six
mouths sometimes accomplishes marvels for a girl
just turning eighteen. Nina left the impression
on all her friends, as on Roger, of unformed girlhood, awkward and self-conscious; but the grub
remains such to outward vision up to the moment
it slips the chrysalis sheath and expands its wings
as butterfly. When Mrs. Clarke and her daughter returned to Garrison, it was apparent to all who
saw that the chrysalis stage was over. Nina had
scarcely tried her wings as yet, but she had learned
she had them. The unripe girlhood of a few
months before had passed like an ugly dream.

Beauty in a woman brings a sense of power which
more substantial traits arouse in a man; but with
Nina it looked as if this power were not to be put
to foolish uses. When she looked in the mirror
and saw the changed reflection of herself, she felt

no special elation or vanity, only gratitude. She had felt alone and helpless before; now that people were beginning to notice her more and say kind things about her, it meant that she might find some place of real trust and usefulness among them, perhaps.

Nina's beauty was of the full-flowered type that startles at first glance, yet that does not satiate. Her rather large figure had lost its angles and presented a succession of curved outlines that melted into each other as she stood or moved about, with an effect like music. The dark eyes showed sensibility and intelligence, the drooping lids giving them a dreamy expression. Her coloring would have been too rich had not much of the old shyness remained, which now seemed to cover her with a veil of maidenly purity. Her manner was at once frank and appealing, and unaffected as a child's.

If Nina's beauty had discovered a trace of coarseness, her mother would have been more displeased than gratified at the change in her. As it was, she did not allow gratification to overcome prudence. On her return the young girl had taken the town by storm. Tongues wagged, and conniving brains began to plot. Society in Garrison had received a new impetus, and all the dangers of young bellehood began to assail Nina. Mrs. Clarke yielded to the current graciously but discreetly. She was not going to vulgarize Nina by excesses of any kind. She might suit the standards of Garrison as she was, but not her mother's. Nina must continue her studies. A few months before she had fully intended to send her to an Eastern college, but now that she had blossomed out in this unexpected fashion, that scheme seemed impracticable. She looked about, therefore, for the best means of private instruction within reach, and Professor Hunt's services were again pleaded for. Regular masters were employed for the languages and music, a judicious degree of social indulgence was to be permitted; but for the substantials Nina was put unreservedly into her former instructor's hands. Roger had not yet met Nina when this arrangement was made. Estella had seen her, and had spoken rapturously of the change in her, but the subject had interested him little. He was reluctant to resume his charge in this direction, but saw no way to avoid it.

"Take her," her mother said, "and do what you like with her. Put her back into mental arithmetic if you want to."

"Mental arithmetic," he exclaimed. Did she not know mental arithmetic was the crowning imbecility of our educational system?

"Is it? Nina will be glad to hear it. I will admit I have a preference for a course in English. I don't know whether I ought to tell you, but she dreads to begin with you again. She is terribly afraid of you."

Roger was not wholly surprised at this, but her words made less impression on him then than at a later period, when he recalled them.

"Teach her to think, if you can," the mother went on, "to have a mind of her own. If she was n't my daughter, I should say she was the most tiresomely docile creature on earth. I would give half her amiability for a little more self-assertion. I don't mean I want her to equal you in that respect."

"You think I am self-assertive?"

She laughed. "You are as meek as Moses when he slew the Egyptian" —

"Did n't the Egyptian deserve his fate?"

"Very likely. But to get back to Nina. As I was saying, she is too good-natured. Any other girl would have had her head turned with the fuss made over her at Cape May last summer, but she seemed only to enjoy it, without letting it spoil her."

"I don't understand," said Roger, frowning a little as he always did when Mrs. Clarke got on to her society tone. "You hoped it might spoil her a little?"

"How dull you are! I only want Nina to have some strength of character. I don't know who can impart it better than you," in a tone that implied flattery and blame at the same time. "You can at least teach her not always to agree with people." He smiled faintly.

"If a girl can't learn to say 'No,'" she went on, "I don't know what will become of her. Nina is just the girl to accept the first man that offers himself. She would n't want to hurt his feelings."

"You wish her to marry, then?"

"I should think what I said indicated the opposite," was the rather sharp reply. "Marriage will take care of itself, with a girl like Nina. I have always been opposed to early marriages. You have an artistic temperament and are romantic, so I suppose you approve them?" She paused for an answer but he was silent. "I did not marry until I was twenty-seven. If I had accepted my first offer, I should be living in a Connecticut farmhouse, and doing my own washing."

"Isn't a woman willing to do her own washing if she loves a man?"

"She courts the opportunity."

"I am trying to guess," he said, after a minute's silence, "whether you wanted to accept him."

"You may guess as much as you like."

"Is it your experience that marriages made late in life are any happier?" he asked, lingering on a subject that interested him above all others. She laughed and shrugged her shoulders, snugly incased in shining black satin. She understood his disposition to sentimentalize in some directions, but flattered herself she knew how to keep it in check.

"I don't know, I am sure. My own case has been pretty bad," with another ironic laugh, "but I shouldn't like to generalize on that."

"At least there is some measure of innocence and true feeling entering into young marriages, on one side or the other," he said, with some warmth.

"Innocence that stands for ignorance."

"I sometimes think you are very worldly-minded."

"You may think so always, so far as I am concerned. I certainly mean to improve all my opportunities. That is the reason I ask you once more, 'Will you take Nina?'"

"I will take her," he replied briefly.

"Thank you; and when can she begin? To-morrow?"

It might as well be to-morrow as later, he thought, and assented. She thanked him again.

"You are very kind." The subject dropped there, and the talk flowed to other channels. There was a business side to the arrangement, which was deftly managed by Mrs. Clarke, and never alluded to by either of them. At proper intervals Roger received a check, generous, but not vulgarly large; of a proportion suited to the circumstances of the case, and gratifying the æsthetic tastes of both donor and receiver.

XI.

THE relation between the two girls naturally
suffered a change after Nina's return. The difference in their ages, which seemed unimportant before, was now very apparent. The two had stood
side by side in their studies, where Estella was not
in advance, and the latter did not easily submit to
the altered aspect of affairs. Hitherto she had felt
that she gave quite as much as she received in this
acquaintance, and had even been conscious at times
of a patronizing feeling towards her friend; now
it looked as if the right of patronage lay on the
other side.

When Nina returned home, at the close of the
period of summer transmutation, Estella hastened
to meet her, but was quite abashed at the vision of
the tall, distinguished looking young woman, who
came forward to speak to her. Not that she found
anything to complain of in Nina's manner, which
was cordial and kind. She stooped down and kissed
her friend, who somehow in this new juncture
seemed about half her size; then bore her away
to her own room to talk with her undisturbed, and
show her the new dresses, jewels, and other treas-
ures accumulated in the season's absence, and at-
testing the dawn of a new era.

It was perhaps because Nina made so many well-intentioned efforts to please, that Estella, sensitive and observant, resented them. Conflicting feelings struggled within her, admiration, jealous pain, and growing surprise. In spite of her friendliness, Estella knew that Nina also felt the changed situation between them. She was both hurt and puzzled, and showed a shyness quite new to her. She looked as uncomfortable as she felt, and was conscious of making stupid replies, listening to her companion's talk with an indifference that looked like envy. Mrs. Clarke came into the room while the two were together.

"You find Nina changed?" she said to Estella, noting the young girl's mystified look.

"I think she is very beautiful," Estella replied, in a tone at once devout and mournful. Mrs. Clarke gave an easy laugh, and Nina, who had lost none of her former sensitiveness, blushed.

"Never mind, my dear," her mother said, with well-meant kindness. "Any girl of reasonable size has a great advantage over a big creature like Nina. She can go quietly along with her studies, and do everything more thoroughly. Nobody expects her to act the grown woman before she is nineteen."

"Oh, for that matter, I don't know that any one has ever expected anything from me," Estella replied, with a little petulance. Mrs. Clarke's words grated on her, she hardly knew why; but that lady was apt to praise people in a way that brought out all their defects.

"I am sure Estella has always had the advantage of me," said Nina. "She is far ahead of me in her studies."

"Yes, Nina thinks you are quite a prodigy," the mother said, in continued good will; but Estella was not in a mood to be grateful for the compensation that might lie in a taste for mathematics and Latin roots. She longed for some more material sign of power. She felt sore and humiliated, the more so that she knew Nina had done nothing to arouse such feelings; she could find no way to restore self-respect except by praising Nina in the highest terms.

"She is so beautiful, mamma," she said, seated on the edge of her mother's bed, — Eleanor kept her bed a good deal in these days; "I never dreamed any one could be so beautiful." She ended with a sigh impossible to repress, and her mother smiled.

"You must bring her in to see me."

Estella shook her head, not in denial of this request, but in foreboding of matters that lay deeper.

"Nina can't care for such an insignificant little thing as I am, any more." Her mother looked at her attentively.

"How long has Estella Hunt regarded herself as insignificant?" she asked.

The girl flushed and looked convicted. She was indeed too much her father's child to make self-depreciation natural.

"You must remember that Nina is two years older than you."

"She did not seem to think she was so much older, last spring." To herself Estella added that she was ten times older than Nina in some things.

"You both had to find it out some time. Was n't Nina pleasant this morning?"

"Oh yes; she is n't a bit spoiled. She tried her best to make me feel as if I were eighteen too," laughing dismally.

"Don't wish away your youth, my child. It will pass quickly enough. Nina is a good girl, I think."

"Of course she is good. That is what I don't think is fair. She ought to be satisfied with being beautiful. You don't think I.'m jealous, do you, mamma?" bending anxiously over the bed.

"I think you are too sensible to let yourself be jealous."

"Thank you, mamma. I am so glad you are willing to give me a little time. I don't mean to go on this way much longer; you 'll see how beautifully I 'll bring myself round. I 'm not jealous," she added, more seriously. "I should like Nina to have all she wants. I hope she will be different from me; she deserves to. I should be ashamed to feel in any other way. Only," lapsing suddenly from this height, "I shall be lonesome," and she sighed again.

"Shall you, dear? I hope not," her mother replied, with an anxiety that seemed rather out of proportion. Her eyes rested on the young face near her, so sensitive and imperious, with a look of wistful concern and question Estella had noticed before. She forbore to tell her mother many of her small troubles, because of the undue importance the latter attached to them; she was apt to take them harder than the girl herself did.

"What a silly thing I am!" Estella exclaimed, springing to her feet. "I shall not be lonesome either. What do I want of Nina Clarke or any one else, so long as I have you, you dear old darling mamma?" bending over and kissing her. "Now I 'm going into the kitchen and make you the loveliest bowl of celery soup — I mean a bowl of loveliest celery soup," with a laugh. "Jane will be cross, but I dou't care. She 's getting to be a perfect tyrant. Even papa is afraid of her."

When Estella returned from this commission, she found her father in the room. He had just returned from the morning visit to his neighbor which had bound him to another term of service as Nina's instructor. The impulse to confide his feelings to Eleanor was very rare, but the sense of injury was too strong to be kept to himself. Estella placed the tray containing her mother's light repast on the stand by the bed, then turned and listened a moment to what her father was saying.

"Then Nina and I are to study together again," she broke in, in a pleased tone. "I am so glad."

"Indeed, you are not to study together," her father replied. Both mother and daughter looked their surprise at this.

"Is n't Nina willing to study with me any

more?" Estella cried, her sensitive pride quickly springing into flame again.

"It is I who am not willing," her father said. "You have got to work." These words were spoken with an emphasis that implied a distinction the girl at once understood, and which was rather flattering; still she was disappointed.

"What is Nina going to do?" she asked, with a pout.

"Nina is going in for the usual lady-like accomplishments."

"Why can't I go in for the accomplishments too?"

"You will learn the multiplication-table first."

Estella knew what that meant. Nina was particularly dull at figures. She began to feel rather sorry for her friend.

"Can you spare the time for separate lessons?" Eleanor asked, looking at him sympathetically. She knew he was unusually busy just now, finishing a new book. Estella, seeing her mother was not yet ready for lunch, took the tray back into the kitchen.

"Of course I cannot spare the time."

"Then why not explain to Mrs. Clarke? She ought to excuse you when she knows how busy you are."

"I consented to take the girl because we need the money," was the blunt reply. This was not strictly true, but it served as an excuse to work off his irritation. He had consented to receive Nina because he did not wish to displease her mother. Eleanor looked at him in surprise.

" I told you some time ago I had met with some losses, and you must know our way of living is expensive." The words sounded worse than he meant they should, and Eleanor, who had learned to hold her feelings in check, knew they were inspired more by the moment's irritation than a feeling of special complaint against any one; yet they could not fail to make her uneasy. She remembered about the losses Roger spoke of, but had not supposed the result was serious.

"If we must economize, I am sure we can find better ways than that," she said. "We can discharge the doctor. I have wanted to speak to you about it before. There is no need of his coming."

"Who said anything about the doctor?" Roger asked, with quick offense. "Do you think I complain of such things?"

"No, dear, no. It is only because there is no need of his coming. He cannot help me. And I cannot bear to be a useless expense to you."

"We will drop the subject, if you please," he said in a displeased tone.

"I did not mean to hurt you, Roger. Don't be so harsh and suspicious of me" —

"It is you who are suspicious of me. You might think of me as a man of honor, if you no longer care for me."

"If I did not care for you, Roger, could you

have the power to hurt me so? I only said what was true,"—cause enough for speaking, usually, in his mind, — "the doctor can't help me. Nobody can help me " — her voice breaking. Roger remained silent, while her breath came in quick labored gasps, prelude to one of those hysterical breakdowns he so disliked.

"Nobody can help me," she burst out again, letting the full tide of feeling sweep over her. "Not even God, else he would let me die. I don't wonder you grow impatient, Roger."

This was another of those outbreaks of impetuous speech she had learned to control during late years, not only unintended, but belying her real wish and thought, and ending in quick remorse almost before the words died on her lips; but the one who heard them stored them up in an embittered memory, where they served to harden conviction and strengthen pitiless resolve anew. Roger turned white with anger.

"If you think me such a coarse brute as that, I had better leave you," he said; but that was now impossible. She had reached the climax of the nervous spasm in which such scenes ended, and he was obliged to go to her assistance. The attack was short but violent, and she lay spent and white on her pillow, clinging still to Roger's hand.

"Forgive me, dear," she whispered. "I did not mean to vex you." He did not answer, his face keeping still its look of stern self-injury.

She looked at him yearningly.

"It is hard for you to forgive, is n't it, Roger?"

"We have had enough of painful discussion, Eleanor. Shall I give you a drink?" She waved away the glass he took from the stand with a faint motion of her head.

"You are hard, Roger, you are hard."

"I am trying to be just."

"Oh, I know what you call it, but I could not treat you so, Roger. If I were the strong one, I should not be so careful to keep my strength; I should not care whether I was consistent or not. And if you were the weak one, and needing anything from me, a loving word or look, you should have it, whether I felt it or not, if I had to peril my soul for it." She was growing excited again.

"I do not understand you." This was true. "You are agitating yourself without cause. I am sorry I do not please you."

"Was he sorry?" she asked herself. "Was he ever really sorry for anything." For it had long seemed to Eleanor, in spite of her strong desire to be just, that Roger was never so much grieved over any loss or disappointment, however real, as newly confirmed in a proud belief in himself. Genuine grief contains the element of a deeper trust and sense of dependence than any he had manifested even when he loved her most.

The nurse entering the room soon after, Roger left it. The sick woman turned her head on the pillow and closed her eyes, and when Estella again entered with the little tray, she signed to her that her mother was asleep, and the girl again quietly left the room.

The money losses Roger spoke of were the result of a business venture quite out of keeping with his usual habits, and not likely to be repeated.

The real estate speculation, which had built up the fortunes of Garrison, developed into a positive mania now and then; and it was during one of these periods of commerical greed and excitement that Roger had been bitten, but with medicinal effect, since the result had shamed even more than it angered him. That did not, however, prevent him from holding in stronger dislike than before his neighbor, Thomas Clarke, who had advised him against the venture.

Roger had sought advice from this quarter with great reluctance, not daring to do without it; yet with the feeling that for a man like himself merely to ask counsel from another, of the mental calibre of Thomas Clarke, ought to procure the kind he wanted. When the advice proved of a different order, he considered himself justified in rejecting it, both for the manner in which it had been given, and the motive he chose to fancy might lay beneath.

The Eagle Company, of which Thomas Clarke was president, was the oldest and wealthiest real estate concern in Garrison, with a fame and credit that extended far beyond. From time to time new syndicates arose, waned or prospered, but the Eagle continued to lead. The latest of these new enterprises was known as the Swampscott, which had purchased a large tract of lowlands adjacent to the town in another direction from which the Eagle's investments lay; one which the Eagle had overlooked, the leaders of the rival company said, which it had looked at and passed by, said the friends of the older firm. Yet Swampscott was not without its possibilities; even some of the directors of the Eagle had been heard to admit that. Once let the tide of suburban emigration set that way, and stock in Sunrise, the name of the little village the Eagle had founded, would sensibly depreciate. Popular opinion wavered back and forth between the rising promise of the new and the established merits of the old; and commercially the town was divided into two factions. Older and more cautious heads argued that if Swampscott were really worth while, the Eagle would have got hold of it before this, while younger speculators were confident in the belief that the Eagle could n't get hold of it. Some of them thought it time that rapacious bird was taught to keep its claws off from something. Roger Hunt was among these.

There was something intolerable to him in the social autocracy of a man like Thomas Clarke, who boasted he had not received even a common-school education, yet who patronized his betters, and recognized no merit or distinction in another he did not possess himself. Though he would not labor directly to bring it about, the downfall of such a man, he could not but feel, would be an act of wholesome moral discipline, and a benefit to the entire community.

The excitement grew, and party feeling ran higher each day. Meantime the Eagle kept up its usual habits, here as in its native wilds, — looked at the sun without winking, and fixed an attentive eye on its unconscious prey below. Thomas Clarke went about with his hands in his pockets and a face about as communicative as the iron door of his combination safe. Roger's irritation against him increased with the compulsion he felt himself under to seek his help; and the two men greeted each other with a strained politeness, the morning the former called at the office of the Eagle. The president frowned when he learned his visitor's errand, then masked his face with an inscrutable expression, pulling at his gray mustache and twirling slowly in his revolving chair.

"What do you ask me about Swampscott for?" he began, after a pause, when Roger had finished. "The Eagle does n't own so much as a mayweed out there. And she 's got consid'able property of her own she 'd like to sell."

"It is Swampscott property I came to inquire about," said Roger with a touch of hauteur, rejecting this hinted offer in another direction, as he chose to consider it, and made, he thought, in the worst possible taste.

"Confound the fellow! What does he mean by coming round here with his infernal airs?" the other exclaimed mentally.

"I thought I might get your personal opinion, which, in a matter of this kind,"—Roger spoke with intentional slowness here,—"would have its value. But if it's unprofessional for you to speak on the subject"—

"Oh, unprofessional be hanged! The Eagle," and the speaker inflated his broad chest with a deep breath, "says what she thinks of a thing of that kind when she does n't invest."

"She could invest then, if she wanted to?"

Thomas Clarke looked at his visitor cunningly.

"Well, she thinks she could; she may be mistaken, though."

Roger found himself devoutly hoping she might prove so. "The wisest are mistaken sometimes, of course," he said aloud, to fill in the pause.

"No doubt. The Eagle's be'n here goin' on twenty years now, and she ain't made no mistakes yet; but I suppose some folks 'd say that only makes the time shorter when she will."

"Then I understand you advise me not to invest in Swampscott?" Roger asked, bringing the discussion back to its definite object.

"I don't say I don't advise you to invest."

"You don't choose to invest yourself?"

"Oh, me," waving such comparisons aside loftily. "I 've bit off all I can chew, already." Roger was disgusted.

"See here," the other continued more seriously, and swinging himself round to face his visitor squarely, "suppose I should tell you I don't think

Swampscott 's worth twenty-five on the dollar, and it was to turn out dif'rent; how 'd you feel towards me? I suppose somebody 'll make something out of it."

"Then there is a chance in it?"

"There 's a chance in the desert of Sahary if you know how to operate it. How much do you know about real estate any way?"

"Nothing," Roger replied, in a tone that thanked heaven for it. "I happen to have a few thousand to invest, that 's all; and I thought if I could put the money safely away somewhere, and let it lie idle for a time."—

"You 'd wake up some morning and find it had doubled itself three or four times over. Perhaps you will."

"I see that I am detaining you," Roger said rising from his chair.

"I 'm sorry if I 've offended you," the other replied, rising also, "but don't you see I 'm not the man you want to ask about a thing of this kind. I 'm an interested party." A quick flash of suspicion darted across Roger's face. He was the most literal man. living in some things, despite those higher qualities of imagination his friends praised so highly.

"Come now," the other went on, "I guess you 'd made up your mind what you was goin' to do before you consulted me. Folks gen'rally have, I notice. You think it 's only my candid opinion you want."

"Certainly, that is all I want."

"Well, it would n't sound candid if I was to give it; it 'd sound a mighty sight worse."

Roger's vexation increased, and so did his suspicion.

"Is it true," he asked with an unpleasant suggestion in look and tone, "that if Swampscott goes up, Sunrise goes down?"

A deep flush colored the other man's face, and he set his heavy jaws together firmly. He was touched in a sensitive spot.

"You 'll find plenty of damned fools who 'll tell you so," he said angrily.

It was now Roger's turn to take offense.

"I don't understand," he replied cuttingly. "They are fools for thinking so, or only damned because they do?"

The other gave vent to a snort of impatient laughter, and Roger feeling that it was hopeless to try to get anything more from this quarter, and indignant with himself for coming at all, made his escape into the street.

The president of the Eagle projected a few unspoken anathemas after his departing visitor, and returned to his desk with a vexed and troubled countenance. He foresaw Roger's loss as distinctly as next morning's breakfast, and the knowledge that it would be largely deserved did not lessen his own feeling of accountability. He reflected that his wife would be even more disturbed than he was if she knew of this visit, and resolved not to tell her; which was probably the reason she learned all about it within a few days.

"You should have refused to give your opinion at all," she said, in an annoyed tone, after the first questions and exclamations were over. They were taking an evening drive, returning from the stock farm.

"I did n't give him my opinion; that is, not d'reckly."

"What did you tell him?" she asked anxiously.

"Oh, I kind o' parried him," he replied, leaning forward to brush a fly from the horse's flank.

"Parried him! Parry a man like Professor Hunt — you!"

She did not mean to be disrespectful, but the image her husband's words called up was one the most liberal fancy failed to entertain. "You had better have spoken outright, and said what you thought."

"Anybody but a darned literary crank 'd 'a known what I thought," was the testy reply. "Darned" was the severest expletive Mr. Clarke indulged in before his wife, who suffered this and other mild lapses without rebuke.

"You can't teach a man like Hunt anything. What hand the Lord did n't have in making this universe he did, and he could 'a took the whole job if he 'd been asked. He did n't mean to take my advice anyway. That 's the reason he asked it."

"You have always disliked him."

"Well, that ain't seemed to hinder my letting you run after him a good deal," he replied with a mixture of jocoseness and discontent.

"Don't use such expressions. I don't see why he should go to you on such a matter."

"Who else should he go to, I 'd like to know," his professional pride aflame. "If there 's anybody in Garrison knows more about real estate than Tom Clarke does, I 'd like to see him."

"I don't mean that; I mean it was in such poor taste. I can't bear mixing up social and business relations in that way."

"There ain't much mix, 's far 's I 'm concerned. He won't be wanting any more advice from me, for a spell. But I hate to see a man lose good money, even Hunt."

"Dear me! Will he lose his money?" Mrs. Clarke asked in genuine concern. "What makes you so sure he will lose?"

"What makes me sure the Mississip' will go on running towards the Gulf next week, same as she 's doin' now? The trouble with them Swampscott fellows is they hain't got the capital. You 've got to have capital to operate with, in the real estate business."

Mrs. Clarke sighed and said she supposed so. She had but a vague idea of what was meant by this "operating" power of capital, and was faintly suspicious at times of things which, had she time to look into them deeper, she might have disapproved of. . But she never had time to look into them. As has been said, she and her husband gave each other a wide freedom, she resigning to him the entire management of those money concerns she knew nothing of, yet was so dependent on; he yielding to her in all matters of a social and domestic nature. He humored her even where he did not understand her, as in her taste for the society of a man like Hunt; regarding it with much the same good-natured tolerance he did her fancy for Persian rugs and a six o'clock dinner served in courses. He himself preferred old-fashioned Brussels of the biggest and gayest pattern, and still cherished a primitive relish for a dinner of boiled vegetables; but he looked up to her as a superior being on some points, respecting without envying those mental accomplishments which added new lustre and power to the wife of a man in his position, but were not necessary in the first person. At the same time he loved her with that romantic fondness which the American husband, even of his busy and self-engrossed type, regards the choice of his early years.

XII.

Estella Hunt had inherited much of her father's mental courage, though as she grew older she sometimes failed to sympathize with the ideas fostering it in him. This difference showed itself in one way, at about this time, in a wish of hers, long cherished before spoken, to attend church. She was growing rather sensitive over the many points of difference between themselves, as a family, and their neighbors. The sense of isolation was increasing, which even the knowledge of the natural, and to a degree flattering, causes leading to it, such as her mother's long illness, and her father's studious habits, could not entirely do away with. These were not sufficient in the young girl's mind for imposing other obstacles to natural intercourse with the world about them. This exclusiveness, she began to see, brought many disadvantages, which she was unwilling to submit to without a struggle. She had been brought up almost as rigidly as a girl in a convent, and her desire to go to church was but part of her keen young interest in life and her kind.

The subject of religion was not often discussed in the household; but Estella knew her father agreed as little in the general judgment here as elsewhere.   Her mother's views she was unable to determine, but the long years of uncomplaining suffering she had witnessed, and her goodness, led her to think she must be very religious.   One day at Mrs. Clarke's she overheard some one speak of her father as an "infidel," but Mrs. Clarke had corrected this statement, and declared he was only an "agnostic."   Estella did not know the difference, and shortly after, one morning when she and her father were in her mother's room, she asked him to explain it.   "Infidel" he told her was a purely relative term: "A Christian is infidel to the Mohammedan form of faith as the Mohammedan is to the Christian.   An 'agnostic' is one who simply refuses to dogmatize about things he does not understand.   'Agnosticism' means 'without knowledge.'"

"Then are you an agnostic, papa?"   She gathered as much from the unprejudiced definition he had given her.

"Not at all."   Roger's basis of opinion in these matters would have been difficult to define, even to an adult understanding; being a compound of Hegelian mysticism and modern science, with a liberal dash of Fichte's doctrine of the ego thrown in.

"Some of the best minds are agnostic and infidel, Estella," her mother said.

"That is what Mrs. Clarke said; then I don't see why they should be used as terms of reproach."

"They are not by intelligent people," said her father.

"Don't you call Rector James intelligent?"

"What do you know of Rector James's views on these subjects?"

"I heard him preach, last Sunday. His subject was 'Modern Infidelity.'" Roger gave a short contemptuous laugh.

"I let her go," said Eleanor, looking at him anxiously. "She wanted to go. If I had known"—

"Pooh! let her go." It would be strange, he thought, if he could not counteract the effect of a Rector James's teachings.

"Oh, papa! May I go to church, really?"

This was putting the subject in a more general way he was not prepared for, and he looked at her with a slight frown.

"What do you want to go to church for?"

"Because other people do."

"That is a very poor reason. Do you think association with a man like Mr. Abbot would be so improving?" Mr. Abbot was a defaulting bookkeeper in a large establishment in town, who had narrowly escaped the penitentiary; he was also a prominent member of Rector James's flock.

"I don't see what that has to do with it," Estella replied. She seemed disappointed, and looked appealingly at her mother.

"I think mamma would be willing I should go," she said hesitatingly.

"No doubt," and Roger laughed harshly. "She certainly likes doing as other people do," in a significant tone Eleanor alone could understand.

"Once she tried to do something different, but she 's been repenting of it ever since."

These words of dire and cruel import would not have been spoken, perhaps, had not Roger still been under the influence of his newly-aroused resentment against Eleanor, besides feeling fresh cause of vexation with her this morning, over some household matter gone wrong, — an insignificant affair, save that it had caused him considerable personal annoyance.

Eleanor, who was pale before, turned whiter still, and clasping the arm of her chair, half rose to her feet.

"Roger!" she exclaimed imploringly. It was absurd, she knew, but she was wildly afraid at such times, when such words of dark and threatening allusion fell from him, that he would expose her to their child. The dread of Estella's discovery of that deed of her past hung over her like Damocles' sword. Should this frightful knowledge ever reach her, and she read her judgment in her daughter's face, Eleanor felt its work would be mercifully swift and instantaneous, like the lightning's stroke. Her own would be the easier part; she should die. But Estella must live. Not a day passed in which she did not pray the cruel truth might never reach her. Surely she had a right to pray for that, not for the lessening of her own punishment, simply that the innocent might be spared. Estella looked from one to the other with a puzzled face, though such scenes were not wholly new to her. It was impossible she should understand her father's words, but she felt pained and a little indignant on her mother's behalf.

"I think other people had better try to be like mamma," she said. "I don't know what she can have to repent of, unless it's her goodness, and if it's that she'll be kept busy," going towards her and bending over her, fondly drawing the little shawl she wore closer about her shoulders.

"If you think people need not repent, papa," turning towards him with a little pertness, and recalling other things she had heard him say on this point, "then I need n't mind taking your gold pen yesterday and spoiling it."

"Estella, I have told you many times not to go into the library when your father is not there," said her mother reprovingly.

"I don't care how much she goes into the library," said Roger. "You may ' repent ' or not," he added, to Estella, "but I cannot afford a new pen, and will deduct the amount from your next allowance." The girl shrugged her shoulders.

"I had better have said I repented."

"For that matter you 'll generally find it easier to repent of a thing than to accept the consequences."

Eleanor bit her lips to hide their quivering. Something caught in her throat and brought on a fit of coughing, which wrenched the thin frame without mercy. Estella flew to her side, and clasped her in her strong young arms. Roger stepped to a table

and poured a mixture from a bottle into a wine-
glass, but the nurse, hurriedly entering at that
moment, took it from him and carried it to the
patient.   Feeling his presence superfluous, he left
the room.

Estella remained at her mother's side, assisting
the nurse with deft and willing hands until quiet
was restored, and her mother breathed freely once
more; winning, as she had before, the hired attendant's praise.

"You 'd make a good nurse yourself, Miss
Stella."

"Oh, no," laughed the girl; "not unless I loved
all my patients as I do my first," bending forward
and kissing her mother.   "But I should like to be
a doctor, and ride about the country, giving people advice, and collecting the fees."   She laughed
again, and drawing a chair, sat down at her mother's side, taking her hand and gently stroking
it.   The nurse, Mrs. Saunders, left the room, and
Estella grew thoughtful again.

"Mamma, why does papa blame good people for
their faults so much more than bad people?"   By
"good" people Estella meant those who made public profession to be such.

"You don't always understand your father, Estella."

"Well," said the girl with a sigh, "I don't see
why it is any worse for Mr. Abbot to have been
dishonest and cheated his employer than it would
be if he were a free-thinker, like papa."

"Surely, my dear, you think people should live up to their professions. Deceit is a sin in itself," a shadow falling on her face.

"Yes, I know."

"Not that I mean to say Mr. Abbot is deceitful," her mother added quickly. "I do not know him."

"You dear mamma! If people waited for you to find out their faults, they 'd have an easy time."

"I don't know that Estella Hunt has always found it so."

"No," with a smile, "but I don't count. I don't understand either," coming back to the subject that occupied her, "why papa has such a contempt for the 'average' opinion, as he calls it. Are n't most of us average people?"

"Your father has a very self-reliant nature. He looks into things more deeply than most people do."

"I suppose that is the reason he likes being in the minority. I heard him tell Mr. Clarke once that he had never yet voted for the party in power. Does that mean the party in power is always wrong; or that it is wrong because it is in power? What good can the other one do if it never gets in power? Oh, dear! I get all mixed up thinking about it," and she laughed dolefully.

"You must talk with your father on these subjects, my dear," but this was advice the mother knew was not easy to follow.

"I 'll stop talking with you any way. You

must rest," and Estella rose. Stepping behind the invalid's chair, she pressed her foot on a spring and lowered it gently. She then adjusted the pillows and prepared to leave her. Bending above her, she asked one more question.

"Do you object to my going to church, mamma?"

"Not if your father is willing; not if it does you any good."

"I don't know whether it does me good or not. I only know it seems to do me harm to stay away. I don't see the use of being so different from everybody else, and I can't think religion is all a sham, as papa does. I am sure if I were religious I should be a better girl."

"You misunderstand your father," her mother said, repeating the substance of her first reply. "And you are a very good girl, as it is. Run away now, dear. I must try to sleep," and with the exchange of a kiss, Estella left the room.

In the long seclusion of her sick-room, Eleanor had had opportunity to reflect on many things, especially on the far-reaching questions of love and marriage, which, aside from the peculiar circumstances of the case, were of keen interest to both Roger and herself, though they had long ceased to discuss them together. Roger's views remained unchanged, but were difficult to summarize. He believed as strongly as ever in man's first, supreme right to happiness, regarding most obstacles to its attainment as purely arbitrary, or springing from human cowardice. He was as innate a rebel now as at nineteen, with nearly the courage of that period; nor was the disposition to invent and test new theories of his own wholly outgrown.

He admitted that the most daring experiment he had tried had failed, but was ready to show by a subtle process of reasoning that this failure was due to no lack of merit in his original purpose. Its cause lay outside himself, as it did outside just expectation and reason.

Eleanor, obliged also to admit the failure, knew well where Roger placed the blame. The blame was hers. The grief and despair which this knowledge first caused had partly died out, not because of failing sensibility on her part, or lessened power on his; but consciousness had simply become dulled to the thought of Roger's disappointment in her, as certain parts of the body had grown used to pain. Somewhat calloused as she had thus grown to his changed opinion of her, she never had any feeling of retaliatory blame or sense of injury. Perhaps it was because she had always been an underling of fate that she had so little power of resentment. She knew Roger so well that she could even see a certain sort of justice in his condemnation of her. She admitted now, as she had years before, the strength of the self-consistency that ruled all his actions, and the weakness of a nature like her own, continually halting and wavering on its course. Her strength had begun to fail her from the first. She acknowledged this humbly, without complaint against any one else. One thing only still hurt as much as it puzzled her, that Roger should count her failing strength as failing love.

It was hard to understand Roger's theory of love. What is love? she asked herself, over and over. The love of man and woman, what is that? Roger seemed to mean nothing else, when he talked of love. All the main friendships of his life had been with women, and he was more or less a lover in all such friendships, which he had not ceased to cultivate altogether since he married Eleanor. But to Eleanor's feeling, refined through physical suffering and mental conflict, love was daily losing its personal aspect, growing into something much larger if more vague, at once more near and far removed. Without knowing it, it was the religious thought of love which was slowly filling her soul. She had learned much from Emerson's poem, "The Initial, the Dæmonic, and the Celestial Love," which she read many times before she understood it, feeling newly sustained and convicted with every reading.

> But God said,
> I will have a purer gift;
> There is smoke in the flame.

These were the lines that repeated themselves in memory and condensed the poem's lesson. She had called Roger's attention to it, who pronounced it a piece of transcendental moonshine; yet he also

was an admirer of Emerson, whom he continually
quoted in support of his own advanced and independent views.

To Eleanor the poem taught the progress of the
spirit from lower, material forms of love to the
highest, from earthly passion to heavenly calm and
beneficence. That was enough! The distinction
between love as passion and love as aspiration
grew clearer to her. In most souls, finitely cir-
cumstanced, they dwell together in endless struggle;
in a few rarely-conditioned lives, warm but stain-
less, they blend into one. A piece of heaven is
dropped down to earth in the homes that crystallize
about such loves, the records of which have become
historic; but Eleanor knew now that Roger's and
hers was not to be counted among these.

She never went so far as to claim that hers was
one kind of love, Roger's another; she was content
to trace the workings of the two principles in different natures. She need not have feared, however,
to pronounce Roger's an example of passional love,
for it was what he would have eloquently defended,
with logic the more persuasive that his worst enemy could not have said it sprung from vulgar instincts. Love to him meant absolute absorption
in its object. Dr. Holmes's simile of the double
stars, revolving about each other, living in each
other's reflected light, satisfied him wholly. It
expressed much to Eleanor, also, but she remembered another law, primary and antecedent, which
these happy double stars, as well as those that move

in single state, must obey, guiding their common revolution around some central sun. It was this thought of love, springing from a sense of loyalty to something higher than itself, that Eleanor was reaching after.

How, then, did she so mistake? is it asked. Because to a nature, timid but aspiring, like hers, the daring thing, the forbidden, done in attempted mitigation of known suffering and wrong, may well seem the only true thing. Experience is costly, especially with the timid, and to Eleanor it had seemed for a time to threaten moral beggary. This was another proof of Roger's fatuous theory that love is sufficient. She had tried to believe this, to act on it, but she now saw that such a conception of love belongs but to a single stage of human experience, and helps very little to solve the great problems of life and destiny. She no longer believed with Roger in man's right to happiness, but she was learning to trace Nature's wish to bestow it, so poorly understood and aided by her human child. Happiness, to her, must be defined in terms of mental peace and calm, but to Roger it must still assume some form of emotional excess.

From Emerson and from another source, much humbler, Eleanor had received the help she needed. From Nurse Saunders, as she was familiarly called, who was also, except for Estella, the sick woman's principal companion.

There was nothing in the appearance of Mrs.

Saunders to excite romantic expectation. After the death of her husband she had sold the farm and moved to Garrison, taking up the vocation of nurse. She had been reluctant to assume her present position, preferring, with utilitarian wisdom, to take care of people who expected to get well; but consenting to take the place temporarily, she became so much attached to her charge that she stayed on. The duties were not heavy, though constant, and Roger paid her liberally. Apart from the relation of the sick-room the two women soon became excellent friends.

Mrs. Saunders was uneducated, save in the district-school sense of the term, but not illiterate, being a diligent reader of the daily paper and an inveterate reader of novels. Here the tastes of the two differed. Most of Eleanor's reading was of the higher order of poetry; she seldom opened a work of fiction, perhaps because truth had proved so much stranger in her case. She listened with amused and dreamy interest to her attendant's accounts of the made-up people she had formed last acquaintance with, and gathered from certain words that fell from her lips from time to time that she had had some unusual heart experiences of her own. One day Mrs. Saunders's narrative took a personal turn, and Eleanor learned something of her history. They had been discussing a new novel, of which the reader had given her listener an outline.

"Her first lover died, and she married this other

man to please her folks, her ma more especially. He was a good man and of more 'count than the first; but you think she did wrong, ma'am?"

"I don't wish to judge her," said Eleanor, who sat in half-reclining position in the large wheeled chair. "There should be no marriage without love."

"And you don't think that kinder respectful feelin' she had for him could take the place of love?" the nurse inquired, with a touch of wistfulness.

"No."

"You think first love is the only true love?"

"I would n't say that."

"Well, that 's what most of the folks who write the books try to make out. It 's different, I 'll admit, more upsettin'. That 's the reason, I expect, folks think it 's stronger. But there 's more than one woman lived to be thankful she did n't marry her first love." She paused a moment. "I did n't marry mine," she added. Eleanor looked at her with new interest.

"You did not love your husband?" she asked softly, with a faint accent of reproach.

"Not at first, ma'am. I was like the girl in the book. She was a city girl and had b'en to Europe; I d' know 's I 'd ought to make such a comparison," she added apologetically. "I married John Saunders to please my folks."

"Then your first lover died?" Eleanor said in a sympathetic tone.

"No ma'am, he did n't die; he deserted me."

"Deserted you!"

"He denied it afterwards," the speaker went on, as composedly as if she was reciting one of her written stories, and indeed she had about the same impersonal feeling for it now. "At least he apologized," she laughed as the word dropped from her lips. "I mean he tried to explain it away. Said he went away because I was too good for him, that I had stricter notions 'bout things than he had, and that he knew he never could live up to 'em. Said he knew it would be hard on me for a spell, but I 'd thank him afterwards. Wa'n't that funny, ma'am? But it did n't look very funny to me then."

"Do you mean that you believed him?"

"I guess I did n't really believe him, but I wanted to believe him. He talked that kind of soft and artful — 'Dolf Graham always could — he got me to feelin' more sorry for him than I ever had for myself. I guess that 's what he set out to do."

"Then why did you marry another man?" Eleanor asked in the same tone of reproach. Nurse Saunders looked at her with a puzzled face.

"Why did I marry John Saunders? I 'd been married to him pretty near two years when 'Dolf Graham came back."

Eleanor looked more astonished still at this. Here was something she had not expected, which lent a new and vivid interest to the subject.

"And did he want to take you away?" she asked, leaning forward in her chair and holding her breath for the reply.

"Take me away? Who? John?"

"No, no, the other one, your lover. Did he want you to go away with him, and leave your husband?"

Nurse Saunders straightened her tall, gaunt figure and looked at her patient as if in doubt of her sanity.

"I don't think I understand, ma'am. What kind of a woman do you think I be? 'T was bad enough my lettin' 'Dolf Graham say a word to me that day I run acrost him in Mis' Peckham's orchard. Mis' Peckham 'd said I could have all the early pippins I wanted, if I 'd pick 'em up off the ground. Apples was very plenty that year. You think I 'd let a man propose such a thing as that to me?"

"I—I did n't mean to offend you."

"That 's all right, ma'am. You did n't know John Saunders," she added excusingly. "No woman John Saunders wanted to marry 'd ever shame and disgrace him like that. Besides, ma'am," and the homely face was suffused with a tender warmth here, "I had my little girl then. A child 'll generally keep a woman right, if nothin' else does."

Eleanor's eyes rested in troubled fashion on her folded hands, and she murmured a faint affirmative.

"Men 'll desert their children — some men will — but women won't, at least, not often."

"It is quite natural," said Eleanor, in a low tone, "that a mother should think more of her child than the father. She has cared for it from birth, — and before. There is very little a man can do for his child, especially when it is little. Sometimes he is situated so that it becomes almost a stranger to him. We should not be too hard on him then, I think. It seems as if Nature meant the mother to be more to the child than the father is."

"Mebbe she did. Then she's carried out her intention; the men have helped her," with a grim smile. "'T wa'n't that way at our house, though. Our little one took to her father, first thing. He was always a dandlin' and pettin' her; and if she took sick, it was he who 'd want to take all the care of her. Used to kinder put me out, sometimes. But then everybody liked John. Folks was always comin' to him for advice, and when they was in trouble. Yet he was one of the quietest men ye ever see, too."

"You are quite sure you did n't love him?" Eleanor asked smiling.

"P'raps I did, but not the way the books explain; sometimes I think it don't matter if I did n't, and there 's other feelin's worth as much in marriage as love, and more sure to bring peace and happiness. That 's the p'int I 'm comin' to. There wa'n't never much romancin' between me and John.   I did n't never have that quivery, all-go-to-pieces kind o' feelin' with him I used to have every time 'Dolf Graham came near me.   I used to be jealous if 'Dolf spoke to another girl, but I wa'n't never jealous of John.   P'raps that was because I knew John did n't care about the girls. I could trust him.   Nobody trusted 'Dolf Graham. You look puzzled, ma'am, and no wonder.   I 've give up tryin' to think it out myself.   All I know is 't was lucky for me I did n't marry 'Dolf Graham.''

"And you were happy with your husband? "

"Yes, ma'am; though there wa'n't never much philanderin' between us, as I say.   I knew John was a good man; and after you 've made your choice in marriage you 'll stand by it, if you 're the right sort.   I could n't help feelin' account-able to John, some way.   His good name was mine, his honor and comfort was mine, too.   I was bound to help him keep 'em all.   I knew John 'd cut off his right hand for me; and I knew he trusted me as much as I did him.   John would 'a' died before he 'd deceive any one, and I could n't deceive him. That 's the reason I had to tell him 'bout 'Dolf Graham, and my meetin' him that day in Mis' Peckham's orchard.''

"You told him that? "

"Yes 'm.   I had to tell him.   Seems if my only help lay that way.   I knew 'Dolf wa'n't none too good to throw himself in my way again, and I 'd be silly enough to let him, perhaps, if nobody knew. You see I was kinder hangin' on to John in my

thoughts even when I was wrongin' him, same as
you do to God. I don't mean to be irreverent,
ma'am, but the Bible itself says you can't know the
love of Him save through the love of his creatures.
Then there was the child; she was John's child,
too, you know. Seems if I couldn't never lift
her out of her cradle again, and her a lookin' up
to me, laughin' and stretchin' out her arms, till I 'd
told her father everything. So I told him."

"Was he angry?"

"Yes 'm; but that wa'n't the hardest to bear.
It was his bein' so hurt and surprised. He looked
just sick, and shook all over for a few minits. I
could see that he blamed me, at the same time he
tried not to, 'cause I 'd b'en honest and told him
everything. He knew the meetin' was an acci-
·dent as far 's I was concerned, but I guess he
did n't think it was much of an accident on the
other side. I did n't neither."

"Were you afraid he would hurt him? — that
John would hurt 'Dolf, your lover, I mean," Eleanor explained as the other did not seem to understand.

. "I 'd rather you would n't call him my lover,
ma'am, in that way," Mrs. Saunders said respectfully, but in a tone that brought the color to her
mistress' cheek. "John was my lover, too. No.
I wa'n't afraid of his hurtin' nobody. I don't
know whether John ever said anything to him or
not; all I know is 'Dolf left them parts, and we
did n't see anything more of him."

"And you never had any regrets, any troubled thoughts about him?"

"No, ma'am, not after I 'd told John. Seems if I 'd committed myself then, like, as if I 'd got through all that foolishness and begun over again. I 've sometimes thought I wa'n't really married to John till then, till he knew the worst of me, and had forgive me and took me back. And now I want to know ma'am," coming back to the point she had started from, "whether, when a girl has to choose between the man she loves but don't respect, and the man she respects but don't love, she ain't a lot safer choosin' the last?"

Eleanor smiled. This was evidently the lesson Nurse Saunders had gained from her own life-story. Love, to her, remained the vexatious, contradictory feeling she had found it in early youth; the quiet, trustful feeling she had for her husband, something quite different. Eleanor saw there was some mental confusion here, but she learned anew how essential it is that love should contain some element of moral worth.

Love, with its first illusions destroyed, its transforming power lost, what remains? she asked herself. Will the "respect" Mrs. Saunders praised so highly, the wish to be just, mutual kindness and forbearance, take its place? The prospect here opened was not cheerful, yet Eleanor had tasted a love that disappointed more than this. She could only conclude that love, like truth, in its human application, must express itself in terms of human failure and incompleteness. It reigns pure and absolute only at its source. Yet because it reigns there it is found everywhere, though distorted from its true shape, often appearing in forms that mock and belie it. All men are lovers, up to their degree; the conjugal, the paternal, the social impulse, each is but a phase of one divine emotion filling the universe. Every form of hate, wrongdoing, and suffering must sooner or later feel its healing touch.

Thus Eleanor reasoned, dimly and unhelped, within herself. She was growing far more a lover than Roger ever had been; but she was no nearer pleasing him.

XIII.

THE mental steps by which Roger's first feeling of contemptuous disparagement towards his pupil, Nina Clarke, changed to a more favorable one need not be described. The change was the natural result of the association of two minds, one of a self-effacing and worshipful order, the other masterful and fond of being worshiped. Incapacity loses half its meaning when it makes frank recognition of itself; and Nina's meek and tireless efforts to 'overcome her deficiencies, the fact that she never tried to make extrinsic qualities serve in the place of more essential ones, could not but in time more than fill the place of missing brilliancy and self-assertion. This native humility did much to ennoble a character that might otherwise have appeared commonplace.

For a time after their renewed acquaintance Roger judged her as superficially as he had always done. Her beauty made no impression on him save to irritate and create suspicion against her. Nina looked forward to the lesson hour with much the same mingled feelings of dread and longing to please as when she studied with Estella. Strangely enough, or perhaps not strangely, since fear, we are told, is the basis of worship, these feelings never lessened admiration in this direction. Her teacher was still to her a superior order of being.

Nina Clarke's large and silent nature was just the kind for romantic imagination to dwell and rove about in. What her mother called dullness was in truth a spirit of brooding gravity, absorbed in problems only dimly defined to her young consciousness, yet filling it with keen anticipations of joy and pain. It was not his literary pretensions alone that made Roger the subject of so much speculation to herself and others, but his retired and solitary life, the unique character and habits of the entire household, shadowed by sickness, and a kind of mysterious privacy no one seemed ever to have gained the exact secret of.

Had Roger once suspected his pupil's feeling towards himself, his own would have speedily changed; for the admiration we arouse in others is apt to excite a similar feeling in return, among the most self-absorbed. Mrs. Clarke's open regard for and pride in him, as a friend, he understood and valued, though sensible at times of the burdens it involved; but the daughter's silence and ready embarrassment he construed, as others did, into signs of mental deficiency. So far was he from surmising the real nature of her feeling towards him that he had charged her with that gravest fault of all, to a man of his disposition, utter lack of appreciation, springing, he thought, from ingratitude and slow wit. One day he learned his mistake.

Nina had been reading aloud a selection from Chaucer. Her usual timidity was heightened by the difficulties of the text, and the performance was very bad. Roger listened with poorly concealed impatience, correcting in nearly every line, until the strain on nerves and temper became too great, and he broke out into petulant rebuke, accompanied with a few words of stinging sarcasm and ridicule, which aroused a feeling of indignity even in Nina. Smarting with a sense of injury and her own deficiency, she mustered all her courage and rose to her feet, trembling at her own boldness.

"It is too trying to you to have to teach me, Mr. Hunt. I shall ask mamma to discontinue the lessons." Roger was amazed, and looked at her a moment without speaking. She stood erect before him, but she did not look at him, and was visibly discomposed.

She was very beautiful. Her furred cloak had fallen from her, and her tall, well-formed figure was clearly outlined against the window and the brilliant winter landscape beyond. Her face was shadowed by the large hat she wore, covered with drooping plumes. Roger noticed these details, but cared less for them than for something else, the indefinable charm of womanliness hanging over all, never noticed before. He seemed to be seeing his pupil for the first time. Until now he had thought of her, chiefly, as Estella's companion; now he saw her as a woman, — a light that could not fail to interest him.

A witty observer of the Gallic race has said that some woman is always uppermost in a Frenchman's mind; Roger was true French in this respect. He felt the thrill of old emotions as he looked at Nina, and recalling the words he had just spoken to her, he was uncomfortable; but he would not yield his ground too quickly.

"Nonsense! " he said, with attempted lightness. "Sit down. We have not finished yet."

"Excuse me, sir, I would rather not try to finish." She spoke without resentment, but with a settled discouragement of tone that sounded more resolute than it was. Roger's surprise grew, and his interest was strongly piqued. Mrs. Clarke's words, "She is terribly afraid of you," returned to him. He rose to his feet.

"Now it is you who are unkind," he said, in a gentler voice than she had ever heard in him before. "I was rude to you, I know. I forgot myself; I sincerely beg your pardon."

Nothing could have astonished Nina more. That Mr. Hunt should speak to her in this manner, seem really to regret what he had done, and seek her forgiveness was incredible. A deep flush spread over her face, the eyes grew darker with grateful emotion, and filled with tears.

"Will you not sit down again?" he asked, in a still gentler tone, and she sank slowly in her place.

"Now we will begin again," he said, reseating himself, and speaking in his cheerfullest manner. Nina, mindful of his interests even then, glanced towards the clock.

"I am afraid the time is up, sir."

"Never mind the time! I will read and you shall listen," and he took up the book. He found the passage he wanted, and began. Roger was a good reader, and like all such, fond of the exercise. He had an agreeable voice, and Nina felt the beauty of the measured lines in their musical utterance, gathering the meaning in a vague, pleasurable way.

"That was very beautiful," she said at the close.

"Could you understand it?"

"I don't know," flushing and hesitating. "I seemed to understand it, every word, when you were reading it, but I—I am afraid I could not tell much about it now." She looked at him timidly, in fear of reproof, but he smiled indulgently.

"Chaucer was a great old boy," he said, tossing the book on the table. "We have had no poets of his size since."

"Not even Shakespeare?" she asked.

An hour before such a question would have been received with scornful impatience, but Roger's amiability remained undisturbed.

"We don't count Shakespeare, you know. He stands by himself, always."

"Yes, of course," she said apologetically. "It was foolish in me to ask that."

"In one sense they were alike; they both lived out-of-doors."

"That is just what I heard mamma say once about Browning," said Nina, pleased with herself for this apt remembrance.

Roger shrugged his shoulders. Mrs. Clarke was leader of the Browning "craze," as its detractors called it, in Garrison, a movement Roger sympathized with as little as most early lovers of the poet, who had made their own discoveries, and were little influenced by the sudden fame which a later generation had bestowed on him.

"If you want to read Browning, don't do it in a Browning class. Some day I'll read you something."

"Oh, thank you," was the reply spoken in a fervent tone. She rose, drew her cloak around her and stepped towards the door, her teacher rising and following her. He placed his hand on the latch to open it for her, a new attention, that embarrassed almost as much as it pleased her.

"So you thought I was rather cross?" he said, smiling and still keeping his hand on the door. She colored and was silent.

"You should hear me scold Estella sometimes, if you think I am severe with you."

She had, and had thought Estella's lot not the hardest; but this memory grew dim now.

"I should not mind being scolded like Estella; I should take it as a proof of interest"— This was not just what she meant to say, and she stopped in new confusion. He looked at her a moment.

"I take as much interest in you as in Estella," he said boldly.

"Oh, sir, you could not, I am sure." Nina's "sir" was very enticing.

"Not of the same kind, perhaps," he explained, in an easy tone. "Estella is a child. I suspect you have been afraid of me all this time; you think me a great bear," and he smiled teasingly.

"I think you are very good to be willing to teach me at all."

"Then if I am to continue, you must promise not to be afraid."

She flushed more deeply than before.

"Is it a bargain?" he asked, and extended his hand. She placed hers shyly in it.

"We are to be good friends, then," as he held it a moment.

"You are very kind, sir." He was about to open the door to let her pass through, when one on the other side of the room was opened, and Estella entered.

"Oh, Nina, I was afraid you had gone!" Her father looked at her with a slight frown.

"Estella, I wish you would learn to enter a room with a little more ceremony." She looked at him in surprise. She had never received such a reproof before, and with only Nina Clarke there; she could not understand it.

"I only wanted to ask Nina if I might walk home with her," she replied with a little pout.

"Of course," Nina answered, "I shall be very glad to have you."

The tone was cordial, but a little forced. Nina really wished to be alone to think over the events of the morning, the remembrance of which held her in a dream-like state throughout the day. She replied rather abstractedly to some of Estella's remarks, thinking she seemed younger than she ever had before, while Estella felt, as she often did of late, that she had lost her friend entirely.

Though Roger did not look forward to the next lesson as Nina did, he retained a distinct impression of her, of a new order, and welcomed her cordially. After this he did a large share of the reading himself, and the lessons took on a less formal and more companionable tone from week to week. Nina seemed to have lost all power to vex or weary her teacher. She was too young and inexperienced to inquire deeply into the change, feeling only the new unexpected happiness it brought.

It was characteristic of Roger that having learned to tolerate his pupil he should at once begin to idealize her. Through the innocent aid of books and under the pretense of study, not wholly a pretense, the readiness to admire and believe on one side, the hunger to be admired and believed in on the other, with a feeling of some real loneliness in each, the relation between these two grew closer.

From the reading of Chaucer and Spenser it was but a step to the reading of authors nearer their own day, and from that to bits of his own composition, explaining them and even soliciting her judgment. When Nina demurred and shrank in alarm from this test of her powers, her unsophisticated judgment was partially reassured by Roger's telling her that it was not the judgment of the wise

and learned a writer often required, so much as
that of the average mind. "Now, if you understand and like this little thing of mine," touching
a pile of manuscript on the table, "I shall feel
that the general reader will do the same. Then the
publisher will take it."

The lesson hour was often encroached upon by
conversations of this and a similar nature; but to
her mother's eyes Nina had never seemed to make
as rapid progress as now. There was a buoyancy
in her manner, and at the same time an earnestness
of purpose she had not noticed before. There were
other ways in which it was found Nina could help
her teacher. Roger had lately resumed his studies
in the line of Indian relics, in which the em-
bankments on the river at Garrison were so rich;
and the two fell into the habit of taking long walks
together to collect specimens, which it soon became
Nina's task to assort and label. Mrs. Clarke noticed this new direction of her daughter's studies
with some surprise, but without criticism, being
gratified at this evidence of a taste for solid instruction. It did not matter so much what particular
studies were followed, she told herself; it was the
general contact with and influence of a mind like
Professor Hunt's she most desired. She was getting her wish here.

At Nina's suggestion Estella accompanied them
on one of the earliest of these walking excursions,
but only once. Things were growing sadly out of
joint with Estella, and she was rather glad, except

for the dread of parting from her mother, that she was to go away in the fall, to begin her university life at Monroe. She had been pleased at Nina's invitation to go with them, but she had not been ten minutes in the company of her father and former playmate before the old feelings of distrust, bewilderment, and girlish pique seized her again. Her father paid no attention to her whatever, and Nina's efforts to be kind and include her in the conversation made her resentful. Angry and jealous, in a way she did not herself understand, she would not pretend to interest herself in the excursion's object, seating herself on the bluff, and looking moodily down the river, letting her father and Nina wander away by themselves. They were unusually successful in their search that day, Nina finding an interesting fragment of an ancient pipe-bowl that pleased Roger much. She was radiant with happiness and the physical exercise when they climbed back to Estella's lonely perch, seating themselves near her to rest and look over their spoils.

Estella listened in surprise at the new tone in which Nina spoke to her father, as respectful as the old, but confident and familiar. She even ventured to jest and dispute with him a little; while her father, she noted with greater surprise, seemed to encourage this freedom. She could not understand it, and had never felt more lonely and forlorn. Her eyes smarted with the effort to keep back the tears. Nina spoke to her, but she could not answer, and rising, walked away.

"You see how it is," Roger said in a low tone to his companion, a shade creeping over his face, as he glanced in Estella's direction and then back at her: "I have no one to help me but you."

Nina's heart beat high with pride in such praise. It did not occur to her that Estella had not been well treated. On the contrary, she was conscious of having made several attempts to interest and include her in their talk. As for Estella's father, she pitied rather than blamed him. Remarks of a similar nature had been dropped in her ears before this, hinting at unknown trials borne, soliciting sympathy. She was coming to believe that her teacher did not receive that aid and consideration from those nearest him which his commanding merits called for. His life was shadowed by something more than sickness. Thoughts like these were vague and half-formed as yet, but they were shaping. Young trust and innocence were receiving their first taint, showing scarcely more than the blue bloom of the grape, and adding a new grace, seen now only in the form of youthful sympathy, the generous desire to please and be of service.

"I think papa likes Nina better than he used to," said Estella to her mother, shortly after the walk to the river.

"I am very glad," the other replied composedly. "That will make it easier for him to teach her."

"Oh, he doesn't seem to mind teaching her. Nina is helping him arrange his cabinet. Why does papa never ask me to help him?"

"Perhaps he did not ask Nina," said her mother suggestively, "perhaps she offered." Estella colored. It was true she had made as few overtures here as she had received. Her father's collection of Indian curiosities did not interest her in the least. She would soon have wearied of any care or duty in this direction. She had neither Nina's patience nor amiability, but that did not prevent her from coveting the rewards these traits gained in others.

The lessons were broken up at the holidays and for a short time after, Mrs. Clarke taking Nina with her on a visit to Chicago, where she wished to do some shopping, renew acquaintance with some old friends, and enjoy a taste of the city's intellectual privileges. The season was at its height. Irving and Ellen Terry were at one of the leading theatres, John Fiske was booked for a lecture before a rising young institute, there were clubs innumerable which stood ready to open their doors to her, and the stores were full of tempting bargains.

Nina received the news of this journey with little of a young girl's usual interest. Her tastes and habits were always quiet, and just now home seemed far more attractive than any other place. Her mother's animated account of the sights and advantages they were to enjoy tempted neither sense nor fancy. Reluctantly, and with visible regret, she informed her teacher of her mother's plans.

"Going away!" he exclaimed. "And what am

I to do, pray?" He spoke half-playfully, but with a serious accent too.

"You will have all your time to yourself now."

"And you think I shall like that?" He asked her some questions about the trip, its length, the time of starting, etc., still with that air of injured surprise, and loneliness already begun. He let her see plainly that he should miss her in many ways, affected to believe she was on her part glad to go, and reproached her cruelty beforehand if she did not return to her place as speedily as possible; all this in a half-paternal tone, that the girl tried to listen to frankly and unabashed, but which raised in her a faint feeling of alarm, so that she wanted to run away. She was beginning to be afraid of the man before her, but in a new way. His deep dreamful eyes held the same magnetic spell for her others had fallen under, his voice vibrated along her heart-strings, his strong, compelling presence filled the room, and her thoughts when she was away from him. Words were spoken that made her cheeks burn, yet whose overt sense was quite harmless, making the blame of any other seem to spring from guilty imagination.

Where the guilt was she was too troubled and confused to know, but the sense of it was growing.

XIV.

THERE were those among Roger Hunt's acquaintance who believed him to be a consummate actor. Even his old friend, Kitty Somers, used to incline to this hypothesis at times. This was because, with all his impulsiveness, he was the most self-observant of men. Careless as he often was of the impression he produced, he nevertheless always understood it. The long estrangement between himself and Eleanor, covered with an unfailing courtesy of speech and manner in the presence of others, so that a four years' inmate in the household like Mrs. Saunders never suspected it, was the result of deliberate resolve, never forgotten, and adhered to more proudly every day. Impetuosity was blended with utmost caution. Self-consciousness was always uppermost, as it probably is with the most trained actor; and gave the impression in many quarters of cunning deceit. "Take my word for it, Lucy," Thomas Clarke had said in his early acquaintance with their neighbor, repeating the opinion many times after, "the man is a fraud. He's the sleekest hypocrite I know."

"Don't speak so coarsely, Thomas. I'm sure Professor Hunt is the last man to be accused of hypocrisy. He's unpleasantly honest, I think.

He does n't try to please people as much as you do, even."

Her husband smiled at this, taking it as a compliment, as she meant he should.

"If he had n't had the luck to inherit a little money," he grumbled, continuing the subject, "he could n't earn his salt."

"There are a great many excellent people in the world who cannot make money. It's vulgar, estimating people's worth in dollars and cents."

"Perhaps it is; but a man should show he has got something better, then."

"Professor Hunt is a scholar, a literary man. I don't see why you are so prejudiced against him," she added for the hundredth time.

"I ain't prejudiced against him. He fills his place, I suppose. All I mean to say is he'd rattle around like a dried pea in a quart measure if he tried to fill some other people's."

She did not attempt to argue this point, to show how the misplaced pea might prove something besides its own diminutiveness, the emptiness of the receptacle holding it; but closed the discussion with a repeated expression of gratitude that so accomplished a man was their neighbor and Nina's teacher. She added that Nina seemed to get on with him better, of late.

"I guess he won't hurt Nina much. We pay him for his services. I'd have to be pretty hard up to accept favors from a man like Hunt."

"You think everything can be settled with money."

"No, not everything, Lucy," he said, drawing near and putting his arm, lover-like, about her waist, a somewhat snugger armful than when she was a girl. "I ain't forgot the woman who showed she had some faith in me when I was a green youngster, and not worth a hundred dollars. I would n't trade you for all the bonds and mort-gages." This was gratifying, and seemed to present a favorable opportunity for a request she had expressed before.

"I wish you 'd give up business and retire. We have more than money enough now. Then we could all go to Europe for two or three years."

"What on earth should I do, hangin' 'round Europe? You 're not going to marry Nina to some broken-down count, I hope."

"How ridiculous! I mean it is time you re-tired."

"Not any Europe for me. You and Nina can go, if you want to; I 'm goin' to stay here in Gar-rison. They want me to run for the legislature again, but I don't know as I want to bother about it. I guess I 'll turn it over to Charlie Perkins," another moneyed power in the town. "He wants it pretty bad; and I suppose it 'd about tickle Mis' Perkins to death."

Nina was homesick the moment she entered the carriage that was to take her to the station. The train whirled her swiftly along, past snow-covered fields and long stretches of leafless forests; but her thoughts flew backward, and she scarcely noted her surroundings. The sights and sounds of the great city, when she reached it, fell on senses muffled in remote thoughts. She followed her mother about like one in a dream. Forbidden thoughts, vague images and desires that both uplifted and shamed her, filled her mind.

Roger Hunt had asked her to write to him, but some monitor within had forbidden it, and it may be taken as a sign of the hopeful struggle going on in the young girl's breast that she had so far obeyed the latter. One day she returned to the hotel at which they were stopping to find a letter from him. —Mrs. Clarke had friends in the city, but never made a convenience of them. —Was her guardian angel asleep, or only the more forbearing, that she who had scarcely been from her mother's side should at this moment happen to be alone and unobserved? Nina's nature was as childlike in some things at nineteen as at nine. She had never received a letter before she dared not show her mother, as something told her she must not this one, before she opened it.

Its length alone would have excited her mother's wonder, though it dealt for the most part with impersonal topics, discussed in a tone of plaintive melancholy Nina was becoming familiar with. It also contained a list of books the writer asked her to purchase for him, and which might be made to serve as the letter's ostensible object. Attached was a postscript of different tenor. It ran thus:

. . . "Out doors it has done nothing but rain

since you went away; the sun has not looked through the study-window once, and he is right, there is nothing here worth looking for. A certain chair by the table looks very empty. Old Chaucer has whispered to me that he is as lonely as somebody else is, and has been punished for his presumption by being put back on the shelf."

Nina crumpled the letter in her hand and sank trembling into a chair. She had gone to her room, and locked the door. Pride and shame struggled fiercely in the young girl's bosom; her mind was in a whirl. Had mere friendship the power to agitate her thus, enslave fancy, arouse accusing conscience? As she sat there lost in frightened and remorseful thoughts, she heard her mother enter the outer room, approach and try the door, then call to her in surprised tones: —

"Nina, Nina! — are you there? What in the world have you locked the door for?"

Rising and thrusting the letter in her pocket, she opened the door.

"What is the matter?" Mrs. Clarke asked, in a rather anxious tone, as she noted her daughter's pale and worn appearance.

"Nothing; I — I was tired a little, and thought I would lie down."

"What have you been crying about?"

"I have not been crying," was the quiet reply, truthfully spoken. Perhaps it was the effort to keep back the tears gave her eyes that bright strained look. Mrs. Clarke gave utterance to a discontented exclamation: —

"Lie down, of course, if you are tired, but I don't understand why you give out so easily, — a great, strong girl like you!   You can't stand half as much as I can, now.   I don't believe you are enjoying your visit at all."

"Oh yes, I am.   But you know I never did like a large city very much.   It tires and confuses me so — especially Chicago."   Her voice took on a tone of slight querulousness at the end.

"Well, you 're very different from me, then. There 's no place in the world like Chicago, I think, not even New York.   It puts new life into me every time I come here.   I can't see how your father ever happened to pass it by and locate in a place like Garrison.   We might just as well be living here as not, in one of those handsome residences on the Lake shore."

"I 'm very glad he did not," said Nina, with a little obstinacy.   "I like Garrison much better." She had removed her hat and wrap, and stood before the glass putting her hair to rights.

"I thought you were going to lie down," said her mother.

"I think I won't now, it is so near supper-time."

"You must change your dress. You know we are going to see Irving to-night in 'The Bells.' "

"Why is.n't this good enough?" the girl asked discontentedly; "we shan't see any one we know."

"What difference does that make? You should wear what is suitable.   What is the use of bringing a trunkful of dresses, if you are always going to wear the same one? Put on your garnet silk, and get out your white hat and some light gloves."

Nina would have much preferred her black silk and other things to match, but she was allowed little voice in such matters.

It was the cause of much maternal pride to Mrs. Clarke, when she and Nina took their seats in the front row of the parquet circle, that her daughter was as handsome and had as city-bred a look as any of the other young women present. She looked about her with a gratified and expectant air, though as Nina had said, they knew no one. But Mrs. Clarke liked to feel herself a part of so brilliant a gathering as this, picturing in fancy the important rôle she might be playing here had destiny treated her just a little differently. Nina's mind was engrossed with importunate thoughts arising from the remembrance of the letter, which she seemed to feel burning in her pocket, where she still carried it for safety's sake, trying to reach a determination to destroy it.

She gave but mechanical interest to the play in the opening scenes, not catching the plot. Her mother had seized it at once and turned to her animatedly when the curtain dropped,

"Isn't it wonderful! I knew the moment he came on the stage it was he who had committed the murder. I hadn't read the plot either. You could tell it by the scared, trembling look he had, even though he was in his own house. Wonderful!" she repeated.

"Who?" Nina asked, uncomprehendingly. "What murder?"

"Why, Irving, of course; 'Mathias' I mean. Don't you understand?"

"I never can understand the first act of a play," was the rather irritated reply.

"They were talking about a murder that had been committed years before. This is the anniversary. Mathias is the murderer, but no one suspects it. He did it for the money, and has kept the secret all this time."

Nina understood now, and when the curtain again rose watched the movement of the play with new interest. As it proceeded, and she began to comprehend the struggle of tortured conscience in Mathias, this interest became painfully intense. During the mesmerizing scene she forgot her surroundings entirely, leaning forward in her seat, with shortened breath, her face paling and flushing, her eyes fixed intently on the great actor. The rest of the audience were nearly as spellbound as she, but two or three who sat near noticed her, looking at her curiously and smiling. Her mother pressed her foot against hers with a warning touch, and Nina started guiltily and fell back in her seat.

Mrs. Clarke was enthusiastic over the evening's performance. "The most wonderful piece of acting I ever saw," she exclaimed, as they drove back to the hotel.

"Acting!" Nina repeated, half under her breath. "It did not seem like acting."

Mrs. Clarke laughed.

"We must see him Saturday in 'Much Ado.' They say he's almost as good in comedy. Then we can see Terry too." But Nina could not think of the actor in his own person, and cared nothing for his reputation in comedy. It was the image of the sin-stricken Mathias that still held her; she was still in the thrall of those terrible closing scenes. Oh, the dreadful weight imposed on the heart by a guilty secret! That was the play's lesson to Nina. Does this extreme application of her text excite a smile? Let it be remembered that the soul's strength is better proved by reactive bounds backward from temptation than by any easy, unhindered ascent towards goodness. Nina's trouble was the greater that no one could help her bear it. She must fight her battle alone, as the soul's real battles are always fought. She felt the strength to fight now. Alone in her room she drew out the letter and tore it to fragments, then threw them into the grate and watched them smoulder slowly into ashes on the dying coals. She drew a long breath, that ended in a sob. She was very tired, worn out with fatigue and excitement. The play still filled her mind, and kept her awake until nearly morning, but to strengthen and exalt now, rather than alarm and crucify. When she rose in the morning she had reached a decision. Her mother would combat it, she knew, but she felt able to resist her mother.

It was with reluctance that she made ready

to attend the matinée on Saturday, and she was full of regrets afterward. Nina's serious nature, doubly in earnest just now, did not take kindly to the comic side of things ever; and to her it was a simple travesty, very painful and not at all amusing, to see "Mathias," as she still called him, for the actor's make-up disguised him here as little as before, dressed in a slashed tunic of blue silk, engaged in foolish love-making with Beatrice. The glory of his first appearance, the almost religious halo with which she had invested him in grateful imagination was quite destroyed. It was a very creditable performance, she supposed. Her mother had been highly amused, and talked enthusiastically of both the accomplished actors, but Nina felt it would have been better if she had seen the first only once. Not that her resolve was lessened; she remembered and repeated it to herself many times a day. It began to look more difficult, she did not feel quite so strong as at first, still she told herself she meant to execute it.

Mrs. Clarke looked for a call from her neighbor the Sunday after their return, but he did not come. Monday was lesson-day, but Nina, keeping herself occupied with small household tasks, let the hour pass, apparently without notice, and was found by her mother in the sewing-room upstairs.

"I thought you had gone for your lesson," she said in a surprised tone. "It is half past ten. You must go at once. You know how it annoys Professor Hunt when you are late." Nina made no movement to obey. She was not afraid of annoying Professor Hunt. She turned and looked at her mother; the color faded from her cheeks, and she trembled: —

"Mamma, I don't want, I mean — don't you think — Need I take lessons any more?"

There was an accent of pitiful entreaty in her words, had there been ears to hear. Her mother looked at her with a displeased face.

"Nina, you try me out of all patience! I hoped you would n't disappoint me again. All your life I have had to urge you to study. I am ashamed to think how far you are behind other girls of your age. Lately you have done better, and I was beginning to hope you cared a little."

"I do care, mamma," speaking with difficulty. "I care very much. It is n't that. I will go on by myself."

"How can you go on by yourself? That is nonsense! You would get tired of it, as you did of your music."

"I will begin my music again, mamma, and practice faithfully. I will do anything you wish, if — if only " — She could not go on.

"I don't want you to go on with your music. You 've no talent for it," her mother said bluntly.

"I have no talent for books, either," was the humble reply.

"That is foolishness. Mercy knows I don't expect much of you, Nina, but I should think you would have a little pride. You need n't think be-

cause your father is rich and you are good-look-
ing ” —

"Mamma!" exclaimed the girl in hurt rebuke of
words flung in her face like a taunt.

"A girl needs something besides money and a
pretty face, in these days," her mother finished.
Nina laid down the small feather duster she had
been feigning occupation with, and looked at her
mother; the few inches she had gained over her in
height seemed suddenly doubled. Mrs. Clarke felt
a little uncomfortable.

"What do you want to give up your lessons
for?" she asked querulously. "Is Professor
Hunt cross with you?"

"No; he is very good to me." Already Nina's
heart had taken swift flight to the little study,
a quarter of a mile distant, away from this hard,
ambitious mother. He was awaiting her there now,
she thought, wondering at her absence, — he who
never sneered and mocked at her as her mother
did. The times when he had done this seemed as
far off as the period of her dolls and skipping-
ropes.

"Well, I know he can be disagreeable enough
when he chooses," her mother went on in more
mollified tone, "and I know he hates teaching.
That ought to make you appreciate your privileges. I can't bear to have you disappoint me so,
Nina."

"I disappoint you a great deal, I know, mamma;
I always have, but I will try not to any more. I

will do whatever you wish." She went out of the room. Her mother looked after her with a baffled expression. Soon she came downstairs, dressed to go out, and left the house without speaking. Mrs. Clarke sighed when she heard the door close. She loved her daughter according to the love a nature like hers had to bestow. For a mother whose expectations were of so just and reasonable an order, she suffered a good many trials, she thought.

Nina walked swiftly down the slight decline of the street that led to the Hunt cottage. Her heart beat fast with double excitement, the hurt, mingled with some anger, given by her mother, and the wish to reach her destination. She now longed to see Mr. Hunt again. Her heart burned with a sense of injustice, then glowed with happier warmth as she thought of the welcoming look and smile awaiting her. How could she be wholly stupid and commonplace, if a man like Mr. Hunt cared for her? And he did care for her! Just now she exulted in the thought. She threw her fears to the winds. The sense of injury and desire for self-justification bore down every other feeling.

With cheeks glowing from contact with the cold air, and eyes alight with expectation, she opened the study door and stood a moment on the threshold. Roger, who had been moving impatiently about the room, was at the farther end. He turned quickly at the sound of her entrance, but did not move to meet her, standing in his place and looking at her reproachfully. But Nina seemed not to fear the reproach. Her heart leaped at the thought that he had been impatiently waiting for her. For a few seconds' space, she, too, kept her place, just inside the door, her eyes returning the full, deep look in his. Then she moved towards him.

"I am late," she said, and unclasped her cloak.

"On our first day, too," Roger said accusingly.

"I — I 'm sorry," she replied. "It 's too late for a lesson now, but " — She did not know how to finish, and throwing back her cloak, seated herself in her usual place.

Roger came slowly towards her. "Are n't we going to shake hands?" he asked. She laughed, colored, and gave him her hand, but this more formal greeting seemed superfluous.

"How natural everything looks!" said Nina, glancing about the room, and feeling the necessity of saying something. He let his glance follow, then return to rest on her.

"Yes — now."

He seated himself opposite her, and a short silence ensued.

"Why did you not answer my letter?" Roger asked at length.

She blushed and looked confused.

"Were you displeased with me for writing?"

"Displeased!" she answered, collecting herself. "Why should I be displeased? It was very good in you to take the trouble."

She then added some remark about being busy,

etc. "Mamma kept me running about so," she ended with a childish accent.

"You don't like running about, then?"

"I detest it." There was a manifestation of uncommon energy in this speech, which seemed to amuse her listener.

"Then you're not sorry to get back to Garrison?"

"Sorry? I am glad. I should like never to go away again."

"That's good. Tell me now what interested you most in the city."

"What interested me most?" she repeated mechanically. She looked at him absently a moment, realling the main events of her trip. "Oh," drawing a deep breath, "it was Irving's 'Bells.'"

"Irving's bells?" he repeated in a mystified tone. He seldom read the papers, and if he had heard of the English actor's visit to this country, had immediately forgotten it.

In a few words Nina described the play. Now she was on the subject, she was glad to talk it over with him, present all its difficulties for his solution. Roger listened, but plainly with more interest in the speaker than her narrative.

"A strange choice of subject," he said, when she paused. "One of those pieces of morbid character study the stage is so fond of presenting nowadays. If I had been there, I could have proved to you that you cared nothing about it."

"Oh, it was not the play," exclaimed Nina; "it

was the acting. He made you feel it all so, the fear, and the awful remorse he lived in, day after day, when every one thought him the most happy and honored of men.''

Roger smiled at her enthusiasm.

"I could not get rid of it for days, it took hold of me so. I did not sleep all night." Here a vivid blush swept across her face, as she recalled other and more immediate causes of this wakefulness.

"Not sleep all night!" cried Roger. "That proves the thorough badness of the play, at once. True art never has a disturbing effect; its mission is to soothe and please. Can you imagine any of the old Greeks lying awake after a representation of the Alkestis?"

Nina smiled, pleased but embarrassed. The habit her teacher had lately fallen into of assuming her equal understanding of allusions of this kind, drawn from the remote and abstruse studies he so delighted in, was part of the growing wonder and happiness of this new relation. No wonder Nina found compensation for her mother's slighting words in the·treatment she received here.

Had she been as well informed as her companion's question implied, she might have questioned him in turn, on the probable effect of the performance of the Medea and the Choephori; but as it was, Roger kept the talk in his own hands.

"Remorse is as unhealthy a sentiment as it is unreasonable," he went on, now on one of his favorite themes. "The man who spends all his life regretting something is an intellectual weakling."

"Yet if one has committed a great wrong — a crime?"

"He was guilty of murder, you say?" Roger asked, raising his eyes meditatively to the ceiling, as if debating the degree in which such an action could command honest regret.

"A terrible murder. It is horrible even to think of it," she replied, with a shudder.

"For all that he should have stood by his deed. That shocks you," he added, as he noted her look of surprise. "He should either have acknowledged it at once, and accepted the consequences," —

"Oh, yes, I understand you now," she interrupted, with relief.

"Or," without heeding her, "he should have buried it so deep below all consciousness and mem-ory that even sleep would have no power to resurrect it."

Her look changed to one of pained perplexity. She felt the force of this kind of reasoning, but it did not satisfy her.

"Irresolution is a vice in itself," Roger went on. "A man had better be strongly in the wrong than weakly in the right. That is one of the lessons your Browning teaches," he added with a smile.

"He is n't my Browning; he is mamma's."

"Very well; then she can't object to my reading you something of his. I promised to read you something, some time." He rose and took a volume from a shelf in the "Poet's Corner." "Let us see now, if you can understand it," he said, reseating himself. "You can't often understand Browning the first time, you know. That's his great merit. That's the reason he has crowded Shelley and Keats off the shelves. Listen, now," and he began to read "The Statue and the Bust."

His reading made the poem as clear as any one's could; and Nina caught the meaning fairly well, but was evidently troubled over it.

"Now tell me what it is all about," Roger said, when he had finished, closing the book and laying it one side. "Give me the outline of the poem." Nina flushed and demurred, but he insisted.

"Well," she began hesitatingly, "the bust represented the lady whose husband had kept her imprisoned in the castle of the window where it stood." She stopped, and they both laughed.

"Window of the castle," she corrected herself.

"'Whose husband had kept her imprisoned in the window of the castle,'" Roger repeated. "Go on. We're getting along famously. Soon the interpretation will be as obscure as the poem. Then we shall have proved ourselves true disciples."

"I told you I could not do it," leaning back in her chair with the least little pout. Once words like these would have sent her home in tears, but now their force was quite dispelled.

"And the statue, what did that represent?" he pressed her.

"Oh, he was a soldier, and an officer in her husband's service; and they — they cared for each other," with lowered eyes, and fingering the beaded ornament on her sleeve nervously.

"He was her lover, you mean?"

"But they never saw each other till the day of her marriage," she said hastily, groping about in her mind for some excuse.

"Yet they loved each other. What next?" keeping watchful eyes upon her.

"And — and they planned to escape, but things kept happening, so they never did; and every day the lady would look out of the window to see him ride past, and he would look up to see her. They should not have done that," she added in comment.

"Why?"

Nina looked at him in surprise. But it was not because he meant to dispute such a point he questioned her, only to see if her own thoughts were clear, she reflected.

"They should have gone far away, and resolved never to see each other again," in a little tremor.

"Quite correct," said Roger, in a tone she did not quite understand. "But would that have destroyed the wish to see each other?"

"I — I suppose not, sir."

"And is it not the wish to do a wrong thing, if you call this wrong, that affects the character as much as the action itself?"

"Do you mean it would have been as wrong for Mathias merely to have wished he had the other man's money to pay off his debt with, as to have murdered him?"

"Who was Mathias?" Roger asked, with a slight frown.

"The man in the play."

"Oh, yes. It would n't have been as hard on the murdered man, perhaps, but the effect on the character of Mathias would have been the same if he kept revolving the thing in his mind" —

"Oh, sir, but he would not. He was a good man, only he was dreadfully tempted. But he would have mastered and killed his wish, I am very sure."

"Those two in the poem did not; they neither overcame their wish nor executed it. They should have done one thing or the other; because they did not they were properly punished by being turned into stone. Browning thinks so, too," and he quoted the line about "the unlit lamp, and the ungirt loin." "The critics have made a fine fuss about this poem. They call it immoral; but it is the hesitating lovers who were immoral. They had better have carried out their wish a hundred times."

"But that would have been a crime," said the girl, in a low, frightened tone. Roger turned his full, lucent gaze on her.

"What is a crime?" he asked. She looked surprised, reflected a moment, then slowly shook her head.

"Simply a term of classification; a legal means of separating one class of actions from another."

"Wrong actions?" Nina interposed.

"Well, wrong actions, then," throwing his head back impatiently. "But you must remember the term is often applied in the most arbitrary fashion. Many a man's so-called 'crime,' for which he is paying the penalty in a prison-cell, is of far less importance than the unlabeled rascality of hundreds of others who live in peace and safety outside; and on the other hand," he paused and drew a deep breath, "many another man may have been accused of committing a crime against society, when his action in no way concerned that precious humbug, and which sprung from the noblest and purest motives."

"Oh, yes, I know that," said Nina, sympathetically. She supposed her teacher was speaking of cases like Galileo and John Huss, and other victims of advanced opinion, whom the world had punished with rack and thumbscrew. She knew his sympathy for every form of social oppression.

Roger was about to continue, when the little clock on the mantel struck, sounding the half hour after twelve. Nina started guiltily to her feet.

"I have stayed too long!"

"I am sorry you have found it so."

"Oh," she replied with a deprecating glance and blush, "I only meant I did not know it was so late." She picked up her gloves, and turned towards the door, where she bade him good-by, meeting again a glance she could not support, and passed outside. She had spent nearly two hours in the little study, but it had not seemed an hour. Not a word had been said of the lesson, an omission both had noticed, but neither had spoken of.

XV.

ROGER had intended to send Estella to the university the coming September, but after correspondence with the authorities at Monroe he decided to have her go six months earlier, in order to profit by certain advantages in the preparatory course which he could not offer her at home.

This decision, when it was announced to Estella and her mother, gave a little shock of surprise to each, but Eleanor bore it more quietly than Roger had anticipated. Estella was filled with consternation at the prospect so suddenly opened before her. The thought of leaving home, when it was still far off, had aroused a feeling of girlish expectation, but now when it was so near, imagination had no chance to play with it, and only the painful reality was left. She must leave her mother, and live alone among strangers! She had looked to support her mother when the time of parting came, but it was rather her mother who cheered and strengthened her. Apart from the hardship to herself, Estella had a sense of disloyalty in leaving her, a feeling that she was deserting one in great need.

Estella had grown more sensitive to the home atmosphere of late, and an undefined trouble filled her breast whenever she thought of her father.

She had always known her father was peculiar, but when younger this peculiarity had only impressed her as superiority, acknowledged even by those who did not seem to like him; but later it had struck her at times as manifest weakness, — eccentricity. She had been put in a position once or twice where she was forced to see him not simply as different from other people, but ludicrously different. It had never been a hardship to her that she could not love her father with that demonstrative fondness other girls displayed; but it would go hard with her if she were ever to lose her respect for him.

As for Eleanor, the trial of parting was as severe as she had ever anticipated; she suffered beforehand all the loneliness of the days that were to come, but at the same time she was glad that Estella was going, that she was to leave home for a time. Some of these reasons were newly discovered to herself.

The relation between Roger and their child had always been a subject of engrossing anxiety to Eleanor. She desired above everything to preserve the instinct of filial respect in Estella. In mental quickness and self-dependence she was her father's child. She was the only member of the household, and so far as her mother knew in their circle of acquaintance, who had the courage openly to oppose her father and hold her own against him; but she had done this as yet only in ways that evinced youthful daring, and which amused more than displeased

him. The subservience he received in other quarters he cared little for here; and he had always
encouraged natural behavior in her, such as he himself practiced. But Eleanor knew there were limits to the opposition he would suffer, here as elsewhere. The possibility that his daughter would
ever become his critic, in any serious way, never
crossed his mind, but it had crossed Eleanor's.
Wifely feeling was the main motive of conduct with
her still, notwithstanding the discouragement it had
received. She could bear it better to have Estella
fail in duty towards herself than towards her father;
and — strange paradox — if the right sentiment
could be preserved only by separating them, she
could willingly, almost gladly, bear the pain of it
for herself.

An incident had occurred a week or two before
Estella's departure from home had been determined, which partly explains this state of mind.

One spring-like morning late in March, Eleanor
awoke, feeling stronger than she had for a long
time. The sunshine flooding the room had an almost summer warmth in it, and new life seemed to
pulsate through her veins. She rose from her bed
and with the nurse's assistance dressed. The effort
tired her less than she had thought it would, and
she longed to test her strength in some new way.
She had not been outside the sick-room for weeks,
and it now seemed like a prison. A daring wish
arose within her to see Roger in his study. She
put it away, but it returned. Her cheek flushed as

she thought of it, and her heart beat with happy anticipation. She never thought of displeasing him. On the contrary, with that fatuous power of self-delusion which loving natures possess, and crucify themselves with anew every day, she thought he would be pleased. He had sometimes made her feel that she yielded too easily to the physical weakness that was destroying her. It would be a proof to him of returning strength and courage on her part. The thought soon gained complete possession of her, but she knew she must execute it alone. Estella was in town and safely out of the way for an hour, and she devised an errand to keep Mrs. Saunders in another part of the house for a while. Alone, she made a great effort and rose to her feet, steadying herself a moment, then walking with slow uncertain steps, stopping to rest now and then, out of the room, across the intervening hall, to the library. When she reached it, excitement more than the physical effort had tired her, her limbs trembled, and she feared to fall. The door was closed, but the absorption of the two inside prevented them from hearing the slight noise she made in opening it, and she stood unseen on the threshold a moment.

The picture that stamped itself indelibly on her brain was innocent enough in its main details, but one she understood the full import of.

Nina was seated at the table, her back to the door, and writing at her teacher's dictation, who stood near her, his hand on her chair, his face bent nearly to the level of hers. Some word of his had caused her to raise her face to his, so near that his breath stirred her hair. Eleanor caught the look of rapt feeling, shy, eager, grateful, which suffused the young girl's face. She could not see Roger's, but she could guess its expression well enough. She longed to escape, but it was impossible, and she clung to the door-casing for support. A slight sound caught Nina's ear, who turned and saw her, uttering a slight scream of fright, then quickly checking it. Eleanor indeed looked like a ghost, in her long white draperies, her face ghastly with returning weakness and the knowledge of her mistake.

Roger too had turned quickly, and the face Nina had seen so calm and tender a moment before changed terribly.

"Eleanor, what does this mean?" In his surprise and displeasure he forgot to go to her assistance, and remained looking at her sternly.

She tried to smile, and cast an apologetic look towards Nina.

"I — I only wanted to surprise you, Roger; I felt so much better this morning, I — I" —

The room began to whirl about her. Nina's face, frightened, and with a look of pitying wonder, tinged with guilty consciousness besides, and Roger's, stern and accusing, floated out of sight. She reeled, and reached out a hand blindly.

"Oh, she will fall!" cried Nina. It was she who sprung to her assistance, her arms that caught and held the swaying figure, then helped it to a chair, kneeling beside and half supporting her.

"This is the greatest piece of folly I ever heard of," Roger exclaimed, after Eleanor had partially recovered, and sat leaning back in her chair, white and exhausted. "Where is Mrs. Saunders?" and he stepped to the door and called her in a voice of sharp command. "I shall discharge her, if she does n't attend to her duties better than this." He stood looking down on his wife gloomily.

"What in the world were you thinking of?" he asked, in the same tone as before.

"Don't scold her," Nina said, glancing up at him, from the place she still kept at the sick woman's side. He turned abruptly away.

"I — I 'm sorry, Roger," Eleanor said faintly. "I ought not to have come, I know. Don't blame Mrs. Saunders, please. She did not know " —

A fit of coughing interrupted her. She pressed her handkerchief to her lips, and when she took it away, Nina saw a spot of red. She uttered a low exclamation of fright. Eleanor's eyes rested on her with a strange, yearning look the girl never forgot.

"It is nothing," she said. "I am sorry I interrupted you. I won't do it again."

Mrs. Saunders entered at that moment and Nina rose to her feet. Roger briefly explained the situation in a tone that conveyed a plain rebuke for her negligence. "We must get her back to her room at once."

"I 'll manage that, sir," the nurse said, and approached her charge to lift and carry her away.

"No — no," exlaimed Eleanor, shrinking from this exposure of her weakness. "Don't carry me; I can walk." Mrs. Saunders helped her to her feet, Roger trying to assist, but awkwardly, and soon desisting. The nurse put one strong arm about the sick woman, and led her slowly to the door.

"Let me help," said Nina, darting impulsively forward.

"There ain't no need, Miss," the other replied, and in a moment they were gone.

Nina stood looking after them a moment. Turning, she saw Roger. He had thrown himself into a chair, burying his face in his crossed arms on the back; but she scarcely heeded him. She put on her hat and cloak hurriedly and stepped to the door, where she paused and looked back.

"I — I am going now, sir." He raised his face. It was the picture of melancholy despair. He looked at her a moment.

"Why are you going?" he asked.

"It is nearly time," glancing at the clock. It said they had still twenty minutes; they had consulted it very little of late. He bent the same look of mournful reproach on her.

"Why not speak the truth? Why not say you are going because you are displeased with me?"

"Displeased with you !" she repeated falteringly. He rose and came towards her.

"You are displeased with me, and you have a right to be. I behaved badly." He paused, and a deep sigh came from him. "But it gave me a terrible shock!" His voice sank, his eyes rested on the floor, his whole attitude spoke sorrowful contrition and self-reproach. He said truly; Nina had been painfully surprised, a quick sharp distrust of him had pierced her like a knife. But she was more ashamed for herself; she felt like a thief. Yet it was hard to throw off in a moment the influence which had held her so long. With Roger standing there before her, humbled and penitent, waiting her verdict, it was not easy to open the door and leave him. Perhaps it was not real anger that had prompted him to speak so harshly, only bewildered surprise. She stood hesitating.

"I do everything I can," he went on in a discouraged tone. "I make no merit of that. I give her the best of care, try to gratify every wish, yet you see for yourself how reckless and imprudent she is."

The girl lowered her eyes; a pained and irresolute expression flitted across her face.

"She — she wanted to please you, I think. She has suffered so much."

"That is true; I ought not to forget that. I try to bear it always in mind — but I — I have suffered, too." He turned away. She could find no reply and kept silent. Something within told her these were no words to be addressed to her, but she could not help a deep, ignorant pity for the one who spoke them. He turned and faced her again.

"You will not forgive me, then?"

"I"— she exclaimed, blushing painfully. "Oh, sir, it is not I"— She checked herself. "There is nothing for me to forgive," she added, her look falling before his. His eye brightened:—

"Then will you walk with me? I cannot go back to my books—now," glancing towards his desk with a sigh. She hesitated, but saw no way save to comply, which she did, however, with more reluctance than she had ever granted request of his before.

She could not have told how, with no definite appeal on his part, and before the walk was half ended, the current of sympathy had set strongly in his direction again. Without making any direct confidences, he seemed to tell her everything. The tone of intentional self-restraint, the frank admission of his own faults, veiled allusions to some exceptional experience in the past, his exaltation of the sentiment of friendship, all combined to disarm and enthrall his listener. Thus, with her rising scruples partially allayed, sympathy warmed anew, and girlish pride aflame with the knowledge of her own power to help one who needed and deserved help, the walk came to an end.

The discovery Eleanor made in her visit to the study was one former experiences might have prepared her for, and which humiliated her for Roger's sake far more than it could now pain her for her own. She recalled Estella's words about her father's changed feeling towards Nina, and marveled at her own dullness. Early in their united lives she reached her first surprised, shamed, and then jealous knowledge of Roger's susceptibility towards women, his almost exclusive dependence on them for sympathy and near companionship. She tried to reason about and excuse it, even when suffering most from such knowledge, remembering his peculiar temperament, and sustaining herself in the old belief, which she still held, in Roger's purity of motive. She had no reason to believe he had ever been untrue to her in any outward sense; he had only permitted his imagination, which was of a roving order, to wander as it would, engrossing itself with any new object that pleased it. She knew what Roger's excuse for these spiritual flights was, and so potent was his influence over her still, that there were times when she tried to make his excuse hers. If she had not disappointed him, had proved all he wished and all he needed, he would not be obliged to seek companionship elsewhere.

Towards the women themselves, — these stars of Platonic friendship that rose from time to time in the domestic firmament, eclipsing the wife's faithful planet, — even Eleanor's gentle and self-abnegating nature felt some righteous scorn, which even the knowledge of her own frailty could not wholly extinguish. This feeling did not extend to Nina, however, for whom she felt more pity than blame.

Blame of all kinds was coming to be out of place

in one so near the final judgment. Happily, as the spirit slips its sheath of flesh, earthly affairs, even the nearest, lose in importance, recede and fade from sight. The soul feels its own helplessness in the presence of the impending change. It is God's world, he will take care of it, was the prayerful excuse with which Eleanor let one care after another slip from her. She felt sorry for Nina, in a strangely curious and impersonal way, newly discouraged with Roger, quite indifferent about herself, troubled only for Estella. She was, therefore, thankful for the opportunity presented in Roger's decision to send her from home six months earlier than he first intended, to keep her young eyes shielded with ignorance a little longer.

XVI.

HER father went with Estella to Monroe, the latter spending the night's journey in tears, and reaching the end half ill with weariness and grief.

They went to the hotel for breakfast, and then started out to pay a visit to the university. Estella's homesickness increased with every new object that met her view. Her heart sank as she followed her father through the wide corridor of the main building, filled with busy young men and women, carrying books in their arms. . Nothing could be in greater contrast to the quiet surroundings she had left at home than the prospective life that opened before her here. She had never felt so insignificant.

Roger inquired the way to the president's office. A tall, angular-looking man, something of the Abraham Lincoln build, with keen eye and scholarly face, rose to meet them as they entered, giving them a courteous welcome, then turning his attention to other visitors who had preceded them. When his turn came, the president listened quietly to Roger's statement of his business, bent one or two examining glances on Estella, and learning that she was not yet ready to enter the regular course, summoned a boy in waiting and sent him away with a message.

"Professor Hart has charge of the preparatory department," he explained. "I have sent for him."

At that moment a bell rung. "We shall have to wait now until after chapel exercises," he said. "Perhaps you would like to join us."

Roger drew himself up. "Do I understand that attendance on chapel exercises is obligatory?" he asked. The president looked at him with mild surprise, and replied it was.

"I am very sorry to hear it," said Roger brusquely, "very sorry." Estella flushed at her father's tone and the amused looks on the faces of two or three people standing near, who had overheard him.

The president made no reply, regarding his visitor more attentively a moment, then excusing himself and passing out. The others followed, leaving Roger and Estella by themselves. The latter was glad to be relieved from the observation of strangers, but thought it would have looked better if they had gone with the others. Her father broke out into a petty tirade against the absent head of the institution, calling him an "antiquated fossil," and declaiming against the elevation of such men to places of honor and influence. Estella made no reply; she thought the president had a rather kind face, but was not interested.

When he returned, a younger man accompanied him who was introduced as Professor Hart, and Roger and Estella were placed in his charge. As they turned to leave the room, Roger jostled against a young man who had just entered. He spoke a word of rapid apology, but scarcely saw the one to whom it was addressed. Estella noted him more carefully, and the two exchanged a look that gave each a vivid impression of the other. She followed her father from the room.

"Well, Watson, what is it?" she heard the president say, as she passed through the door.

Her father, she was glad to find, seemed rather pleased with Professor Hart. Roger expressed his disapproval, when he learned that the Roman pronunciation had been adopted in Monroe, being as conservative in his literary principles as he was radical in some others; and Professor Hart let him see he sympathized with him. Another ground of mutual interest was found in their common love of science, and dissatisfaction that the university had not planted itself squarely on the Darwinian basis. Professor Hart took them to his laboratory, where he and Roger fell into a long and learned talk on bacteria, during which Estella grew very tired, and felt herself ill-used. When the professor learned something of his new acquaintance's pursuits and identified him as the author of one or two magazine articles he had read with much profit, the relation assumed a still more friendly character. Estella noted the frank pleasure her father felt in this recognition, and was pleased for him. She saw, too, though she was too miserable to care about it, that this discovery raised herself as well as her father in the pro-

fessor's eyes. If the president had, as she expected, conceived a prejudice against her father,
Professor Hart had taken as strong a one in his
favor. As they left the laboratory, she saw a
young man walking down the hall, some distance
ahead of them, and though his back was turned,
she recognized him as the young man her father
had jostled against in the president's office.

"That is my assistant," Professor Hart said to
her. "He will be your teacher in mathematics.
I should like to introduce you." He opened his
lips to call him, but at the same moment the young
man turned a corner and disappeared.

"Never mind; some other time will do as well,"
he said, smiling.

He then gave her father a list of addresses, for
the next duty was to find a suitable home for Estella. Accompanying them to the door, he bade
them a friendly farewell, again expressing to Roger
his pleasure in meeting him.

They seated themselves in the carriage which
Roger had ordered to wait, and were driven through
the wide streets, lined with trees just clothing
themselves in the young foliage of an early spring.

"A very intelligent young man!" said Roger.
"It's a pity he is n't at the head of the institution."

Estella could make no reply. Another wave of
homesickness was sweeping over her. The muscles of her throat ached with the effort to keep
back her sobs, but the tears would gather and roll

in great drops down her cheeks. She shrank back into the corner of the carriage, and covered her face with her handkerchief. Roger noticed her, and felt sorry for her, but forbore, wisely as he thought, to express any such feeling. He talked on indifferent topics, not seeming to observe that he received no answers. The carriage drew up before one of the places indicated on the list. The prospect was not inviting. A small frame house, one of a long block, with a long flight of dirty and broken steps, was what Roger saw when he alighted.

"This won't do, I know," he said, but, bidding Estella remain where she was, went reluctantly up the steps. An untidy servant answered the bell, and looked at him with a vacuous countenance. As the door opened he caught a whiff of mixed and greasy smells from the kitchen below, and saying hastily that he had made a mistake, returned to the carriage, and ordered the driver to go on to the next place.

"There is no use in wasting time here," he said, as he seated himself by Estella. "I don't know what Professor Hart meant by referring us to such a place."

The next presented a more inviting outside, but developed nothing but a small third story back room, with no sun and poorly heated.

"I don't know as I should mind a third story," said Estella, listlessly, as they rolled on again.

"I mind it," her father replied. Her mind was

less occupied with the material comforts he was so careful to inquire into than with painful conjectures on other points, the kind of people she should be thrown in with, the impossibility, she now felt it, of making acquaintance with strangers, of interesting herself in this new life, liking and making it her own.

The third stopping-place looked so attractive that Roger told Estella to come with him, and the two ascended together the steps to a neat brick residence on a quiet street, that wore an air of domestic retirement. A pleasant-faced servant responded to their summons, but disappointed them by reporting her mistress out. On learning she would return soon, Roger asked permission to enter and wait. The parlor into which they were ushered was small but homelike, with signs of refined taste and some degree of culture in its appointments.

"Really, I begin to think we have found something at last," said Roger, in an expectant tone. Estella dropped into a chair, and listlessly waited what might happen next. In a moment there was a rustling sound on the staircase in the adjoining hall, the portière was pushed aside, and a woman entered. She was of middle age, short stature, and a trifle stout, with light hair, and dressed in widow's black, relieved with muslin bands at the throat and wrist.

"I beg your pardon," she began, before she fairly saw them, "but I am Mrs. Black's sister, and if you wish to look at rooms" —

She stopped suddenly. Roger had turned while she was speaking, bringing his face into full light. They recognized each other at once. He stood facing Kitty Somers.

She spoke his name, in extreme astonishment, and stood looking at him. He neither answered nor moved towards her, only looked at her in turn. That he was as deeply surprised as she, and a little agitated, was evident, but it was not for him to make the first move. A variety of emotions swept over her face. What she might have done had they two been alone need not be conjectured; but the surprised look on Estella's face, who had risen from her chair, caught her, and recalled her to herself. She had heard of Roger's marriage, shortly after it occurred, and of the birth of a daughter, so she understood the situation at once. She stepped forward and extended her hand.

"This is a great surprise," she said.

A deep flush of relief and gladness surged over his face. He clasped her hand warmly. She withdrew it and turned to the young girl.

"This is your daughter?" and Roger made the necessary introductions. Mrs. Somers took her hand, and looked at her kindly.

"Your father and I are old acquaintances," she said.

Roger noticed she did not say "friends." A light broke over Estella's face.

"Oh, and did you know my mother, too?"

Mrs. Somers felt Roger's eyes upon her.

"Not so well, yet I remember her quite distinctly, also. She is well, I hope?"

The girl looked at her, her lips quivered, she tried to speak, but could not. Roger explained that Estella's mother had been an invalid for many years.

She turned to him, and asked a few commonplace questions. He answered, keeping a watchful eye on her. Estella, too, looked at her earnestly. She was puzzled, but felt a strong attraction towards this new acquaintance. Would she admit any claim towards herself? Would she like her to stay? Had she liked her father? She thought she seemed a little embarrassed before him, and noted, too, with more perplexity, that he seemed a little afraid of her. Mrs. Somers caught the yearning, wistful look once or twice, and it touched her. The instinct of protection was as active as ever, and already at work.

In a few minutes Mrs. Black entered, and was presented and made acquainted with the visitors' errand. Greatly to her surprise, her father signed to Estella to go and look at the rooms without him.

When he and Mrs. Somers were left alone they exchanged a long look.

"How strange we should meet like this!" she murmured.

"I fear I must assume that to you the meeting is as disagreeable as it is strange, but you need fear no intrusion from me. Estella and I will take our leave presently, and not trouble you further."

Mrs. Somers knew what words like these meant. She knew he wished Estella to stay, but that he did not mean to ask it. She was provoked with herself that her own wish ran with his. Estella's face, with the appealing eyes, red with weeping, and the sensitive mouth, had made an instant and deep impression on her. Years had done little to abate her impulsiveness, and already she loved the girl, she thought. Yet how could she be friends with the daughter, and ignore the father? It was not of himself he was thinking least in this matter, she was very sure. She foresaw difficulties and complications, but for all that the wish in her heart grew stronger.

"Why not let her stay, if she wishes?" She tried to speak carelessly.

"It can hardly be as she wishes," was the reply; then, after a moment's pause, and observing her: "It can only be as you wish." She frowned a little, finding herself in a more difficult position than before.

"Estella is a stranger in the city?" she asked, after reflecting a space.

"An entire stranger." Roger had not thought of this before, but the words were spoken with portentous gravity.

"She has never been away from home before?"

"Never."

"Would — would you like her to stay, — if the place suits her?" This question was cunning, and left them facing each other in a new position.

"That would depend upon what conditions she was permitted to remain," he said, plainly.

"Conditions?"

"I cannot consent to leave my daughter in any place where she is likely to form a disparaging opinion of her father."

"How can you say such a thing!" she exclaimed indignantly. "What must you think of me, I wonder!"

"I think very highly of you, as you know," he replied, in a tone that made her color.

"Why should I disparage you to her? As though the poor girl's happiness did not depend on her faith in you !" she retorted bitterly.

"Estella is an object of commiseration to you, I suppose." She was silent.

"You pity her, as you blame me. You have always blamed me!"

"Of course I. blamed you. We both blamed you, but we did not judge you as harshly as others did. We knew you acted from what you believed to be sufficient motives, but we thought you terribly in the wrong. Afterward, when we heard of your marriage, we were very thankful. We said it was like you; you had done what you could to rectify your mistake."

"Do not give me praise I do not deserve," he said, flinging back his head with the impatient motion she remembered so well. "I never sought to rectify any mistake, for the simple reason that I have never yet acknowledged it was a mistake." She looked at him with a mournful smile.

"You have not changed much, Roger."

"I don't know.   I have laid up a small store of experience,   And if it's any merit in me, I am a somewhat sadder as well as wiser man."

"Ah, then, you did see it was a mistake, that you had taken the wrong way!"

"There have been some mistakes, very likely, but I doubt if we should agree in placing them." She did not understand this, nor care to, and sought an easier theme.

"Tell me about Eleanor," she said.   "I remember how delicate she was.   I never knew her very well.   After—after what happened I reproached myself many times that I had not tried to know her better."

"You would have tried to prevent it?" raising his head.

"Certainly, I should have tried to prevent it, if I could."

"You are very frank, but Eleanor would not have helped you, at least not then.   Afterward, she might."

"Afterward?"

"The qualities you find lacking in me, Eleanor has to excess."

"Ah!" recalling her prediction.   "She has not been happy, then?"

"No one is happy who proves unequal to a great task.   Eleanor failed me!"

"Failed you!"

"It is natural that you should look on her as the chief sufferer"—

"Failed you!" she exclaimed again, but at the same moment held up her hand. Steps were heard descending, and in a moment Mrs. Black and Estella reëntered.

"I like the room very much, papa," the latter said, stepping towards him, and speaking in a tone that conveyed a strong wish.

Mrs. Black wore the gratified look of one about to complete a desirable bargain, and smiled indulgently at the girl.

"We shall be very glad to take her," she said to him. But he made no reply either to Estella or to her. He was looking at Mrs. Somers, quite regardless of appearances. Estella began to look embarrassed, Mrs. Black annoyed, but still Roger kept his eyes on his old friend. She reddened with vexation and a feeling of defeat.

"You had better let her stay," she said, turning towards him, and speaking more coldly than the import of her words warranted. A flash of triumph lighted his eyes a moment. Estella was told she could stay. Mrs. Somers's vexation continued, but she was ready to laugh, too.

"He succeeded in making me do as he wished," she said to herself, alone in her room. "That is Roger Hunt. Estella stays because I asked it; I am the favored one. But why should I care? The girl needs a friend, — all the more because she has a father."

After Roger's departure, she accompanied Estella to her room, where she left her, judging it better to leave her by herself awhile, letting repressed feeling spend its force.

"I know what it is to be homesick," she said. "I shan't pretend it's any easier to bear than it is; but you may take my word for it, you can't always feel as you do now. You're bound to feel better by and by. But that need n't hinder you from having the longest and hardest cry of your life now. I should if I were in your place. I 'm going to leave you now on purpose," smiling into the tear-stained face, taking it between her hands and kissing it. "We 're to be very good friends, my dear. My room is across the hall, and you must ask me for anything you want. We 'll go down to lunch together."

"I don't want any lunch," said Estella plaintively.

"Not now, of course; it 's only eleven o'clock; and not at all if you feel the same way two hours from now." She kissed her again and went out of the room, but left so much of her cheerful presence behind that Estella found it impossible to yield as unrestrainedly to the feelings at work within her as she had permission to do. A little quiet tear-shedding seemed to finish that sort of exercise for the time, and after she had bathed her face and combed her hair she was glad to see her trunk brought in, and to find another occupation in its unpacking. Mrs. Somers came in again and helped her. The two remained together all day, sitting in Mrs. Somers's room after supper, before a small wood fire.

"You are to spend all your evenings in here," she said impulsively. She felt she was behaving rather recklessly, but prompted partly by sympathy, partly by genuine liking, and conscious, too, of considerable curiosity, she yielded to every fresh feeling of kindness that came over her.

"I wonder why mamma never told me about you," Estella said, later in the evening, but Mrs. Somers explained this on the ground of long illness, which must have dimmed many memories of the past.

Roger had noticed that Mrs. Somers was in mourning, and knew that her husband must be dead, but even had he not been more than usually preoccupied with his own affairs, the occasion was one that afforded little opportunity for the usual expressions of interest and sympathy. He still held to his old opinion of the marriage, and the injured remembrance of the last letter he had received from George Somers had never left him.

He left the house in a buoyant and rather exultant frame of mind, having, as he conceived, been able to maintain his own against Mrs. Somers, and compel her respectful treatment of himself. As to the motive which had led her to befriend Estella and show an interest in her, he believed it related to some one else ; that if she were honest, this revived acquaintance was the source of as much pleasure to her as he was willing to admit it was to himself, though she would always, he supposed, keep up the old feint of opposition and pretended disapproval. His old admiration for her flamed into sudden life, even while his irritation against her remained. His blood tingled, his mental faculties were newly aroused by this unexpected encounter with one who had always stimulated his imagination, and whom, though he had never admitted it, he had a stronger desire to please than any one he had ever known.

Mrs. Somers had been a widow four years. Breaking up her home after her husband's death, she had secured a place as newspaper correspondent, and had spent much of her time in travel, chiefly on the Pacific coast and in the Mexicos, going once on a special mission to Brazil. She had been spending the winter with her sister in Monroe and her plans for the future were undetermined, when she met Roger Hunt, and in a way assumed charge of his daughter. The loneliness of her widowhood, without children to care for, was heightened by the fact that she missed her husband in so many ways. He had been not only her lover, but her friend and most congenial companion. She missed him, not simply when she needed counsel and support, but when she wanted some one to talk to, to share a jest, or, perhaps, to differ with.

George Somers's death had been sudden, and had an element of tragedy in it. He had been killed instantly in a railroad accident; but there was the element of another sort of tragedy connected with it: he and his wife had quarreled shortly before he left her. To be sure, they had made up again, and thus ended the affair; but they were still in its shadow when they exchanged their last good-by.

The quarrel was as trivial in its source as the conjugal dispute usually is, the result, mainly, of tired nerves on the one hand, a depressed mood on the other. Some careless word of his had aroused a swift feeling of injury in her, and provoked a petulant reply. Then the gates were let down and impetuous speech had its way; the man's forced coolness deepening the woman's sense of injury, her small jibing thrusts stinging him like nettles. He had left her in tears, with too much anger and disgust still in his own breast to attempt reconcil-iation. Each felt very much abused and very heroic for the space of half an hour; at the end of which George dallied with the impulse to turn back from his office door and reënter his violated home, and Kitty tried to devise an errand that might take her accidentally down town. But the absurd-ity of the affair began now to appear, and they passed the day in miserable waiting. Each looked at the other with a shame-stricken face, when they met at night, then broke into a helpless laugh. The next moment she was in his arms, crying and laughing at once, and, woman-like, abusing herself and declaring she alone was to blame.

"You don't mean that," he said, releasing her. His emotional resources, even in periods like this, proved smaller than hers. She looked up at him with a conscious expression, the tear-drops still hanging on her eyelashes.

"Well, no," she sighed, "perhaps I don't. But George, it is so ridiculous, so perfectly shameful in us! Why do we behave so? But we never will again!" she added hopefully.

He smiled, with a touch of mournfulness. He had been a listener to such devoutly-spoken resolutions before; they impressed him much as a resolve might not to stumble over an unseen obstacle on a dark night. His was not a sanguine nature; she understood his feeling and had learned to read its signs.

"You are such a fatalist," she said reproachfully. "How are we ever to do any better, if we have no faith in ourselves, if we don't try."

"Perhaps we never shall do much better," he replied resignedly.

"Oh, how dreadful! Two such people as we are," — they were a rather superior couple, she thought, — "to spend all our lives quarreling and making up, and about nothing at all!"

"We do not spend *all* our lives quarreling," he corrected her. "As for the making up, that's rather in our favor, it seems to me, and it's better to have no cause for a quarrel than a good one, in such cases."

"I don't see why," she said, rather dully, for her.

"Well, I can't stop to explain now. I've got to go to New York to-night."

"To New York!   To-night!"

He explained to her the business errand that was to take him from home for a few days.

"But why must you go to-night?" she urged. It seemed a kind of sacrilege for them to separate now.

"In order to be there to-morrow."

"I 've half a mind to go with you."

"All right.   You can if you want to."

She reflected a moment, but prudential thoughts overcame this impulse.

"But I shall go to the train with you," she said.

"You had better not.   It is dark, and you will have to come home alone."

"I don't care," she said hurriedly, "I shall go."

She gained little by this, except the chance to keep him in sight, for the street-car was crowded, compelling George to stand on the platform outside, and at the station he was hailed by an acquaintance and kept talking on some business topic until the train was ready to start. They kissed each other and she stood watching as he moved slowly in his place in the line through the gate, and then mounted the car platform. He turned and lifted his hat, and she waved her hand. Then he went inside, and she saw him no more, until he was brought home to her in his coffin.

The relation between these two was peculiar, and not entirely destroyed by death. Lonely as she was, Kitty Somers never felt entirely alone; death having surrounded her with a presence more near and pervading, in some ways, than life had brought. She counseled with George, dead, much as she had with George, living; projected his views against or in support of her own; talked things over with him. They understood and belonged to each other still. No other relation could ever replace this one, whose very imperfections helped to constitute its claim for precedence.

This was Kitty Somers's idea of married fealty, of love's loyalty, which must be preserved whether love be perfect or not. How can love be perfect, humanly conditioned, more than knowledge? It was an idea a man like Roger Hunt would not have understood in the least, nor have professed to respect, if he did understand it.

XVII.

Estella did not settle at once into her new place. Study in a large school-room, and contact with so many people, was quite new to her. Life was not very quiet at Mrs. Black's either, who had several "roomers," as they were called, to mark the fact that they were not boarders, and took their meals out; but Mrs. Somers had persuaded her sister to make an exception of Estella. The constant coming and going, shutting of doors, and sound of gay young voices in the hall, was a complete contrast to the perpetual quiet at home.

"Our house is so still," she said to Mrs. Somers once. "Sometimes the neighbors call, but not very often, because mamma, you know, can hardly ever see them; and papa is always at his studies."

"You studied with your father, did you not?"

"Yes; I was never allowed to go to school. Papa does not believe in the graded system." Mrs. Somers smiled. There were so many things Roger did not believe in.

"That gave you the benefit of better instruction in many ways, I dare say," she replied; "but I always think it a pity that young people should not be with each other."

"I don't think I minded — much." It was not easy for Estella to speak of Nina.

It had been something of a relief to Mrs. Somers that Estella cared so little for society. She was willing to accept the full responsibility of this relation for herself, but hesitated, in a way she could neither quite justify nor wholly condemn, about extending it to others. When this looked cowardly, she excused it by saying that Estella had inherited so much of her father's self-reliance, that she required little from other people; and when this kind of reasoning seemed rather heartless, she argued that the consequences of an áction like Roger Hunt's could not be expected to end with the doer, and went to science and the Bible for justification. Then she turned about remorsefully, and treated the girl with more kindness than before. She became more attached to her each day.

Professor Hart presented the new pupil to his assistant, the first day of her attendance. The latter was seated at his desk, busily writing, and raised his eyes in a rather startled way when he heard his name spoken. He did not catch Estella's name, but his face showed that he recognized her. It was his duty to enter her name in the register, and make some further inquiries about her studies, and Professor Hart left them together.

"I beg your pardon," he said, as he dipped his pen in the ink-bottle, "but I did not understand the name."

"Miss Hunt — Estella Hunt," was the reply.

He started slightly, and the pen remained suspended in his hand, while he looked at her in a way that embarrassed and annoyed her somewhat.

A careful observer might have noticed certain signs of resemblance in these two, in a rather peculiar shape of the forehead, narrow but high, with clearly defined angles. The color of the eyes was the same, but the young man's wore a cloudy and downcast expression, while Estella's were clear and direct in their gaze, like her father's.

"Pardon me," he repeated once more, recollecting himself, but again looking at her closely. "The name arrested my attention. It—it once belonged to my own family; but it is a very common one."

The peculiar expression, "It once belonged to my family," did not strike Estella, but she felt, for some reason, more annoyed than before. It had always been a source of surprise, and some personal sensitiveness in her, that she had never been told she had any relatives on either side. She felt strangely ignorant on many points other girls seemed to possess abundant knowledge of. Nina Clarke, she used to notice, talked a great deal about uncles and aunts and cousins, writing letters to them and receiving gifts at Christmas and on her birthday; but her own connections seemed to end with her parents. She believed her mother had once had a brother, but whether he was dead or living she did not know. The young assistant's words, and the way he looked at her, seemed intrusive, and she was glad to turn away from him and take the seat he assigned her. Several times throughout the day she felt his eyes on her, always withdrawn when they met her own, and her annoyance increased. She thought he was very disagreeable.

"You will be sure to like Professor Hart," Mrs. Somers said to her that evening, inquiring into the day's progress. "He is a great favorite."

"I do not recite to Professor Hart, but to Mr. Watson," said Estella, with some discontent.

"Watson — Watson," the other repeated, thoughtfully. "I wonder if that is n't the young man who called to look at rooms a few weeks ago. Tall, with dark hair and eyes?" Estella reflected a moment.

"Not so very tall, I should say."

"I 'm sure it is the same. He wanted board, so Mrs. Black sent him across the street to Mrs. Richardson."

He was in the neighborhood, then, Estella thought, with a renewal of her former feeling. She learned later that Mr. Watson was helping himself through a post-graduate course by teaching. Unlike Professor Hart, he was not a favorite. On the contrary, his moody and unsocial manners made him an object of some antagonism to many of the pupils, who took pains to vex and tease him. When Estella understood this, she began to feel a little sorry for him, and to take his part. Each preserved a shy bearing towards the other, but in time they grew better acquainted. They met each other frequently on the way to and from school, and one day Mr. Watson joined her. Her first fleeting dislike of him had by this time vanished, and given way to a feeling of kindly interest. To this was soon added pride in her teacher's evident liking for herself, and the distinction she was gaining of being a favorite pupil. The difference in their ages, about eight years, was more noticeable now than it would be later, and made the relation a more flattering one to Estella. At the end of two months they were good friends.

By degrees Estella had learned something, but not all, of Mr. Watson's history; that he had lived alone, without brothers or sisters, in the home of an aunt who had brought him up, but who died when he was in college.

"Then your father and mother died when you were very young?" she said to him, one day, after listening to some of these revelations.

"My mother died when I was eight years old."

"And your father?" He hesitated a moment.

"I lost him some time before." She listened with a sympathetic face.

"I never had any brothers or sisters either," she said simply, and after a moment's silence. He looked at her gravely.

"Tell me something of your home." She replied that there was very little to tell. He gathered the mental picture of a country-like home, resting in an atmosphere of refined and scholarly leisure,

marred only by the mother's long illness.   Rather
ideal, he thought.

Estella said to herself she was a very fortunate
girl to make two such friends as Mrs. Somers and
Mr. Watson.   She had grown more accustomed to
her new life, and was enjoying it.   She had not
forgotten her mother, but pain here was softened
to tender regret.   The right of youth to its own
hopeful outlook was beginning to assert itself.
The light of happy expectation glowed in her eyes,
young joy and trust warmed her heart.

Mrs. Somers watched the growing intimacy between Estella and her teacher with puzzled disapproval.   If a particle of youthful silliness had
revealed itself here, if Estella was not so perfectly
frank about it, she felt she would have known better how to deal with it; but evidently nothing was
further from the minds of these serious young people than a flirtation.   She did not like Mr. Watson very well, she did not know why, and would
have been glad of an excuse to break off the acquaintance.

"She is n't the least bit in love with him," she
said to herself.   "Such a thing never entered her
head.   Yet she always stands up for him.   I suppose it 's because nobody else can get along with
him.   I hope the girl is n't going to develop her
father's passion for being in the minority."

What the nature of Assistant Watson's feelings
for his pupil might be she felt less sure of, and, as
far as he was concerned, less interested in.   He

had a strange way of looking at her, she had noticed, when she saw them together, but his manner
was too grave and composed for a lover's. It
showed his poverty-stricken condition, socially, she
thought, with some irritation, to fasten himself on
a young girl in this way.

In the mean time if any youthful folly were going
on, nothing could tend to correct it so well as a
little timely satire and ridicule; and Mr. Watson
came in for more than one little shaft from this
direction.

"Why does not the man assert himself a little?" she asked Estella one evening, when they
were sitting together in her room, and the latter
had been telling her about the unruly behavior of
one of her classmates that day. "Why does he
let a silly young woman torment him so, and break
up a class? He ought to be ashamed to permit
such things!"

"It is the young woman who ought to be
ashamed, I think," said Estella.

"Very likely, but a teacher must either win the
respect of his pupils or compel it. Mr. Watson
is n't one of the winning kind, I know" —

"You don't understand him, Mrs. Somers. He
has been very unhappy all his life." There was
faint reproach in her tone, and a hint of mystery,
that made the other look at her in surprise.

"Unhappy!" she scoffed. "What has Mr.
Watson been doing to make himself unhappy?"

"It is n't what he has done himself, it is what

other people have done," with more mystery than before.

"That's a very shallow cause of unhappiness. If Mr. Watson has only reached the point where he is repenting of some one's else misconduct, he will do very well."

"If you knew his history, Mrs. Somers, I don't think you would speak like that."

"His history! So Mr. Watson has a history?" She looked at the young girl sharply. What sentimental disclosures had she been made to listen to by this conceited and gloomy admirer? Estella returned the look calmly.

"What has he been telling you?"

"I don't know as he would be willing I should repeat it," said Estella thoughtfully.

"His willingness has nothing to do with it. You are to tell me everything he said to you." The girl looked at her quietly, as before.

"After all, I don't see why I should not tell you." It was plain the springs of obedience were within. "And some of it was so strange," leaning back in her chair, looking meditatively at Raphael's head of Paul on the opposite wall. "I don't think he was to blame for telling me."

"I can tell that better when I have heard what it is. Come," ironically, "what is Mr. Watson's 'history'?"

"Oh, I don't mean he told me all. Only his life has been so different from most young men's. He lost both parents when very young, and was brought up by an aunt. His mother died, but his father, — he has known nothing about him for years. I think he must have done something that brought some kind of disgrace on the family. Mr. Watson did n't tell me just what, but it seemed to distress and anger him so to speak of his father."

"Well, go on," said Mrs. Somers, as Estella paused. There had been nothing very serious so far, but she felt unaccountably nervous.

"There is n't much more. As I say, his aunt adopted him and gave him her name. That is the strangest part of it," she went on, leaning forward, and clasping her hands over one knee. "His real name is n't Watson at all. It is Hunt."

"What!" Mrs. Somers sprung to her feet.

"Just like mine! Is n't that odd?" said the girl dreamily. "What is the matter, Mrs. Somers?" looking up at her in alarm. "Are you ill?" and she rose to her feet.

"No — no. Go on. Yes, it is odd, as you say," and she tried to laugh. "I wish you would open a window, Estella," and she sank weakly down on her chair again.

"Never mind," she said, as the girl rushed to a window, tried to open it, and could not. "I feel better now," but she leaned her head against the back of her chair; her face was white and haggard.

"You are really ill, Mrs. Somers," said Estella, coming back to her side. "We must have walked too far in the hot sun this afternoon."

"Yes — yes, that is it. I will lie down a little while. No, dear, you need n't stay," as the other began to make preparations for her comfort. "Go to your room. I shall be better alone, for a while." But Estella would not go until she had seen her friend lie down, placed a pillow under her head, and thrown a covering over her. It seemed a small eternity to Mrs. Somers while she submitted to these cares. At last Estella turned, reluctantly, to leave her; but reaching the door she heard her name called sharply, and came quickly back to the lounge.

"Estella, you are not to stir out of the house again to-night," and she clutched the girl's hand in hers.

"Why, no, Mrs. Somers; I was not intending to go out," the other said in surprise. " It is nine o'clock." She wondered if Mrs. Somers were going to have a fever. Reluctantly she turned again, at her bidding, and left her.

Alone, Mrs. Somers sprang from her place, throwing the covering to one side, then rising to her feet, went to the door and locked it, and stood still to think.

How could she have failed to identify Charles Watson at once, when she first heard his name? But how could she be expected to do so? She had, in truth, as many others had, remembered Roger Hunt's flight from home, chiefly in its relation to himself and her own disappointment in him. Occasionally the images of the severe-faced woman he had left behind, and the child towards whom she had taken a mother's part, had come back to her, but it had been years since she had thought of either. Fear, indignation, despair, swept over her in turn as the situation unrolled before her.

"It is ghastly! " she exclaimed.

Her indignation darted swiftly from one object to another: first towards Charles Watson. Why had he told Estella his miserable story? What right had he to throw himself on her sympathy in this way? Why was he there — in Monroe — at all? Then she turned against herself. Would she never learn to let people alone; to stop trying to play at Providence? Because a girl had looked at her with appealing eyes, she must go and get herself mixed up again in the affairs of a man like Roger Hunt! Because she knew the girl's history, she must conceive the fantastic notion that she might be able to help avert natural results! She remembered the offer she had received a few days before from the Philadelphia "Peacemaker," to go to Toronto and report the proceedings of the Red Cross Society; and declared she would reverse her first decision and accept it. She would leave on the first train the next day!

Then, ashamed of her childishness, her anger flamed up in another and more just direction, as she remembered the one who had caused all this trouble. As she traced the far-reaching effects of Roger Hunt's action, there seemed a kind of moral enormity in it. What would be his sensations

when he heard of this latest development in the
drama he had inaugurated? Would he care?
Would he be at all disturbed? Would he perceive
his own accountability towards these two young
lives it should be his first duty to protect. She
doubted it, and the doubt whetted her. anger against
him anew. She cried out in her heart against the
law that condemns the innocent to suffer with the
guilty. She longed to make him feel only one
tenth the misery and shame the full knowledge of
himself had power to inflict on others. The desire to punish, to reveal him to himself, to repudiate, and place miles of spiritual distance between
herself and him, filled her.

She seated herself at her desk, and began to
write. Sheet after sheet was filled and pushed
aside. Scorn, rebuke, entreaty, angry protest,
flowed into the written lines. Her excitement increased, and her subject grew in the dimensions of
the moral indignation in which she enveloped it,
until even she began to perceive exaggerated, sometimes grotesque effects. But she was in no mood
to discriminate and choose, and hurried on. She
had put on the black robe of judgment. Let the
recording angel excuse and plead for Roger Hunt,
if he was so inclined. She had done that for the
last time.

At the end she leaned back in her chair with a
long sigh of exhaustion. Then she gathered the
sheets rapidly together, folded them, directed and
sealed the envelope. Rising and stepping quickly

across the room, she touched a bell-button in the
wall.

"Post this letter to-night," she said to the servant who answered it.

"If I could be so foolish as to repent, it would
be too late now," was her thought.

As she reflected on what remained to be done, she
saw she had performed the least important duty
first; the letter to Estella's father might have
waited, the question of Estella herself was immediate and pressing. How to prevent Charles Watson from imparting any more of his personal history
to his willing and sympathetic listener — that was
the point to be settled, and at once. Mrs. Somers
decided here that the hardest way was the easiest,
as well as the surest. The next day was Saturday;
she would get rid of Estella, and send a message
to Mr. Watson, asking him to call on her.

Something tugged at her heart-strings, and just
before undressing she slipped out of her room into
Estella's. It was dark, and she could only see the
outline of the dark hair streaming across the pillow. The breath of the young sleeper came and
went lightly, and one could fancy she was smiling.
The tears rushed to Mrs. Somers's eyes. She bent
over the bed, an immense pity swelling in her
heart. Ah! the innocent suffering of this world,
she thought again, and recalled the words thought-
lessly spoken a few hours before, which now seemed
so shallow, about the unreality of the suffering
that does not spring from our own mistakes. It

was true in a sense, of course, but what is the use
of trying to teach such lessons to the young? Mrs.
Somers herself felt very old as she stood there.
She thought again of Roger Hunt. What was he
doing now? Conning a Latin sentence from Lu-
cretius, or counting the pieces in an ancient bit of
mosaic, proud of the distinction such lofty pursuits conferred above other men, looking piously
to heaven and a grateful posterity to reward him.
She was glad she had written the letter. Going
back to her room, she extinguished the light and
crept into bed, but not to sleep, any more than on
a certain night eighteen years before.

The next morning she carried out her plans very
successfully. Estella was out of the house, and she
sat in her room awaiting Mr. Watson. Up to this
time she had given very little thought to his connection with the case she had taken in hand, and felt
free to disclaim all accountability in this direction;
but she was conscious of compunction rising in a
new quarter when he entered. She had thought
of him before as an unfortunate and rather disagreeable young man, whose failing popularity was
due, she suspected, to his own morose and difficult
temper. Now she could not but look at him somewhat differently, though she meant to keep feeling
strictly in hand, be very cool, and if necessary a
little severe with him. This was simply a matter
of moral economy; the young assistant, she was
willing to admit, deserved sympathy, but hers was
promised beforehand to some one else. She fortified

herself in this resolution by the thought that Mr. Watson was a man, and could take care of himself.

The first thing she noticed, as he stood with uncovered head before her, was a resemblance to Estella, but as she had never noted anything of the kind before, she ascribed it to a freaky imagination. It suggested, again, however, that he, too, might have claims to assert. It would be impossible to treat him as if he were an enemy.

He responded slowly to her invitation to be seated, while the puzzled look on his face remained. She placed herself opposite him, and a moment of rather awkward silence followed.

"I sent for you," she began at last, "because I wished to speak to you about a matter of importance." She paused, and he bowed gravely, without proffering any response.

"Important to yourself, I mean," and paused again; but this time he only waited.

"Estella — Miss Hunt — has been telling me something you recently told her." He flushed, and moved uneasily in his chair.

"Pray do not think I mean to intrude on matters that do not concern me," she added, "but I — I feel you ought to know something of Miss Hunt's history."

"Why did she repeat what I told her?" the young man broke out. "It was a violation of confidence."

"Excuse me, but do you think you have a right to impart confidences in such a direction? She did quite right to tell me. I stand here in the place of her mother. Estella is very young. The sympathies of such a girl are easily aroused; so easily, you will pardon me for saying that I cannot understand what satisfaction any one in your position can derive from them."

This was not at all the line she had expected to take. The angry blood swept like a wave over his face, and he rose to his feet.

"I beg your pardon, madam, but you are using language and attributing motives to me I cannot permit myself to hear and be accused of. It is impossible any one should understand my motive in speaking to Miss Hunt."

"That is where you are mistaken," she said quietly, feeling more kindly towards him, now that she had tried the edge of her first irritation against him. "I understand your motive perfectly."

He smiled bitterly.

"I understand it better than you do yourself, perhaps. Sit down again, please." There was a gentle authority in her words that compelled attention, but he hesitated and looked at her distrustfully.

"If you sent for me merely to warn and reprimand me," with an icy smile, "we may consider the object of my visit accomplished."

"Nonsense! What right have I to reprimand you? It is not of you I am thinking." This had a rude sound, and she corrected herself. "I mean I am thinking of Estella. I am very anxious about

her. I want you to help me." He looked surprised and newly perplexed at this, and slowly
resumed his seat.

"How well do you remember your father?" Mrs.
Somers asked, after a few minutes' waiting. He
looked at her with more surprise still, and renewed
distrust.

"I have a good reason for asking," she continued. "I knew your father."

Her heart beat fast. To her excited fancy it
seemed she need tell no more. Surely he would
be able to put two and two together.

"You knew my father!" he repeated, and continued to look at her.

"I knew him very well. He — he was a friend
of my husband." Here she paused mentally to
cross and objurgate herself. ("There! Go and
lay it at poor George's door, who is in heaven, and
can't help himself.") "I knew your father and
your mother both," she went on aloud. She looked
at him keenly at this reference to his mother, but
was unable to conjecture what memories it aroused.

"I have long since ceased to think I ever had a
father," her listener said, after a brief pause.

"Do you mean you have heard no news of him
in all these years?"

"Nothing; I wish to hear nothing." She did
not heed this.

"Then you did not know that after your mother's death, your father married the woman who
— that he and Miss Thaxter were married?"

His lip curled scornfully.

"What difference does that make?"

"I did not say it made any difference. Please do not think I am defending him. They were married, and had a child, — a daughter." She caught her breath again, and waited; but he looked at her with dull eyes. His mind was less occupied with what she was saying than with painful memories of his own.

"After they were married they returned to this country. The little girl was born over here, I believe."

"All this is nothing to me, madam," he said, moving impatiently.

"But think; you may meet him some day. Nothing is more likely, in these days, when everybody goes everywhere. Can't you see what I mean?" she asked with an imploring accent, leaning towards him. He drew back and turned a little pale, but even then less with any suspicion of the specific thing she had to say, than from a sudden sense of impending evil.

"Suppose he were to come here," she urged, "to see Estella."

"To see Estella!" He looked at her blankly. "My God! You mean"— He sat staring at her, stiff and motionless.

"Oh, I am so sorry for you," she broke out, the tears rolling from her eyes. "I would give the world to spare you." He rose dizzily to his feet, keeping his hand a moment on his chair.

"You mean that, then?" he said in a low voice.
"Her father is mine. We — we are " — A singular expression flitted across his face.

The tears continued to stream down hers as she looked up at him. He stooped mechanically and took up his hat from the floor, then turned towards the door.

"You must not go yet," she cried. "We must decide something."

"What is there to decide?"

"About Estella." She rose and went towards him. "She knows nothing of this, you must remember. We must never let her know. That is the reason I have told you."

"You did right to tell me. Do you mean Miss Hunt knows nothing of her father's first marriage?"

"Nothing. If she were to know that, she must know the rest. It would kill her. She is devotedly attached to her mother. If she were to learn anything against her " —

Her listener reflected a while, with bent head, and serious face.

"You need have no fears for Miss Hunt on my account," he said, raising his eyes to her. This pleased her, but was not quite definite enough. She began some words of sympathy, but he checked her with his hand.

"What shall you do?" she then asked.

"Do?"

"I mean, shall — shall you go away?" She was

a little ashamed of the question, and the wish it implied, but it would come.

"Go away! Why should I go away?"

"Shall you see Estella, then?" A slight frown creased his forehead.

"Why should I not see Estella?" he asked.

"It would impose too severe a restraint on you. You would be unable to keep things to yourself." The old bitter smile rose to his lips.

"I have kept things to myself all my life."

"But if her father should come!"

He had not thought of this, and reflected on it a minute. "It will make no difference. We shall not see each other."

"But he knows," she replied quickly, and for the first time felt a little conscience-smitten about her letter. "I—I have written to him," she added. He looked at her with new bewilderment. This struck him as a singular confession from one so careful to extort promises of secrecy from other people. At the same time a half-defiant gleam lighted his face. She knew what it meant; he would not object to meet this father.

"The consequences be on his own head, then," the young man said harshly. She pitied him, but she was a little displeased too.

"I see. You wish to be avenged. You think only of yourself; you will make a scene and a scandal. You care nothing for Estella."

His face grew grave again. He was silent a moment. "I will think the matter over," he said, and left her.

"What brutes men are!" Mrs. Somers exclaimed to herself, when alone once more. "Always wanting to spring at each other's throats!" With this superficial irritation she relieved the deeper strain the interview had caused her.

If regrets for the letter she had written returned to her, they were useless. Fate or Providence, it soon seemed, had not left things to her management entirely. That night at supper, Estella told her she had written a long letter to her mother, relating to her, as she had to her friend, Mr. Watson's story. It was strange Mrs. Somers had not thought of this possibility, but she could not think of everything. She was by this time tired out, helpless and hopeless; ready to wash her hands of what might happen next. She said to herself that Destiny might rule hereafter. Her own jurisdiction seemed drawing to a close.

XVIII.

THE life of the Hunt household moved on still more quietly after Estella's departure. Roger made regular visits to his wife's room two or three times a day, shutting himself the remaining time in his study, paying an occasional social visit to his neighbor, Mrs. Clarke, and one or two other friends.

To his observation there seemed little change in Eleanor, but to the more watchful eyes of Mrs. Saunders, she was losing strength daily, though by slow degrees. She had not risen from her bed since Estella went away, and passed hours in that half-waking trance in which the body lies numb and passive beneath the action of wasting physical forces. The only thing that seemed thoroughly to arouse her these last weeks was Estella's letters. She kept the one last received near her until the next one came, and Mrs. Saunders often noticed her lying with her hand under the pillow clasping the little missive that symbolized the strongest tie which held her to earth.

Eleanor had been a good deal agitated when she learned of Roger's meeting with Mrs. Somers, and that Estella had been left in her care. She was deeply grateful, though unable to learn from

Roger, who spoke with much reserve on the subject, just what construction to put upon her action. She had expressed a desire to write Mrs. Somers and thank her, but he had promptly discouraged this. As Estella's letters reached her, and she saw how much she was coming to regard this new friend, she grew not only reconciled to the necessity of parting, but thankful for it. The need of further effort on her part even here was slipping fast from her, the duty of living growing smaller.

Roger's absence from home, when he took Estella to Monroe, had been so short that the lessons with his pupil suffered no interruption. The days were growing warmer now, but Nina's interest in her studies did not flag. She had never again expressed the wish to discontinue them, and her mother was highly gratified at the change in her, the results, she believed, of her own wholesome discipline. The walks to the river were kept up, and Nina was growing something of an expert in ancient arrow-heads and picture-writing. The season was also taken advantage of to begin a course in botany.

One day at the close of the lesson, when Estella had been absent from home nearly two months, Nina extended an invitation, in her mother's name, to dine with them the following Saturday, with a small company of friends, "to meet my uncle Mortimer," she explained.

Roger expressed his thanks, but frowned a little, also.

"I don't like dinner-parties," he said.

"Mamma is very anxious you should meet my uncle. He is her youngest brother; we are all very proud of him."

Roger smiled and asked the reason why; but did not pay much attention to the answer, gathering only that the gentleman in question was a successful journalist in a large Eastern city.

"Suppose I forget it?" he asked teasingly, when she renewed the invitation. She pouted a little.

"Then mamma will be greatly disappointed."

"I should like better to know how mamma's daughter will feel."

"You will have to come, and find out that for yourself," she replied; a rather happy retort for Nina, at which they both laughed.

"I will help you to remember," she said. "I will mark the day." She took a pen from the desk, with the freedom she was now coming to feel in these surroundings. "Not in black ink," she said, drawing the pen back from one side of the double inkstand, and dipping it in the other, then drawing a red line round the date on a printed calendar near by. "There, now you can't forget."

"I might, if I did n't know who put it there," he said. "We ought to mark all the Mondays and Thursdays in that way," he added.

"Why?" asked Nina, with her ready flush.

"It is n't necessary, though; they are red-letter days as it is." The flush deepened, and she laid down the pen.

"Shall I tell mamma you are coming?" she asked, turning to go.   "She will be sure to ask."

"Tell her yes, if I can sit by you," he replied in the same bantering tone.

She shook her head.   "I am sure she will not consent to that.   She always puts me at the lower end of the table."

"She does!   Where will she put me, then?"

"You will be at mamma's left, I should think. Of course my uncle will be the principal guest," she added, apologetically.

"Well, I 'm used to that," said Roger.   "The theologians consigned me to the left hand, long ago.   That is the place of punishment, you know," he explained to her.   He was often obliged to explain, things here, that he would have found it a severe trial to elsewhere.   Nina laughed.

"It is not so at a dinner-party; it is the second place of honor."

"Indeed!   And what are the duties of the lucky occupant of the second place of honor?"

"I don't know," thoughtfully.   "I think, perhaps, mamma may·have you take out the rector's wife."   Roger made a wry face.   The rector's wife belonged to the order of women he especially disliked; she reminded him of Mrs. Hamilton.

"Rector James is to be there, then?"

"Of course; and I — I am afraid I have made a mistake.   I think the second place may be given to him.   He is the minister, you know."

"Then it will be his place to take out his wife? Serves him right!"

"Oh, no," laughing again.

"Any way, I shall be a little nearer the lower regions — where you are!" Her ever-returning blush came back at this, and she opened the door.

"You are very wicked to-day," she said, and made her escape.

With some inward grumbling Roger dressed to go out on the evening named. He looked into Eleanor's room a moment to tell her where he was going, then walked leisurely up the hill to his destination. One of the numerous minor protests by which he kept the spirit of social revolt in exercise was seen in his hatred of a dress-coat; so he appeared as Rector James did, in a long frock garment, and, with his slight physique, and intellectual countenance, looked even more priestly than he did. If Nina had given him her uncle's full name he did not recall it, nor had he been sufficiently interested even to notice the omission. He wore his usual look of mingled abstraction and indifference as he entered the parlor, and which his hostess found discouraging.

Mrs. Clarke stepped forward to meet him in a trained gown of crimson silk. Near her stood her husband, trying to look at ease in his evening costume. He greeted Roger with mixed hauteur and carelessness, to let him see he neither liked nor was afraid of him. Farther down the room stood Nina, dressed, in white, and talking with Rector James, but throwing a quick pleased look in the new guest's direction. The guest of the evening was standing near, but with face partly hidden, conversing with his latest introduction. Mrs. Clarke placed a hand on his arm and he turned towards her. Roger saw and recognized him first, and was thus prepared, by a second's warning, for whatever was to come. The other started perceptibly when he saw Roger, and heard his name. It was Mortimer Gray. Other guests appearing, the hostess' attention was immediately engaged. The two men looked at each other squarely an instant, a flash of defiance in the eyes of one, indignant asking astonishment in the other's. Then they bowed, and Roger, more excited than he had been for a long time, but maintaining perfect outward calm, turned away.

He rebuked himself sharply that he had not provided against this embarrassment, and threatened danger besides, by inquiring more carefully about the man he had been asked to meet; but his pride was aroused now, and he resolved not only to stay, but to show himself as indifferent to the situation as he would like to feel. He had had a rather small opinion of Gray in the old days when he used to meet him in the Plato class, and it would go hard with him before he showed any signs of fear or concern now. He passed around the room, greeting the other guests with more than usual cordiality.

Mrs. Clarke verified her daughter's predictions by whispering to him that he was to take out the rector's wife, but he found Nina on the other side.

She blushed with pleasure when she discovered the conjunction, which was a surprise to her, and to be accounted for only by the fact that a young gentleman accompanying her uncle on his Western trip was her escort, and had been given the place on the hostess' left, the rector being assigned the second on the right. Roger sat nearly opposite the guest of the occasion, but the circumstance did not seem to disturb him in the least. He was more than composed, the most brilliant and talkative member of the company, turning the attention, more than once, of those who sat at a distance to look and listen to him. He told anecdotes, entered into a lively scrimmage in words with the rector, taking care 'to keep it good-natured, covered the ladies near him with mingled badinage and gallantry, made the rector's wife laugh at things she did not approve of, and would have to do mental penance for afterward, whispered words of delicious nonsense into Nina's ear, distracting her attention quite from the young man on the other side, who, it was plain, would have been glad to have her to himself; in short, made himself the life and hero of the evening. If the host of the occasion had understood the situation he would have conceived a new admiration for his guest; he would have said that he at least meant to die game.

The guest of honor was quite eclipsed, but seemed not to know it, playing his part poorly. From difficult attempts to talk he lapsed into long periods of silence, playing with his food, and looking at Roger, who never looked at him in return, yet noted his slightest movement. Mrs. Clarke was agreeably surprised with Roger, but a little disappointed with her brother, and made several attempts to draw him out, but to no avail. Nina looked at him delightedly. When Roger drew near his hostess to say good-evening, she thanked him warmly for coming. She felt the success of the occasion was due to him.

"I know dinner-parties are a great bore to you," she said. Her brother stood near.

"Oh, no, not always; one sometimes finds an unexpected sauce to such things which whets appetite."

"I wish you would tell me what it was this time. I would have it always. It was n't the mayonnaise, I suppose."

"No, though that was very good, too."

" Thank you; I know you are a judge of those things too. I want you and my brother to get acquainted," she went on, turning to include her solemn-faced relative in the conversation. "Professor Hunt," she continued to him, "is the only literary character Garrison can boast of. We make a great deal of him,—spoil him a little, I sometimes think. He has written some books. They are so learned that few of us understand them, but that only makes us the more proud of them."

"Don't tell him the rest," said Roger ironically. "Don't tell him I 'm kept in a cage and marked 'dangerous.' "

"Oh, he would have found that out anyway," she laughed. "These newspaper men are so clever — they know everything beforehand."

"Not always, my dear sister," Gray replied, finding himself in a position where he must say something. "I can assure you the unexpected happens to us as often as to other people, and has sometimes a stupefying effect."

"What is that you are saying, uncle?" said Nina, who had been hovering near, and now came towards him, running her hand confidingly through his arm, and looking into his face with a smile. "That newspaper men are stupid? I shan't let you slander yourself like that."

"Not just that," he replied, "only that they sometimes require time to get used to their surprises."

The sight of her daughter reminded Mrs. Clarke of something she wished to say to Roger.

"Is it 'talking shop,'" she asked him, "if I request to have Nina's lessons given up during her uncle's visit? She wishes to see as much of him as possible, and his stay with us is so short." Roger suspected that it was less the uncle than the uncle's younger friend, whom Mrs. Clarke had been very gracious to at table, that formed the motive of this request. He bowed rather coldly, and said it should be as she wished, of course.

"I don't see why I should give up my lessons," Nina exclaimed, in a disappointed tone. "Uncle Mortimer does n't want me with him all the time,

I 'm sure." She glanced at him affectionately, but he looked at her gravely, putting his hand over hers that still rested on his arm.

"I cannot see any too much of you, Nina."

"Then if you are willing we will take a week's vacation," Mrs. Clarke said, paying no attention to this by-play, and Roger bowed again and took his leave.

The next morning their neighbor came up as a natural topic at the Clarke breakfast-table. Mrs. Clarke still remembered with gratification the help he had been to her the evening before, and spoke of him with high praise.

"Why do you call him 'professor'?" her brother asked.

Mr. Clarke laughed. "Lucy gave him his title." His wife colored.

"I 'm sure he deserves it," she said. "He is a university man, and has studied all his life, besides."

"From what university did he graduate?" Gray inquired. He wanted to learn just how much his relatives really knew of this man.

"I don't know; some Eastern institution. He has lived abroad a good deal. His wife is an invalid — consumption. They say she is failing fast. That reminds me I must try and get in to see her."

"Are there any children?"

"One, a daughter. She is away at school now. She and Nina used to study together, though Nina is two years older. I don't know what we should have done with Nina if it had n't been for Professor Hunt. He has been most kind, and Nina has improved wonderfully under his instruction."

Mortimer Gray glanced at his niece as her mother was speaking. There was a bright flush on her cheeks, and her eyes were dropped to her plate.

"So Professor Hunt is your teacher," he said to her later, as they sat in the library together. "What are you studying?"

"English literature," she told him. He pressed his inquiries farther and learned she had begun with Chaucer and had now reached the dramatists.

"Do you like poetry?"

"I did n't much until I began to study with Mr. Hunt." Nina knew her teacher liked this simple designation better.

"You have still a good deal of ground to go over, if you have only reached the dramatists."

"Yes, sir; but Mr. Hunt reads to me sometimes from the modern poets."

Her uncle asked which ones. She reflected a moment. There was "Atalanta in Calydon," he had read part of that to her once; and Edgar Poe — Mr. Hunt was a great admirer of Poe — Moore's "Lalla Rookh," and a little from Keats. A unique list, her listener thought.

"Anything from Wordsworth or Tennyson?"

"I don't think he cares much about them. He thinks Tennyson is overrated. Once he read something from Browning."

"Ah, Mr. Hunt is one of the Browning devotees."

"Oh, no; he makes fun of them."

"What poem did he read to you?"

"'The Statue and the Bust.'" Her uncle looked at her in surprise.

"That is a rather strange selection," he said.

"Do you mean it is an immoral poem?" Nina asked anxiously. "Mr. Hunt says that is what some of the critics think, but he does not agree with them."

"No, I should n't call it immoral; but it is one that can easily be put to immoral uses." Gray pulled his beard thoughtfully a moment.

"How long do you intend to continue your studies with Mr. Hunt? Are you not going to school again?"

"I think not, sir; I don't want to go now."

"I thought your mother intended sending you to some college."

"Yes, sir, at one time; but I grew too fast, and I was so much behind. I cannot learn quick, like Estella."

"Who is Estella?"

"Estella Hunt, I mean."

"Oh, yes. What kind of a girl is she?"

"A very good girl," was the conscientious reply, "and very bright; the brightest girl I know. Study is like play to her. Her father has taken great pains with her."

"You and she are good friends, then?"

"Yes, sir," coloring. "That is — Estella is much younger than I am, and she is away at school now."

Her uncle rose and soon after left the house, taking a long walk by himself.

Mortimer Gray's clean and upright type of manhood showed in his physical exterior. The auburn beard covered a skin clear and white as a woman's, eyes of pure blue looked straight before them. They had none of the piercing brilliancy of Roger Hunt's, but wore a calm and steadfast look, showing a courage that was not dependent on noisy bluster, or any sensational effects. His moustache nearly covered his lips, which were a little too red for a man's, but defined a mouth kindly and strong in its expression.

There was nothing in the world this man so hated to do as to hurt any one. A spirit of wide benevolence governed the least of his actions. He was never unhappy except when called on to pass judgment on another. One reason why he liked his calling as a journalist was that it put him in such impartial relation with his fellows. Professional bias was possible here as elsewhere, but not a necessary adjunct of his vocation. As a lawyer, a doctor, or a minister, even, he must look at men from a distinct point of view. Each of these callings he was ready, with his native modesty, to pronounce greater than his own, yet he liked his best, for the genial and even frame of mind he fancied it preserved him in towards the rest of the world. He had neither to adjudge, dissect, or save his fellow-creatures, only to observe and record them.

Yet with this unpartisan spirit he had a contempt for all kinds of meanness and human deceit. He hated sin, though, more than the sinner. He did not wish to injure Roger Hunt, nor even to judge him. He thought of him without rancor or a tinge of pharisaical pride or scorn, but with distrust newly deepened. Of singularly pure and blameless character himself, a combined Bayard and Galahad in the eyes of his friends, he saw himself full of faults, which forbade too strong condemnation of others. He had seen Nina and her teacher together, however, and he had determined to act in some way, but quietly. He remembered the sick wife, and the faint, fleeting interest he had once felt in Eleanor Thaxter in his own behalf. He was happily married now, with a troop of boys and girls around him, but he remembered it. He thought of the innocent daughter also.

He did not forget that Roger, too, had claims. Some immunity from wrong-doing had been gained in the mere passage of time, the flight of eighteen years, an honorable if late marriage, and the high respect, honestly earned since then, in the community in which he now lived. Yet something must be done, and he must do it. He resolved to do it quite alone. Neither his sister, much less her husband, could help here, for Gray wished above everything to avoid a sensation. He wished only to put an end to the relation between Roger Hunt and his niece. Coming back to the house, he wrote a short note, and went out on the street again to find a messenger; for this was a matter he did not care to intrust to one of the servants of the house.

Gray's letter was not a surprise to the one who received it, who nevertheless felt affronted by it. It simply requested an interview on a matter of common interest to them both. Roger threw it on the table with an exclamation of anger, then remained, standing in sullen thought until a sound from the boy who stood waiting recalled him.

"There is no answer," he said sharply. The boy turned with a slouching motion towards the door. When he reached it, Roger, looking at him distrustfully, spoke again.

"Where are you going?"

The boy turned partly towards him again, and spoke in a drawling tone.

"I was to bring the answer to him, nobody else, the man said, so I s'pose I 've got to tell him just the same, if there ain't none." He wore an aggrieved air, evidently thinking there ought to be an extra dime for so useless a job.

"You need not go back," Roger said. "I will see that the answer is delivered."

"Them wa'n't my orders," said the other sulkily. Roger looked at him, in his soiled and ragged clothes, and put his hand in his pocket. The boy watched him narrowly, but Roger drew it out again, empty. He had his own notions of honor, and they were not so bad. He could defy high heaven in the pursuit of a chosen object, but he could not crawl in the dirt.

"I will send an answer by mail," he said. "Tell him that, if you like."

This was but a weak postponement of the inevitable, he felt; yet, as it was sure to annoy some one else, he found satisfaction in it. He had judged rightly; the message did irk Gray, though he told himself he would have done better to be simply amused by it; but his sense of humor was not strong. The answer by mail, when it came, simply said that the writer would be at home Tuesday evening at eight o'clock. That meant another postponement of twenty-four hours, but Gray was a patient man.

Roger compelled himself to go through his usual routine of work, not leaving the house until towards evening, but in spite of himself he felt nervous and excited. Passing the Clarke mansion he met Nina, who stopped to speak with him. She saw that he was in one of his depressed moods, the inevitable accompaniment of high talent, she had come to believe, commanding respect as well as sympathy.

"I had a bad dream, last night," he said, in reply to some inquiry of hers, and in a sad, far-away voice.

"Tell it me," she said; but he shook his head to express the futility of description.

"I was surrounded by darkness, and quite alone. All my friends had fled from me; some because they were afraid of me, others because they no longer believed in me. A few still believed, but were

kept away by others. You were one of those."
The color came and went in her sensitive face, her
heart beat fast.

"I am sure, sir, I shall always believe in you."

"Will you?" and he looked at her mournfully.

"Why should I not?" He shook his head the
second time, in sign of more mystery.

"I am a doomed man, I sometimes think. Because I can stand alone, I must. What would I
not give for one true heart, that I could trust utterly, that I know would never forsake me; but
when a man asks for that, he asks for heaven."
The girl trembled, and turned away.

"See, now, it is coming true already. You are
afraid of me and anxious to get away."

"Oh no, sir," turning towards him again.

"Promise me, then, it shall not come true, that
you will believe in me, be my true friend, always?"
He held out his hand. That seemed an easy promise, and she put her own within it.

Mortimer Gray, pacing up and down in his
sister's library, came to the window, and looking
out, saw them. Though they were at some distance, something in the attitude of the two struck
him and sharpened his distrust, but he was aware
he was in a prejudiced state of mind here. Mrs.
Clarke, sitting near, noted him, and rising, approached the window also. Nina had left her
teacher and was coming towards the house.

"Is that Professor Hunt?" she asked in some
surprise and a little disappointment. She was

wondering why Roger did not call on her brother, and was growing a little vexed at his neglect. Whom did he think was good enough for him to associate with, she wondered. Journalism was not literature, she knew, but —

"Why did n't Professor Hunt come in?" she asked Nina, when the latter entered the room.

"I asked him," was the reply, "but he excused himself. He is not feeling very well, I think."

"He keeps himself mewed up in that library from morning until night," Mrs. Clarke said discontentedly. "He does n't deserve it from me, but I believe I 'll send over and ask him to spend the evening with us." Nina left the room.

"Not to-night, sister, if you please; I have an engagement."

Two hours later a servant ushered Gray into Roger's study. The two greeted each other formally, and Roger asked his visitor, coldly, to be seated.

"Thank you," said Gray, "but as my errand need not be a long one, and as I must assume this visit is not wholly agreeable to you, I had better remain standing, perhaps."

"Why should it be disagreeable to me?" Roger asked, with quick suspicion.

"Pardon me, but we waste time, it seems to me, to deal in any disguises. You must surely have guessed why I asked to see you."

"Not so well but that I will leave you to explain."

"I will do so at once." But having reached this point Gray hesitated. It was a difficult and delicate task he had undertaken; he wished to execute it with all the nicety gentlemanly honor and taste demanded. He was conscious, also, in a dim way, of wishing to justify himself to the man before him, even while seeming to attack him.

"I should like you to believe, first of all, Mr. Hunt," he began, "that the duty of this visit, as I conceive it, is one I would gladly have put aside. I can assure you that I lament, as much as you do, the circumstances that have thrown us together in this way."

"I am as far from lamenting them" — Roger began, in his former tone, but a quiet glance from the other checked him.

"We shall get on faster," Gray repeated, "and relieve ourselves of each other's presence sooner, if we are perfectly frank. For myself, I admit this meeting is unpleasant" —

"Why did you seek it, then?" Again Gray's eyes rested on him.

"If you have come here to threaten me, then you should know I care nothing for your threats. If you have any evil designs against me, you will execute them, I suppose, and without any hindrance from me."

Gray mused on this a space. It looked as if the speaker spoke the truth, and was as indifferent as he seemed.

"You have the courage of your opinions, I know,

and your own sense of honor, I do not doubt. May I assume, then, that my sister Mrs. Clarke, and her family have the same knowledge of your past life that I have?"

. "You may assume what you please," scornfully. "Why do you not ask them?" a moment later.

"I have considered that," was the quiet response, "but I am loath to resort to such measures before I am compelled to."

"You are not prompted in such consideration by any feeling for me?" Roger said, ironically.

"By more, perhaps, than you would willingly believe. I have no word of condemnation to speak of your past, Mr. Hunt; I am more desirous to understand my fellow-men than to judge them. But I ask you, are you doing the fair and upright thing in keeping up this intimate relation with people who know so little of you?"

"You wish to break off my connection with your relatives, and if I do not agree to your demands you will reveal what you think a damaging secret in my past life! I leave you to judge for yourself the character and disposition of a man who seeks an interview with another in his own house for such a purpose. You will find I am not a man to be intimidated. I say to you, sir, that I consider such conduct no better than a piece of villainous blackmail! You may do your worst!"

"That is your final word, is it?" Gray asked, taking up his hat from the table where he had laid it. He had watched Roger curiously during this outbreak, and though he detected some signs of bluster, he thought, very likely, he meant what he said. Any way he had had enough of preliminaries. "I will not trouble you further," he added, and turned away. Before he reached the door, Roger spoke: —

"What are you going to do?"

"I have not yet determined."

A less intelligent man might have found some weak ground for hope in a reply of .this kind, so candidly spoken. Roger did not.

"You mean to strike at me in the dark, then?"

"I came here in the hope of avoiding any action that might have that construction put upon it, of reaching some basis of just agreement. I wish to act with you, not against you." There was a moment's silence, while Gray stood waiting.

"What is it you wish me to do?" Roger asked shortly.

Gray stepped back a pace or two. "I do not ask you to break off all connection with my sister's family. That would be impracticable. I only ask you to regulate it. I wish you to discontinue teaching my niece." Roger threw a quick suspicious glance at him.

"I see," he exclaimed sarcastically. "You have other designs for her."

"Other designs!" Gray repeated, in a puzzled tone.

"You wish to marry her to your young friend!"

The total unexpectedness — the brazen effrontery

or stupid ignorance which could dictate such a remark, staggered Gray. Was the man a fool, he
asked himself, or a downright villain? Roger saw
that he had overshot himself and reddened with
mortification.

"Why should I give up teaching Miss Clarke?"
he asked, with recovered boldness.

"Suppose we agree not to discuss that point,"
said Gray. "Suppose we say it is only because I
ask it."

"And you expect me to act on a reason of that
kind?"

"I do not know whether you will or not," said
Gray, and looked at him attentively. A bright
spot was glowing in each cheek, his blue eyes
emitted a keen light, seldom seen there, his nostrils whitened. He took a step or two towards
Roger.

"When a man of low, animal instincts," he began, in a low tone, "deliberately plans a woman's shame and ruin, we know how to describe his
action. We call it by an ugly name, and know
how to deal with it. But for the man who, under
the guise of friendship, is satisfied to reap a victory
of another kind, yet quite as deadly — when he
aims to seduce the imagination only, to blast a
young girl's spirit, kill all her innocent thoughts,
worm himself into affections he has no honest use
for, pollute her soul — for that man and his conduct the word has yet to be coined."

"That is enough!" cried Roger. He was white

with rage, and shook like a leaf with something besides rage. No one had ever spoken to him like this, and he both feared and hated the man who had done so. It was as though he had suddenly caught a horribly distorted image of himself in a mirror held up for that purpose. He did not believe in its truthfulness, he denied the likeness, but it shamed him, nevertheless, more than he had ever been shamed before.

"You reveal your own nature, not mine," he hotly declared. "It is you who cover innocence with foul suspicion, who turn light into darkness, the fit abode of minds that peep and pry and make dastardly charges as yours does."

"We have had enough of this," said Gray, wearily. "Will you grant my request about my niece?" Roger looked at him. "Let us have no more words, please. A simple 'Yes' or 'No' will suffice. — I fancy you mean it to be 'No,'" he added, as Roger still looked at him with proud disdain, and he made another movement to depart.

"It would be 'No' a thousand times over, now and throughout eternity if — if I had only myself to consider." The speaker's voice broke, whether from real emotion or with intention the other could not tell. He dropped down into a chair and covered his face with his hands.

"I am helpless," he exclaimed, raising it a moment after. "If I stood alone — but I — I have a wife and child." He again hid his face. Gray looked at him with increasing wonder and curiosity combined. Was this acting?

"It is because I, too, remembered them that I am here," he said gently.   He waited a moment, but Roger did not raise his head.   Gray then quietly prepared to leave the room.   He considered his point gained, and wished to be magnanimous. He believed this was an enemy he could trust.

"I think we understand each other," he said, as Roger still remained silent.   "I will not trouble you further;" and went out.

XIX.

In the discussion that had taken place at Mrs. Somers's after the flight of Roger Hunt from his home, Mortimer Gray had remarked that he seemed to be a mixture of the hero and the crank. He left him now unable to determine whether it was a mere braggart with whom he had been trying to deal, a downright impostor, or only, as George Somers had called him, an egotist. Soon after he had occasion to suspect that he combined other characteristics with these, and was at heart both a coward and a sneak. Two days after the interview in Roger's study Gray received the following letter: —

Mortimer Gray:

Sir, — I write to say to you that after you left me last Tuesday evening, I bitterly regretted the momentary weakness which led me to make even a tacit show of acquiescence in the ridiculous and presumptuous demand which formed the object of your visit, and which I now reject with all the contempt it deserves.

I should not deem it necessary to inform you of this changed decision had not circumstances arisen which you might otherwise misconstrue. I am about to leave home on a rather extended absence, the object of which is explained in the accompanying letter,. which I inclose for your reading, that you may be under no misapprehension as to my real motive, to show you that my seeming compliance with your request is no real one, nor to be so regarded by you.

I regret to be obliged to speak thus plainly, but I should be untrue to myself not to express once more, in closing this letter, my deep abhorrence and scorn for certain sentiments expressed by yourself in our late interview, and for the motive which prompted you to seek it.

. Respectfully, ROGER HUNT.

The letter inclosed was a brief business epistle from an Eastern publishing house, asking Roger to visit some ancient ruins in California and Mexico, and contribute a series of illustrated articles to a leading magazine. Gray read it and let it slip through his fingers to the floor. He sat musing a long time, an expression on his face that was half irritated, half amused. Finally he spoke.

"Check!" He picked up Roger's letter, folded and replaced it in the envelope, and could fancy he heard a faint rustle of triumph in its pages. His nature was far less belligerent than most men's, yet he had not only a man's love of accomplishing the thing he had undertaken, but of winning acknowledgment of his success from others. It galled him to think that Roger Hunt would never admit any one but himself victor here. The device was perfectly transparent, the end he had sought was gained, but events had so shaped themselves that the man who had been beaten would, Gray knew, go through life proudly denying he had suffered the least coercion, declaring, and perhaps believing — for he now began to see what an immense power of self-delusion there is in a nature like Hunt's — that he had been influenced only by outward circumstances and his own free choice.

"Pshaw!" said Gray to himself, who found his vexation deepening. "What do I care how the man defines his motives, so the thing is done?" But he did care.

That the end he sought was accomplished, he did not doubt. The letter from Hunt's publisher had stated that the journey proposed would probably cover a month. Before the end of that time Mrs. Clarke and her daughter would be on the other side of the ocean, for at least a year's absence, if the former carried out her present intentions, of which she had not yet spoken to Nina.

"After all," Gray thought, as he reflected on the subject, "what can be more ignoble than the wish to extract confession from your fallen enemy of his weakness and your strength? The tactics of war in ancient times permitted a man to spoil as well as defeat his opponent; modern civilization resigns the former privilege to the savage and brigand." He repeated that it was enough the object sought was accomplished, let Roger Hunt theorize about it as he chose.

Roger made preparations to leave home on the following Sunday. He was greatly pleased with the offer he had received, as a sign of growth in that literary reputation which it was his dearest wish to achieve; but gratification of this kind had been overlaid by another, for the sudden escape it offered from the difficulty he had fallen into with Mortimer Gray, and the chance he had not dared hope for to repudiate and defy him, retrieve his own wounded dignity and pride. He sent a letter to Mrs. Clarke, formally resigning his post as teacher, leaving the future unprovided for with any expression of wish or suggestion, and closing with a message of friendly remembrance for his pupil.

Mrs. Clarke showed the letter to her brother and openly mourned the loss they should all sustain. When Nina heard the news, surprise and fear made her dumb, and seizing a book Roger had loaned her as a pretext, she hurried over to the study unobserved. When she returned her eyes were red with weeping, and she shut herself in her room. Roger had used a devil's frankness with her, clothed in a saint's holiness of purpose. "Let there be only truth between us two," was the sub-stance of his talk with her. Vaguely and mysteriously he reminded her of his dream. Evil forces were at work against him — against them both. He could not explain further, he said with a sigh, could not disturb and darken her youthful confidence; but this much she should know, that their

innocent and friendly relation had been observed
by evil eyes, that the reason assigned for bringing
the lessons to an end was only formal, that if he
had not been going away, the end would have
come through pressure of these mysterious forces
at work against them. He assured her he told her
all this because he trusted her, because she had a
right to know, to preserve the beautiful understanding between them, and in secret pledge of their
continued faithfulness to each other.

Nina listened with wonder, distress, and shame.
She could gather nothing from what she was told
except that somebody was displeased with them
both. Her thoughts flew at once to the sick wife.
She was newly alarmed and humiliated for herself,
but most miserable over the thought that Roger
was going away. Pity and admiration were now
doubly increased, exalted with the sentiment of
self-sacrifice. If Mortimer Gray could have read
the strange conflicting emotions at work in that
young heart, and understood the cause, he might
well have questioned himself whether he had accomplished good or evil in his attempt to regulate
the conduct of Roger Hunt.

Mrs. Somers's letter reached Roger Saturday
evening, as he was completing his preparations for
departure the next day. He did not recognize the
handwriting, and the postmark was blurred. Its
bulk, requiring double postage, showed that it was
no ordinary business communication, and he looked

at it with much curiosity, before he cut the end of the envelope and drew out the letter.

He turned at once to the signature, and his face brightened when he saw whose it was. Kitty Somers had resumed a large place in his thoughts of late. Since his return from Monroe he had been seized with the impulse, more than once, to write to her, but the fear of meeting a repulse had withheld him. Now, it seemed, she herself had taken the initiative. That pleased him, and was, he thought, quite suitable. With a gratified look he turned back to the beginning of the letter and began to read.

This expression changed slightly before he reached the end of the first sentence, and soon deepened to a displeased frown that grew darker as he proceeded. Once he started with surprise, when he came upon the news about his son; but as this was told in a way that offended even more than it astonished him, it but increased resentment against the writer. With compressed lips and lowering brow he read on to the end, then threw the letter on the table, and rising began pacing rapidly up and down the room.

He was intensely angry with Kitty Somers. He termed her letter "insolent." Certain words and phrases she had employed returned to him and stung him like scorpions, but less to shame or alarm than to anger him. As for the effect of the news her letter contained, and which formed the writer's chief motive in sending it, the discovery

of his first-born, it was scarcely more than one
of annoyance. Still less was he moved by what
most concerned Mrs. Somers, anxiety for Estella,
or remorse on her account. He gave only passing thought either to his son or daughter. He
could think only of the writer of the letter. All
the vexation and chagrin he had lately suffered
from other directions was for the time forgotten.
The near became remote, the distant the all-de-
sired. Nina Clarke and Mortimer Gray faded
from his thoughts; all he wanted now was to meet
Kitty Somers, to give her his opinion of her
letter and her temerity in writing it, to answer
her taunts and reproaches. To attempt to put his
fermenting thoughts in writing was far too in-
adequate a means of punishment. He wished to
meet her face to face. Suddenly he asked himself, Why not? and at once resolved to make a
little détour in his journey and go to Monroe.
Eleanor had begged him to do this when he first
told her of his projected trip, but he had put her
wish aside. Then too, Roger supposed, as he re-
volved the matter in his mind, he ought, perhaps,
to see this almost forgotten son of his. He had
no unpleasant feelings towards him, and was conscious of being a little curious concerning him;
certainly, he was not afraid to meet him.

When Eleanor learned this new resolution, that
Roger was to observe her wish and go to Monroe,
she was first pleased, then alarmed, the fear that
something had happened to Estella quickly assail-

ing her. He reassured her on this point, briefly and somewhat impatiently.

"Then what is it?" she asked in a weak voice, looking helplessly up at him from the pillow. "I know something has happened, Roger. You are in trouble."

It accorded with his scrupulosity in small matters that so far as he told her anything he should tell her the truth. He might have employed any one of a dozen innocent subterfuges to soothe and reassure her, but that was not his way.

"And if I am," he replied, "it is not about anything in which you can help me."

"Oh, Roger, what is it? Do tell me? Don't leave me in this suspense! If it is about Estella " —

"It is not about Estella. Estella is perfectly well, so far as I know. No, I can tell you nothing more," in reply to another entreating word from her. "I find that some business of importance calls me to Monroe, so I go that way; that is all." He bade her good-by and left her.

Mrs. Saunders was sadly puzzled over this sudden departure from home of the master of the house, on so long a journey and at such a time. She still held to the belief that Mr. Hunt was a good husband, seeing the wife surrounded with all her condition required, and trying to excuse missing care and attention of a more personal order on the ground of long illness and the husband's absorption in his books. He could not know, she thought, how swiftly the end was approaching, and hesitated as to her own duty, half-resolved to speak to him, but this was not easy. Just before leaving the house, Roger repeated the minute directions he had before given her about the different points at which a letter or telegram might reach him. She listened deferentially, but summoning courage to say a word.

"It seems a pity you should have to go, just now, sir, and for so long."

"A month is not very long," he said, coldly.

"No, sir, I know; but I — I think she is failing very fast."

"You are unnecessarily alarmed. The doctor says she may linger in this way for months. He ought to know."

"Yes, to be sure, — the doctor ought to know," she replied, and saw him depart. She went back to her charge, to find her still excited over Roger's change of plans, and to pass a restless night with her.

Roger scarcely remembered Estella was in the house, when he mounted the steps of Mrs. Black's residence and inquired for Mrs. Somers. He met her, however, in the parlor, her books in her arms, just ready to set out for school. She uttered an exclamation of surprise when she saw him, thinking at once of her mother. He had to quiet and reassure her, as he had Eleanor the night before, repeating many times that her mother was not worse, and explaining, briefly, the errand which was taking him from home.

"A month!" the girl exclaimed in some concern. "Is it safe to leave mamma for a month?"

"If I had thought it was not, I should not have left her," her father replied, in a tone of reprimand, and she was silenced. He looked restlessly towards the door, and a moment after Mrs. Somers entered. Constrained again by Estella's presence, she went forward and gave him her hand.

"I wish to speak with Mrs. Somers, Estella," he said, breaking the silence that followed, and while the girl waited. She picked up her books and turned towards the door, but reaching it glanced back.

"Papa!" she exclaimed, stepping towards him. "You are not trying to deceive me? Is mamma worse?" He made an impatient response to the same effect as before, and she turned a troubled face towards Mrs. Somers.

"Your mother is no worse, Estella. Do not be alarmed," and she went out of the room, wonderingly.

Alone with him, Mrs. Somers met Roger's look of angry challenge, and began to suspect what was coming.

"Are we secure against interruption here?" he asked, glancing about the room, separated from the hall and an adjoining one in the rear only by hanging draperies.

"Not altogether," she replied calmly, seating herself where she was, and not offering to lead him elsewhere. He came towards her.

"I received your letter," he began.   As there was nothing to be said to this she waited.

"I shall be very frank with you," he went on. "I shall begin by telling you that I consider such a letter utterly inexcusable on any grounds.   I do not permit any one to address me in such terms as you have employed, not even an old and valued friend like yourself."

"For that matter," she replied, with some sarcasm, "I ceased to prefer any claims of that kind years ago."

"Very well!   That is all the more reason, then, why you should refrain from giving your opinion of me now — unasked."

There was some reason in this, and she sat reflecting on his words a moment, unmindful of their rudeness.   She saw at once how things stood.   She had meant to pierce him with honest shame and remorse, but she had only aroused his resentment against herself.   It was soon plain that he cared not a jot for the main charges in her letter, the principal revelation it contained; he was simply angry with her for writing it, and meant to quarrel with her.   She herself was in too displeased a state of mind to guard herself against him in the latter point.

"I wish to repeat," he began again, in the same manner, "that I consider such a letter entirely indefensible.   I am at a loss to know how any one — any woman" — with emphasis, "could have written it.   There is not a particle of womanly gentleness or feeling in it." A slight color rose to his listener's face.

"What excuse have you to offer for such treatment of one who never injured you?" he ended, in the tone he might have used to Estella.

"Excuse!" she repeated with a singular smile. "I wished to speak my full mind on some points. I am not sorry I have done so."

"Speaking her full mind is no doubt a woman's privilege, but I had given you the credit of being able to refrain when you knew nothing could come of it. What did you expect to accomplish? You should know me well enough to know that I am not easily alarmed."

"I was not thinking of you at all," she replied. He stared in some natural surprise at this.

"I was thinking of Estella." He frowned a little.

"Estella! What harm threatens Estella?"

"It is like you to ask."

"Estella will be surprised, of course, perhaps a little hurt and offended, at the knowledge that she has a half-brother. She would have known it long ago, had it not been for her mother's foolish scruples. I see now how unwise I was to yield to them."

"You mean to tell Estella?" Mrs. Somers exclaimed in an anxious tone.

"How can I avoid telling her?" he asked petulantly. "If, as you say, he is here" — Even Roger Hunt found it hard to speak his son's name.

"It will kill her!"

"You take a very exaggerated view of the whole matter."

"Do you mean to say there is nothing you would spare her the knowledge of? nothing you regret?"

"There are some things I regret; but I deny I have reason to regret any action of mine so far as its motive was concerned. As to results," and he sighed, "I have been able to bear them so far as they affected myself; I am not called on to bear them, I suppose, as they affect others."

"Not even as they affect Estella?"

"Not even as they affect Estella."

She leaned back in her chair and looked at him. "You are a strange man, Roger."

"Not to those who understand me," he answered proudly. She had some difficulty not to smile. The mighty seriousness with which Roger Hunt always took himself was one of the causes, she used to tell her husband, underlying his erratic behavior. He had some sense of humor; she had seen him laugh over Dogberry, and Sir Andrew Aguecheek, but it had never yet served as a help to self-knowledge. In discussing himself, a certain tone of ponderous gravity was always uppermost.

"Tell me, Roger," she said, as these thoughts passed and gave way to others, more serious, "what is the duty of the strong towards the weak in this world? Is it not to help? Does not strength bring responsibility?"

"Undoubtedly; but the duty of the weak is

equally plain.　They should submit to be guided by the strong."

"But the weak do not regard themselves as weak.　We should not wish them to, I think.　We should encourage the stronger qualities in all.　I remember how much you used to make of people you liked, how stoutly you would defend them, how much you would do for them.　You spoiled them sometimes, I thought.　To be sure," with a peculiar expression, "you generally made up for it by your very different treatment of those you did n't like."

"What do you mean by that?" he asked quickly.

"Oh, never mind!　I don't know why we are wasting time like this.　You are one of the most intelligent men I know, in some ways, and the dullest in others."

"That is what you said in your letter," he exclaimed, lifting his head.

"Oh, for pity's sake stop talking about the letter."

"It was just that I came here to talk about."

"What folly!　There is something much more important to be talked about.　There is Estella."

"I do not share your anxiety about Estella."

"There is no need to tell her," Mrs. Somers went on.　"Mr. Watson has been to see me.　He has the same as promised me to leave the city."

"Promised!" exclaimed the other.　"Do you mean you exacted such a promise, in my name?"

"I don't mean promised, but of course it would be better for him to go."

"I don't see why. Whether he goes or stays, he must act on his own wish entirely. I shall see him myself."

"And Estella?" she urged.

"I shall know what to do with Estella. Just now I wish to speak with you. That letter" —

"Roger, how can you be so silly!" and she rose quickly to her feet. "One would think," wheeling and facing him, "that I was the one on trial here."

"So you are."

"Indeed!" drawing herself up. "And what are the charges, pray?"

"The charges are those that spring always from betrayed trust and friendship."

"Friendship! Our friendship ended eighteen years ago."

"To outward recognition, perhaps." She looked at him in astonishment.

"What do you mean?" she asked haughtily.

"When I chose to be my own master, and threw off the yoke society and the world had imposed, the world and your precious 'society' denounced me with virtuous indignation. You tried to do so, too, but in your secret heart" —

"Oh" — The sound was like a wail and angry protest combined. "And if ever I did try to speak an excusing word for you, I am well repaid for it now, — well repaid!"

"You are a woman of unusual strength of character," he went on, unheeding, "but of some

marked weaknesses as well, which it is necessary
some one should point out to you. You think it
was love of truth that made you turn against me.
You pride yourself on your moral courage, but I
call it moral cowardice. I wish you to know that
I stand by every action of my past life. I can
stand alone if need be."

"That is doubtless a great virtue," she· replied.
Her better judgment and sense of propriety told
her this discussion should end, but it was impossible not to answer him.

"Self-reliance is a very good thing; perhaps
there is nothing better, unless it is a little humility. For my part I have learned that other people are, on the whole, as wise and as good as I am.
I admire courage as much as you do. I, too, can
stand alone, but I trust I am guiltless of the vanity that is always courting occasions for that kind
of display."

"Most people select their occasions very carefully. True freedom knows nothing of occasions;
it lives in its own atmosphere, like love. If you
lived in China you would think it your duty to
hobble around on deformed feet, as other women
do."

"Very likely, if I had never seen a woman with
feet of natural size. My mental servility is
proved, I suppose, by the fact that some of my
opinions run counter to yours. You talk of freedom very eloquently, but you have not yet learned
to yield it to another. Where you cannot domi-

nate, you begin to abuse! It was always so. When you were young there was not a friend who ever differed from you on any point touching your interest or self-love but was made to suffer for it."

"You seem to be taking some freedom, now."

"I mean to. You, to talk to me of the power of friendship, of faithfulness!" she added, with heightened color, and in a voice that trembled in spite of her effort to keep it steady; "to prate to me of loyalty, — you, who broke the most sacred ties, who violated your home, deserted your wife and child, placed the stigma of a dishonored name on those who look to you for protection; who even now traduce and complain of the woman who blindly sacrificed everything for you, — you to talk of faithfulness! You do not understand its smallest principle." She paused with flashing eye and heaving breast. He was deeply offended, but if she had thought to arouse any other feeling of shame or self-judgment, she was disappointed.

"You repeat the shallow platitudes of your set and your circle," he answered her. "My actions are beyond the comprehension of minds that reason as yours does. Yours can reason better when it tries. Now I can prove to you " —

"Oh, you can prove anything, I have no doubt, but I am not in a mood for dialectics. Casuistry is n't my forte. Come, I am tired of this, — tired and ashamed," and she waved her hand, to end the discussion.

"Not yet," he replied. "You have said what

you wished to say, have spoken freely and fearlessly, but, I repeat, you have not spoken sincerely." Again that hint of unpleasant suggestion in his tone. "You try to persuade yourself you are angry with me, that you dislike and distrust me, — but you do not." She drew herself up and looked at him steadily. "We were good friends once," in a changed tone, and with seeming hesitancy. "I never could understand just what it was came between us."

"Came between us!" she gasped.

"We understood each other perfectly. There was no one I could talk to as freely as to you. And you — you liked to talk with me. Is it not true?" She clenched her hand and bit her lip, her color coming and going.

"Yes, we were good friends! When I went away, as I have said, you thought fit to join the general outcry against me. You would not stand up against the world, and your husband" —

"My husband! How dare you bring George into a discussion of this kind! He was your friend. He said what he could to excuse and condone your conduct. He had as much courage as you."

"You mistake me. George was a good fellow. He wrote me a letter I never forgave; but I let that pass, now. And you — you acted according to your nature, that is, according to one side of it, the side that is afraid. There is another side, which, properly guided and supported, would be afraid of nothing; but it has been kept in subjection so long to the other and lower that it is doubtful if it ever rises above it now."

"Thank you for the doubt," she interjected sarcastically. She was recovering herself. At first a wild apprehension had seized her that he was going to make love to her. A man can do this when denouncing and upbraiding a woman as well as when openly praising and seeking her favor.

"No, it will never predominate now," he continued, heedless of her sarcasm, and looking at her reflectively. "You will always be about the woman you are, mistaking the conventional for the real, prejudice for conviction, yet cherishing thoughts and an ideal of life very different, which you did not hesitate to avow when you were younger, and which — I speak with unusual frankness, I know — the sight and remembrance of me always awakens."

"Are you a man, to talk to a woman like this! "

"I speak as one freed spirit to another. Yours is not wholly freed, and never will be; yet you understand me."

"I understand nothing. You are a monster of egotism! That is all I know."

"I am a man of some consistency of purpose, if that is what you mean. Come," he added, with a still bolder touch, "if what I have said is not true; if, in spite of all that has happened you do not trust me, and — and regard me with some kindness, why, when we met each other accidentally two months ago, did your looks and words so report you? Why did you not send me on my way? Why did you ask to have Estella remain here with you?"

"Estella! Was it possible to see that poor child, to know what I know, and not feel for her, not wish to be her friend!" She paused a moment, while the full meaning of his words slowly dawned on her. She turned white with outraged womanly feeling. "Why did I receive Estella?" she exclaimed. "Do you mean — Oh, this is too much! We have had more than enough of this. I ask you, sir, to leave me," with an imperious wave of the hand. He colored and opened his lips to speak.

"Not another word," she exclaimed. "Leave me." There was no mistaking her. Even the man before her was unable to support her look, and seemed to grow sensibly smaller in her presence. With a crestfallen air he left the house.

She flew to her room, where she paced up and down excitedly for a few moments, then suddenly stood still. She remembered Estella. What should she say to her? That she had turned her father out of the house? What would he, Roger, do next? Would he remember he had a daughter in Monroe, and that the ostensible object of his visit was to see her? Then if he came to the house again, what must she do, how must she behave? She had something to think of here besides her own insulted dignity as a woman. That

is the inconvenience of tragedy in common life!
The curtain does not fall leaving a long blank of
darkness and silence as on the stage. On the contrary it leaves things about as it found them.
Dinner must be ordered and cooked the same as
before, the appointment kept with the dressmaker.
We must wear as composed and cheerful faces as
though we had not just escaped drowning in an
emotional whirlpool.

Mrs. Somers was not fond of the sensational,
and passed the day in the moral abasement that
naturally follows such a scene, in a mind disposed
to rational behavior. Externally she was nervous
and excited, and kept moving restlessly about the
room. Catching sight of her husband's picture,
a small framed photograph that stood on the mantel, she did a curious thing. Going towards it,
she leaned her arms on the mantel and looked for
a long time into the eyes of the portrait.

"Did you hear him?" she asked at last, silently.
"Wasn't it shameful? Wasn't it ridiculous?
At first I was terribly angry. I am angry still,
of course; but what is the use? One might as
well be angry with the ravings of a sick man!
He has not changed at all! Sometimes I think
nobody ever does change — much, unless it is in
heaven. And he thinks you are a 'good fellow.'"
A low laugh, half like a sob, escaped her, and she
dropped her head a moment on the marble slab.
"But I hope you won't change, even there," she
began again, raising it. "You mustn't get too far

ahead of me. Yes, I know I was foolish, to stay there talking with him so long; but what could I do? I kept thinking of Estella. You don't think I ought to give up Estella? She has n't a friend in the world! I knew you could n't want me to do that. What do I care what such a man as that thinks? What should either of us care?"

She took the little picture in her hands, looked at it a moment longer, then pressed her lips against the cold glass. Her breath obscured it, covering it with a faint mist, which soon passed, however, like the little clouds that sometimes used to arise and shadow their marital skies.

XX.

ASSISTANT WATSON'S pupils pronounced his behavior, the Monday following his visit to Mrs. Somers, more difficult to support than usual. Even Estella noticed it, and found some cause of blame. He avoided looking at her, and made brief answers when she spoke to him. During the half hour intermission at noon, when he saw her approaching the desk, he rose abruptly and left the room. She was a little hurt, but tried to excuse him, supposing something had gone wrong with his work.

Watson, reflecting on Mrs. Somers's wish, while he still did not perceive its necessity as she did, and felt the slight it offered to his own plans and rights in the matter, resolved to yield to it and to leave Monroe. She could not know the practical difficulties attendant on such a change, or she would not have felt so free to suggest it. To leave his present position meant the hindrance and perhaps the complete breaking up of his life-plans.

In the first place Charles Watson was poor. The money left by his father had been invested by his aunt in a concern that seemed to her all the safer, because it was cloaked in a great deal of outward piety. The president was a member in highest standing of the church, and prominent on mis-sionary boards and in similar enterprises. It was said he called all his employés together every morn-ing for prayers. His business was supported by the contributions of his admirers, who were glad to believe they were making a good investment of their money, and serving the cause of religion at the same time. Miss Watson was one of the lar-gest subscribers, but did not live to know the de-ception that had been practiced on her. She died urging her nephew to live a godly life, and to fol-low in the footsteps of the man who, he learned a few weeks later, had squandered every dollar in-trusted to his care. The revelations connected with this gigantic swindle, from which so many others suffered besides himself, and who could far less afford to, gave the young man a deep moral shock. His faith was destroyed in a new direction. Hith-erto it had not been difficult to believe that reli-gious heresy was a synonym for the worst immoral-ity; but now the shame and perplexity of his father's example was balanced by this other discov-ery of betrayed trust. The spirit of misanthropic doubt arose anew, and embittered his entire outlook on life, which seemed now equally barren of hope for himself and belief in his kind.

Coming to Monroe, he had not tried to make friends or social acquaintances, living by himself, and performing his duties in a mechanical manner; inspired by no cheerful prospects, or the desire to please any one dear to him, simply by the necessity to live. He had felt strangely attracted to his new pupil from the first, and though the knowledge that she was his half-sister had been at first a little repugnant to him, that feeling had quickly passed; and another, the right of ownership, the claim to acknowledge and be blessed in this new relation had arisen; so that the duty of denying himself all this, even for her good, was a hard one. It seemed to him, now that he was about to be deprived of it, a sister was of all human ties and relations that which he most craved and needed. He felt, too, he could be of use and service to Estella. She liked him; but there were her father and mother, whom she must love best, of course. The affection he could offer could not be accepted without to some degree displacing and dishonoring other feelings. Mrs. Somers was right; he must not think of himself.

The work of the day ended at last, and he was alone in the empty schoolroom. He sat behind his desk, his head supported on one hand, in an attitude that brought out some resemblance to his father. He was lost in painful thoughts. The noise of the departing pupils in the hall outside had died away, and the building, except for the sound of the janitor moving about in another room, shutting windows, seemed deserted. As he sat there motionless and absorbed, he did not hear the door quietly open, nor note the visitor who entered and paused a moment just inside. As he stepped forward, with a slight air of embarrassment, Watson looked up, and the eyes of father and son met. He knew him at once, and rose from his chair, his dark skin turning to a sickly pallor. He kept his eyes fixed on the approaching figure, but did not speak. Roger, too, waited a perceptible space, after reaching the desk and pausing before it.

"I need not introduce myself, I see. You recognize me."

The one whom he addressed turned paler still. His lips tightened, and his nostrils quivered a little. A tremor of mingled pain and loathing. swept over his face.

"You are my father!" he said at last, with an effort. Roger bowed.

"I only learned the day before yesterday that you were here. If I had known it when I was in town before, I should have sought you out." His son looked at him in dull surprise. He was quite unprepared for the easy, unconcerned tone in which these words were spoken.

"You would have sought me out?" he repeated.

"Certainly. Why not? We meet in a rather strange way, I admit; but I have never cherished any ill-will towards you."

The young man looked at him.

"Thank you."

"Why should I have cherished any unkind feeling towards you?" his father asked. "You were but a child when — when " —

"When you deserted my mother and me," the son finished.

"I never deserted you. I gave you your choice
to come with me if you wished."

"You gave a boy six years old his choice! But
I have never ceased to be grateful-that I knew how
to make one, even then."

Roger paid no attention to this.

"I also gave your aunt instructions to send you
tó me, if that suited either her wish or yours. It
did not surprise me that she did not choose to do
so, to learn afterward that she had deprived you
of your right name, and bestowed that of her own
respectable ancestor in its place. She has done all
she could to prejudice you against me, of course."

"She could not 'prejudice' me so much as your
own actions have done."

"I did not come here to be brought to account by
my own son," Roger exclaimed angrily.

"Your son! I am not your son! I repudiate
any such dishonorable title. We are strangers —
aliens in every fibre. The breadth of the universe
lies between us." His father looked at him with
cold dislike.

"You speak the truth more nearly than you
know, though I was the first to discover it, and
though I came here in the hope of disproving it.
It was because I saw the natural antagonism between us, even when you were a child, that I felt
justified in leaving you. I saw how little alike we
were in anything. You belong distinctly to your
mother's family " —

"I thank heaven," said the young man quickly.

"I gladly stand in my mother's debt for all that I am and have, though I must inherit her suffering, too."

"Her suffering!" Roger replied ironically. "You will please observe that I disclaim all responsibility for your mother's 'suffering'!"

"Do not speak of my mother, sir! Is it not enough that you deserted her, a sick and helpless woman, whom you had placed in the hands of strangers, that you must insult her memory now?" Roger looked at him a moment with a singular expression, in which curiosity, anger, some faint pity, too, played back and forth, with a rising resolve, which he hesitated to execute.

"So that is the story with which your pious aunt has regaled you?" he asked at length, with curling lip. "It is false from beginning to end!" The other started, and stepped towards him with a threatening look, but something in his father's eyes checked him. A cold fear suddenly clutched his heart.

"Your mother" — Roger began again, but hesitated. Even he shrank from the thing he was about to do, but the demon of self-justification had him in his grasp.

"Your mother died in an inebriate asylum!"

"What! Oh, this is infamous!"

"It is perfectly true. I have the certificate of her death, duly witnessed and sealed. Your aunt knew this as well as I. What her object was in concealing the truth from you, I do not know."

Some fatal instinct told Watson his father spoke the truth. There had always been a mystery about his mother. A hundred confirming signs and circumstances rushed back to substantiate what he had heard. The passion died out of his face, leaving only its look of misery. His clenched hand fell to his side. He sank down into his chair and let his head drop on his arms, uttering a groan of despair.

"You might have spared me this."

"So I would, had you spared me. I am not responsible for the foolish delusions others practiced on you. You see, yourself, they have accomplished nothing."

"Nothing!" the other repeated drearily, raising his head. "I know now I have had neither father nor mother."

"I stand ready to be your father, if we can arrive at an understanding." His son's face was turned from him, and he did not see the expression of repugnance that flitted across it. After a few more remarks of a preliminary nature, Roger made him an offer. He had made some inquiries and learned his situation. He now offered to bear the expense of his further studies and settle ten thousand dollars on him. There was but one condition, that he should change his name, and thus acknowledge their relation. This offer was proudly declined. Roger was not surprised, but had the sense of duty performed.

"As you please," he said coldly. "Only bear

in mind I have nothing to conceal here or elsewhere. I rely on the simple truth to support me,
always."

"The truth!" exclaimed the other scornfully,
his first feelings returning. "Who has outraged
truth more than you, profaned everything that is
sacred "—

There was another listener to these words. Estella, who had gone to the laboratory after school,
returning, went towards the schoolroom, ostensi-
bly to get a book, but hoping for a chance to speak
with Mr. Watson. The door had been left slightly
ajar, and looking through, she saw with amazement
her father and teacher talking together. She drew
back, hesitating whether to go forward or to retire,
when the young assistant's words of passionate de-
nunciation reached her ear. She listened eagerly
to what followed.

"That will do," she heard her father say. "I
did not come here to be insulted."

"What did you come for?"

"Simply to learn your own wish and intention
respecting the future. I learn from Mrs. Somers
that you have told something of your history to
Estella."

"You need not fear for Estella. She will learn
nothing more from me."

"You mistake my meaning; there is no reason
why Estella should not know the truth." His son
looked at him with new indignation.

"Do you wish to drive her to despair?"

"What folly! What harm can there be in Estella's knowing that her father has been married twice, and that you are her half-brother? It is not my fault she has not known it before."

"How will you explain this second marriage?" his son asked cuttingly. "Will you tell her the first wife was living, and helpless to protect herself, when you left her in the company of another woman? Will you explain that for more than two years before she became your wife she was your" —

"*Stop!*" thundered Roger, striking his clenched hand on the desk, with a force that made the room ring. But it was too late, the fatal word had been spoken; Estella heard it. The two men heard a low moan, and turning quickly, saw the door open, pushed inwards by a falling figure. The next moment Estella lay unconscious across the threshold.

"Great heavens!" exclaimed Watson, "she has heard us!" He rushed forward and lifted her in his arms, carrying her to a wooden bench near by. He and Roger worked together to restore her, chafing her hands and bathing her face.

"This is your work!" Roger declared, pausing a moment in his labors, and glancing angrily at his son. The latter groaned and attempted no reply. He did not think for a moment of the wicked injustice of such a charge; it rather seemed to him true. The thought that Estella had heard those horrible words of his filled him with anguish.

In a short time the stricken girl opened her eyes, but when she recognized her surroundings, and remembered what had passed, she groaned and closed them again, against the sight of both father and brother.   Her father went out to find a carriage.

Left alone together, and Estella more fully restored, she and her teacher could not look at each other.   Watson longed to implore her forgiveness, but something in that white, suffering face, so young to bear the impress of such woe, forbade him to intrude himself upon her.   They stood mute and helpless before each other, clothed in a common misery, which had not yet the power to draw them nearer together.   Estella could not raise her eyes to his, and he could not have borne their look, if she had.   In silence he helped her gather up her things, and without a word led her outside, down the steps to the carriage, the door of which her father held open.

Only once was a word exchanged between Roger and his daughter as they drove towards home.   The subject uppermost in the minds of both was not one that could be discussed.   Shrinking into the corner of the carriage, Estella covered her face with her hands and gave way to a passionate burst of grief.   Her father let it have way a few moments, then spoke to her, calling her by name, to quiet and remind her where they were.

"Do not speak to me!" she exclaimed, and drew still further away from him.   He bit his lip and looked displeased, but said nothing more.

It was a day of catastrophes.   Just within the door they met Mrs. Somers, who had a telegram in her hand, directed to Roger. She was about to leave the house to find a messenger and send it to him. He tore open the envelope. The message informed him that his wife was much worse, and bade him and Estella return home at once.

Estella, without heeding or seeming to hear this latest news, climbed the stairs slowly to her room.

"What is the matter?" Mrs. Somers asked, looking after her, then at Roger with sharp distrust.

He told her Estella had been ill, and added a stiff apology for his own reappearance. Mrs. Somers at once divined more.

"You have told her!" she exclaimed rebukingly. "Roger Hunt, you are the cruelest man living !"

"I have told her nothing," he retorted angrily.

"Then how did she find it out? Not through Mr. Watson, I am sure!"

"You are mistaken. It was through Mr. Watson she found it out."

"Oh, how shameful!"

"There is no need of wasting time in reproaches. My son and I were talking together in the schoolroom, and she overheard us."

"You said he told her."

"I beg your pardon," said Roger loftily. "I said she learned it through him." She gave it up, and turned her attention to the telegram.

"There is a train leaves at six o'clock," Roger said, consulting his watch. "Tell Estella to be ready. I will call for her," and he took a hurried leave.

Mrs. Somers went up to Estella's room and knocked. There was no response, and after waiting a moment, she opened the door and stepped inside. The girl was sitting on the edge of the bed, her hands clasped tightly together, her eyes staring vacantly before her. She turned quickly at the sound of Mrs. Somers's entrance, then threw out her hands to ward her off.

"Don't come in here, Mrs. Somers. Leave me alone, please." Mrs. Somers went directly to her, sitting beside her, and clasping her in her arms. The girl struggled to free herself, but could not, then submitted, but kept her face turned from her friend.

"Estella! I have some bad news for you. Try to be brave and bear it."

"I know it already, Mrs. Somers. I know everything."

"I am speaking of your mother, Estella." The girl shuddered, and again tried to release herself.

" She is worse ; she is in a very dangerous state. You must return home with your father to-night."

"Home," wailed the girl in a despairful voice. "I can never go home again."

"Estella, listen to me. I know all that has happened; you have had a hard blow. I shall not pretend it is easy to bear, or of little account, but you are not to think of that now; you are to think only of your mother."

"My mother ! " She wrenched herself free, and

stood upright. "Why did not my mother think of me?"

"Estella, that is wicked!"

"Yes, I suppose so," with youthful bitterness. "But I have a right to be wicked now. When people do wrong things, why do they think of themselves only?" she went on excitedly. "Why do they make others suffer, who are not to blame?"

"I shan't try to answer any of your hard questions, Estella," but she did. "How can a wrong action stop with the one who performs it, more than a good one? We don't want the good actions to stop. You are not to judge your mother, Estella," Mrs. Somers went on more seriously. "Remember that. What do you know of life or its struggles? Your mother is your mother. That is all you have any right to think about, now. Has she not always been very good to you?"

The young face quivered. "I could have borne it if she had not: I could bear anything better than — Oh, I wish I could die, I wish I could die!" She threw herself again on the bed, burying her face in the pillow, shaking and sobbing with grief. Mrs. Somers let the first paroxysm pass; then, when she had grown quieter, took her hand and spoke again.

"My dear, listen to me. You have been hurt, cruelly hurt, in a way you will not forget for a long time, perhaps never. But you are a good, right-thinking girl; you can compel yourself to act justly, even at such a time as this, if you try.

You are going to try. I am going to help you. Now listen. Suppose your mother had been suffering all her life from some physical hurt you had just learned about, and you knew it was the result of an act of careless disobedience when she was a child. Would such knowledge change pity into blame, destroy your love?"

"It is not the same," was the quick reply; "it is not the same."

"It is more nearly the same than you know, only you are too young and ignorant to understand. Your mother is a good woman. She deserves all the love and honor you have ever given her. But I can't talk of these things now. Your mother is much worse. She loves and needs you. Come, I will help you to get ready. Your father will be here soon."

"But you are going with me," exclaimed Estella, in new alarm. "You are not going to send me away alone!"

"Alone! You forget your father is here!"

"I cannot go with my father; I want you," sobbed the girl. "I cannot go without you."

Mrs. Somers hesitated. Now that the idea was thus presented to her, she believed she ought to go. Estella was in no condition to be left to herself, or, what was worse, to the care of her father. She remembered her quarrel with Roger, but it seemed too petty to think about now, compared with the need here disclosed. In a moment she had determined.

"Very well, I will go with you."

Roger looked the surprise he felt when he saw two women descend the steps dressed for travel.

"Estella wishes me to go with her, and I think I ought," Mrs. Somers explained briefly.

"I cannot go without Mrs. Somers, papa," Estella added, in a tone that mingled warning with entreaty.

"I shall be glad to have Mrs. Somers go with us," said her father.

She saw that he read this action of hers, as he had others, in the light of his own complacent beliefs, and knew that he took her presence as a distinct sign of concession to himself. The thought stung her a little, but she would not let it deter her from her purpose. To serve and help Estella she was prepared, if need be, to submit to even more disagreeable things than she had yet borne. To let Roger Hunt seriously interfere with this or any other plan of action she considered just, would be to assign him an importance he did not deserve.

XXI

As has been surmised, it was Estella's letter to her mother, relating the interview with her teacher, that had so suddenly loosened life's weakened hold, and mercifully, at the moment when new suffering for an old misdeed was at its height, and remorse too severe to be borne. The greatest dread from which Eleanor had suffered all these years was about to be realized. Her child stood on the edge of the discovery of her mother's shame.

The blow she had received was the harder to bear that it had been so innocently dealt. The horror and anguish Estella must suffer, her swift instinctive revolt from one she had loved best, her own helpless agony, these were the intense, destructive emotions that seized and overwhelmed her in turn. The poor, spent frame could not long endure these spiritual throes. One sinking spell followed another, with one or two violent hemorrhages that threatened to spill life out at once with their red flow. Between, were periods of white unconscious exhaustion, that · looked like death; the grim angel hovering very near, eager for his own.

Mrs. Saunders was as much puzzled as alarmed over this sudden change, and wholly unable to account for it. She had been out of the room when Eleanor received her letter, who, warned of its direful effects, made a superhuman effort, rose partly from her bed and concealed it before her return. From time to time words of faintly spoken delirium dropped from the dying woman's lips.

"Estella, don't look at me like that! Estella — I am your mother!" and "Roger! Where is Roger? — I want Roger!" The doctor had been hastily summoned, arrived and looked at his patient, and signified by a look to the nurse that the end had come at last. It was he who had dispatched the message to Roger, returning to the house and remaining there as much of the time as he could spare from his other duties.

The sky was covered with the pale gray light of early morning when the travelers reached their destination. The doctor met them at the door, and Roger went immediately to the sick-room, Mrs. Somers and Estella stepping into the library to remove their wraps and await his summons. Estella's face had a pinched and frightened look. Superstitious dread, which is the first feeling death arouses in the young, had for the time benumbed other emotions. Mrs. Somers's heart ached with pity for her, as she helped remove her bonnet, but she felt, also, a little distrust, and watched her narrowly. She was full of anxious dread for what might happen next. In spite of her evident agitation, there was something in the girl's cold, stolid look that alarmed her.

"Estella," taking her hand and speaking in a low, urgent tone. "Remember, — she is dying. She must see no difference — she " —

"You need not be afraid of me, Mrs. Somers," Estella answered quietly, and withdrew her hand. They remained waiting.

When Roger entered the room where his wife was, she lay like one already dead, save for the faint, irregular breath. He drew near the bed and looked down on her. Death could not make that face look whiter. Roger's too was colorless. Severe emotions struggled in his breast ; he bit his lips to still their trembling. He stood there, motionless, and there was not a sound in the room to disturb the sleeper; but something in that look of his, which had been her strongest magnet in life, seemed to pierce the mists of death and arrest the fleeing spirit. A quiver passed over her face, a fluttering sigh escaped her, and the eyes slowly unclosed. The film of death was already spreading over the large blue iris, but a look of consciousness soon gleamed through. She recognized him, and spoke his name in an agitated whisper. He placed his hand on hers, warningly: —

"Do not try to talk," he said in a low tone.

She wound her fingers about his, with a hold that was feeble, but which he could not resist, and he sat down on the bedside.

"Don't leave me, Roger," she whispered, and again closed her eyes.

At the same moment, Estella, whose ears were

keenly alive to every sound from that direction, caught something, more with spirit than with sense, made a sign of silence to her companion, and stepped softly to the open door, where she stood listening. The movement was noiseless. Eleanor could not have heard, yet seemed to, opening her eyes with a look of startled inquiry.

"Estella!" she exclaimed in a sharp whisper.

"Hush," said Roger, quietly. "She is here."

"Here." She threw a frightened glance around the room. "She is here — Estella — Oh, Estella."

The imprisoned voice broke from its bounds and escaped in a long, wailing cry. Estella heard it. It frightened, but it also drew her. The long, sweet habit of years was aroused. Obedience sprung prompt and true to guide her. With a low, answering cry she sped across the hall to her mother's room. On the threshold she paused, scarcely a second, not from any waning purpose, only scared back an instant by what she saw; her mother struggling vainly to rise, stretching out weak, trembling arms to her, that seemed at once to beckon and try to shut out some dreaded sight. Again came that wailing cry, like a prayer for mercy: "Estella — Estella."

"Mother — Mother!" she cried, and springing forward caught her in her arms, pressing her passionately to her heart, letting wild tears of pity, self-reproach, and the orphaned loss she now felt for the first time rain down on her face and hair. It was the first time Estella had ever addressed her mother by the stronger, truer term, and the occasion was fit. It was love's baptism and sign of pardoning grace. If joy could kill, Eleanor's spirit would have made complete escape then, with one glad, upward bound; as it was, it only swooned back into another period of unconsciousness.

A half hour passed, when the eyes again opened, this time with the light of full intelligence in their depths. She knew them all.

"Mamma," cried Estella, who was kneeling by the bed, and with a little sob of happiness, "You are better now — you know us."

Her mother looked at her, infinite love and blessing in the look. The doctor glanced at the nurse, and they left the room. Mrs. Somers would have followed, but Eleanor had seen her. An expression of pain crossed her face, and she looked at her appealingly. Mrs. Somers stepped towards her, took her hand and bending above her, pressed a long kiss of sisterly affection on her brow. They looked into each other's eyes, and in that look Eleanor tasted the first draught of something she had longed for all her life, a pure friendship, whose power to understand, console, and strengthen the stronger passion of love often misses.

"You have been so good to Estella; I wanted to thank you," she said, faintly.

"I love Estella," was the reply. "It makes me very happy to be able to do anything for her."

The dying woman gave a long sigh of thankful content.

"Love your father, Estella; take care of him," she said as her look fell again on the young girl, kneeling beside her. The eyes grew dimmer and wandered restlessly. She murmured her husband's name; he bent over her.

"Lift me up, Roger." He raised her in his arms, sitting behind and letting her rest against him. She moved her head until her cheek lay against his breast. In the midst of her racking grief and fright, the thought sped across Estella's brain that never before had she seen her father and mother like this.

"Do you love me, Roger? Say you love me. I am dying, Roger."

Mrs. Somers had turned away, and 'could not see him. If she had, she would have pitied him. He was suffering acutely. His face was blanched and nearly convulsed with the emotions fighting in his breast; but he could not be other than himself, even in such a moment. Perhaps, for a passing instant he wished he could; perhaps he, too, rebelled against that iron in his blood which would not let him yield. His bearded lips rested a moment on her cheek, but he did not speak.

Happily, those who go through the world hungering for love need so very little! A peaceful smile spread over Eleanor's face. Estella sobbed aloud, and called to her mother in imploring tones, but won no answering word or look. The present was dead to Eleanor; so, too, was the nearer past; but the spirit on its flight to the future made one swift backward swoop to the years that were gone. Child and husband had passed from sight; Eleanor was dreaming of her lover again.

"We love each other so," came in faintest accents from her lips. "Roger needs me. It cannot be wrong — when he needs me so." The words died on her lips, the head fell gently forward, — she was dead. The love that had been the supreme motive of her life, caught and held her again, at the last; less to prove its worth than its truth; yet there was one to whom, even here, it failed to justify itself.

Who can estimate a single human deed? If suffering can atone for error, then Eleanor had atoned! If a gentle and trusting heart, misled by its own needs, and the holy wish to serve another, waking too late to its own mistake, yet humbly placing blame only on itself, is worth anything in this world, then Eleanor's story has been worth the telling.

Mrs. Somers stood long by the narrow coffin. The face was not wholly peaceful, as Death so often leaves it. A slight expression of care and painful thought remained; yet there was in it such a look of suffering sweetness, such wells of tenderness seemed covered by those closed lids, that its look was none the less one of benediction.

"She loved much!" were the words in which the living woman summed up her thoughts; and others from the same sacred source came floating across her memory: "A broken and a contrite heart, O Lord, thou wilt not despise!"

XXII.

Mr. and Mrs. Clarke sat at breakfast in their sumptuously appointed dining-room, the second morning after Eleanor's death. This was the day of the funeral, and Mrs. Clarke informed her husband that he must accompany herself and Nina; the occasion being one that demanded the presence of the entire family.

"I did n't know anybody but women ever went to funerals," he grumbled.

"It 's time the men began to observe a few of the proprieties. Of course you must go. They are our nearest neighbors."

"I 've got an appointment with a man from Denver at eleven o'clock. It 's a cool thousand out of my pocket if I don't meet it."

"I thought it was about time that man from Denver was making his appearance," she replied ironically.

"He 's here this time, for certain. Why can't you and Nina go without me?" A servant entered from the kitchen with a plate of hot cakes, and his wife looked at him warningly. At the same time Nina, who was late, came into the room from the opposite side, and took her place, listlessly, at the table. She looked as if she had not slept well.

"Hello, Nina!" her father addressed her, jocosely. "This is the third time you 've been late to breakfast this week. You 're getting on first-rate. Pretty soon you 'll be as high-toned as anybody. I noticed you did n't have any trouble gettin' down to breakfast when young Norris was here. That 's the way with you girls. There was your mother, now, before we were married, she was as sweet and polite as honey. She never corrected my bad grammar then " —

"Thomas!" exclaimed his wife in her severest tone.

He leaned back in his chair, and drew out his watch. "Well, it 's time I was off," he said, but weakened again, when he caught his partner's eye.

"There 's this much about it," he added in an injured tone. "When you and Nina get off to Europe, then I can do as I like " —

"To Europe!" exclaimed Nina. "Are we going to Europe, really, mamma? Do let us go!"

"I did n't know as you would care about it."

"I do care about it. I should like to go right away."

Nina Clarke was still in a tumultuous mental state. She had been longing for the past few days to get away from her present surroundings, to go far from home, where she could think things over quietly, could still importunate thoughts that kept rising against her will, and allay the fever in her veins. Her mother had kept her plans quietly to herself until now. Europe seemed to Nina a heaven-sent boon and means of escape.

"Well, your mother can't start this morning," said her father. "She's in the undertaking business just now; she's got this funeral on her hands." He looked in vain for a sign of encouragement from his daughter to this kind of fun-making, then cast his eyes helplessly towards the servant-maid, who had again entered the room to bring Nina a warm plate, and now beat a precipitate retreat back to the kitchen.

"Thomas!" said his wife reprovingly. "I do wish you would be careful how you speak before the servants."

"Why, then, are they always around?" he asked complainingly. Thomas Clarke liked his estate of social leadership very much, but he found some of its details wearisome. He missed the simpler ways of their early married life, when they ate their meals in unattended privacy, and his wife handed him his cup of coffee across the table, receiving a plate of meat and vegetables in return. Mrs. Clarke pressed her foot on a button and summoned the maid again.

"Tell Peter we shall want the carriage at ten." The maid responded with a respectful, "Yes, ma'am," and went out.

"A carriage to go a block and a half!" exclaimed her husband.

"It is for the cemetery," she explained.

He drew himself up. "Now, see here! I draw the line somewheres. I ain't a-goin' to no cemet'ry."

She looked at him thoughtfully a minute.

"Well, I don't know as it will be necessary," she replied in a conciliatory tone. "Perhaps it will do if Nina and I go there."

"It will have to do," he said, feeling himself grow stronger as the opposition weakened. "I don't see why you can't go to the funeral without me, too," he added, with the same discontent as before.

"Thomas, I am ashamed of you! When we are under such obligations to Professor Hunt!"

"Why did n't you tell me it was the professor's funeral?" he asked, with pretended accession of interest. Nina rose and left the table. His wife looked at him more severely than before.

"I 'd naturally feel more interest, would n't I, if it was somebody's funeral I knew," he said defensively. "I never saw Mrs. Hunt in my life."

There were many others in Garrison who were saying the same; but though Eleanor was so little known, personally, her long illness, the secluded life it had necessitated, and her husband's reputation as a writer and man of gifts, combined to surround her image with something like romance. People who had never caught a glimpse of her spoke of her in hushed and reverent tones. The impression deepened that here had been a life of self-abnegating sweetness, of hidden trial and conquest, too little noted when among them.

After the funeral, Mrs. Clarke called on her neighbor, taking Nina with her. The former gave most of her attention to Mrs. Somers, near whom sat Estella. Roger and Nina sat a little apart, but though his face was turned in her direction, and he kept his eyes on her, she detected signs of absent-mindedness. Twice when she asked him a question he failed to reply, and she saw he was listening to what Mrs. Somers was saying to her mother. When she told him she was going abroad, he had only smiled and wished her a pleasant voyage. At parting he seemed not to remember that he was not likely to see her again, unless he took pains to do so; and she had a heart-sick feeling when she left him that he would not do this. She had been so long accustomed to consider herself preëminent in his thoughts, necessary to him, that she was deeply hurt and puzzled now. It would be long before she could understand of how light and passing a nature the relation now ending had been to him; but it was fortunate that her last feeling about him should be mixed with one of self-injury. She tried to excuse him in her thoughts, but the hurt feeling remained, and even then was beginning to work a cure deeper than its own.

Mrs. Clarke carried her neighborly attentions to the extent of asking Mrs. Somers to drive. The conversation naturally turned upon Roger Hunt.

"You knew him when he was young?" Mrs. Clarke inquired.

Mrs. Somers said yes.

"We think a great deal of him in Garrison.

To be sure, he is not very social, and some people are a little prejudiced against him, on account of his radical views, you know, but it will be a loss to the place if he goes away."

Her listener said Mr. Hunt was a man of many accomplishments.

"I shall always feel under the greatest obligations to him for what he has done for Nina. She studied with him, you know."

No, Mrs. Somers did n't know. She would not have supposed Mr. Hunt would like teaching.

"I don't think he does, but of course it was different with Nina. We are such near friends. Did you know his wife too?"

Mrs. Somers did not ask, "Which wife?"

"How fortunate that he should have run across you at Monroe. It is so good in you to take charge of Estella."

"I am very fond of Estella," was the reply. Mrs. Clarke remembered then that her companion was a widow. She wondered if — but such thoughts were unbecoming. In harmless ineffective talk of this kind the drive came to an end. Mrs. Clarke would have been righteously indignant had she known how near she had been, twice, or rather how far, from making discoveries' she would have claimed she had a right to know; but in Mrs. Somers, as with her brother, she had met one who had a strong instinctive dislike of hurting any one, and felt its reactive indignity as well. Mrs. Somers did not shrink sometimes from offending and even hurting her friends in her own person. She let them see plainly, when she thought it necessary, what she thought of them, but she could not harm them otherwise. Thus Roger Hunt escaped unhurt a second time.

Deeply as Estella had loved her mother, sincere and complete as had been her final surrender to that love, loyal as she meant to be to it still, it was impossible that a deeper loss than Death's, which no grave could cover, and which needed no carved tombstone to repair the memory of, should not be uppermost in her thoughts. To Mrs. Somers it seemed providential that since Eleanor must die, she should have died at this time. Estella could never judge her mother, dead, as she might have judged her living. In a vague, unsatisfied way she saw that her mother had suffered more than she had sinned; but she did not yet see how suffering atoned for sin, still less how it removed the results from those who were innocent. Mrs. Somers's answer had not contented her here.

Estella had cause enough for unhappiness, but the most real grief brings some opportunity for self-indulgence. There is an element of the factitious even in the sharpest suffering; the melancholy egotism of the unhappy is an indisputable fact. This is, perhaps, because the power to suffer affects us like any other form of discovered strength, and increases self-love. It seems to set us apart from others, to remove us from commonplace levels, and to make a distinct personality of us for the first time. This is why too great indulgence in grief is as fatal to character as any other form of indulgence, vitiating judgment, letting imagination rule in reason's place, making true feeling the cause of selfish and weak-minded display.

Mrs. Somers kept a watchful eye on her young charge, and read all her thoughts. There was another, more slight but real, cause of suffering here, which she had foreseen. Eleanor's last words to her daughter, "Love your father, Estella; take care of him," had returned to the daughter again and again, their import darkened by the remembrance they aroused that her father was her father.

The dying should pay more heed to these last words of theirs which impose heavy penalties sometimes! These to Estella, when she recalled them, seemed to shut her within prison doors. Her lot in life was fixed. She must give the years to come to one who would not care for the gift. Her mother had not stopped to think of that; she had thought only of her father. She wished to make her own supreme object in life her daughter's as well, the latter reflected with some bitterness. But what did it matter? What did anything matter — whether she studied any more or not, was ignorant or learned, loved or despised? Love could only mean pity for such as she. She was a disgraced creature, about whom the truth must not be spoken, who must go through

life in daily expectation of meeting some new sign
of scorn or distrust in others. The thought grew
intolerable.

Mrs. Somers sympathized keenly with the young
girl, and admitted the sincerity of her suffering,
but she neither despaired, nor bestowed false sympathy on her. She had often been blamed for
failing sensibility in matters of this kind. She
declined to wear her heart on her sleeve, while
years' exercise of the faculties resident in another
place, the head, gave her an increasing respect for
that organ. She knew women enough, who, in
her place, would have done nothing but mourn and
sentimentalize over Estella, weighting her spirits
still more with the load of their own depressed
fears and forebodings, who would have succumbed
at once to the child's callow judgment that her lot
must be separate and distinct from that of other
girls, that most of life's opportunities were closed
to her, that she must spend her days in trying to
retrieve the errors of others; a duty not the less
imperative that it promised to achieve nothing.

They would have told Estella that though the sin
was not hers, she must sit always in its shadow;
that to refuse to do this would be an act of rebel-
lion against heaven — and society. They would
tell her she must not hope to escape the bonds of
heritage and circumstance, that people do not make
their own lives, but must be content to walk in the
paths prescribed by Providence and human con-
vention. There was science as well as piety in

these conclusions, and theoretically, Mrs. Somers held to most of these prescribed opinions of the good and the fortunate, but she reserved the right of application.

The first thing to do, she argued, was to get Estella back to school and at work, even though the year was so near the close. She wished to do the nearest, most natural thing, first. It was a general principle with her that it is not necessary to reconstruct the universe before sweeping your front steps. More opportunities than were needed were likely to present themselves, with a nature like Estella's to deal with, to talk over her affairs and make an abstract settlement of the case in hand. In the mean time, half the difficulty was met and conquered by proceeding as if nothing had happened that need essentially to change Estella's prospects or future duties. The third day after the funeral, she told Estella that they had better prepare to return the next afternoon.

"I am not going back to Monroe," said Estella.

"Indeed! How is that?"

"I must stay with my father." She spoke with downcast face, not meeting her friend's eye.

"Your father is going away."

"It makes no difference. I cannot leave him. You — you heard what mamma said," her voice breaking.

"You give her words a meaning she never intended, I am sure. Your father would not wish it either, I believe. Have you spoken with him?"

Estella said no. "Why should she not have meant them?" she broke out. "She put him first in everything, as now I must do. But he will not care; he will not care for anything I can do, any more than he cared "—

"Estella!" The girl dropped her face in her hands, and began to weep. Mrs. Somers waited a minute, then drew a chair and sat down beside her.

"Estella, I wish to speak with you. You are not in a condition to see anything pertaining to yourself in the right light; you must, therefore, let others see and think for you. I am sure your mother did not mean you were to give up your work, and not return to your place in school "—

"I cannot go back, Mrs. Somers, I cannot go back."

"My dear child, what do you expect to gain by staying here?"

"I shall be by myself; I shall not have to meet strangers, people who would despise me "—

"When you are as old as I am, Estella, you will know that we are our own worst and most dangerous society when we are in trouble. And as for people despising you, people will have just that opinion of you which your own character and behavior warrant, no other. See now," taking the grief-worn face in her hands and turning it towards her, "I have known all about you from the first, and do I despise you?" smiling at her tenderly.

"You care for me only because you are sorry for me," the girl replied, turning her eyes obstinately away.

"You don't believe that when you say it," said the other, with a touch of rebuke.

"Oh, no — no," leaning forward and throwing herself in her friend's arms. "You are good, but others are not like you. Forgive me, but I am so miserable, I cannot bear to live. No girl was ever so wretched as I am."

"There, Estella, let us stop right there. You are unhappy, and you have cause for unhappiness. Let us admit that; but don't try to measure your grief with other people's, nor with what may come to you in the future. Wait until the cause of your trouble lies in some wrong action of your own. Come, now, suppose it was only some physical disease you were suffering from," going back to a style of reasoning she had employed before. "Suppose you had been very ill, and were too weak to walk, and I wanted to wheel you out into the sunshine. Would you refuse to let me, dear?" Her listener was silent, still keeping her face hidden.

"I don't say I'm going to bring back your old happiness; the old happiness never comes back. I do not ask you to believe anything I say about yourself or any new happiness in the future; I only ask you to trust me."

With words like these the girl was won back to confidence. Her stormy emotions were quieted for a time, at least, and she received the further suggestions Mrs. Somers made with passive quiet.

"But you must speak to papa," Estella said.

"My dear, you are the one to do that." It then occurred to Mrs. Somers that they had been taking a good deal for granted.

"No — no," said Estella, in a voice and manner that threatened another breakdown, "I cannot talk with him. Do not ask me," and Mrs. Somers, though she disliked it much, made her way to the study.

Roger's bearing toward her the past three days had been one of stiff politeness, nothing more, and the had not before spoken with him alone. She dreaded a renewal of old conflicts, and wished to make the interview as short as possible; stating her errand at once and declining the chair he offered her. She told him she must return the next day, and expressed the hope that Estella would accompany her. He listened with impassive face and eyes bent to the floor.

"Estella will return to her school, soon, of course." She did not seem to notice the mental reservation implied here.

"I was sure that must be your wish."

"Do you mean that Estella is unwilling to go back?" he asked, catching an unexpressed meaning in her words.

"Naturally she looks upon her return with some dread."

"Why?"

She recognized the tone, and not wishing to be caught in any more wordy combats, shifted her ground.

"She construes something her mother said into a wish, on her part, that she should remain with you." He thought of this a moment; Mrs. Somers doubted if he recalled Eleanor's words.

"Estella is to go with me then?" she asked again, as he kept silent. He looked at her significantly.

"How can you expect me to place my daughter in the hands of my enemy?" He pronounced the words "my enemy" as if he were some high dignitary of state.

"I am not your enemy, Roger."

"Are you my friend?" She hesitated.

"Probably not, in your sense of the term. Certainly I am not your flatterer."

" I do not seek flattery from my friends; I seek only their confidence."

"It is their misfortune when they cannot give it."

"Indeed, I quite agree with you there," lifting his head. "I would rather be misjudged than to misjudge others."

"So would I," she replied, leaving the application to fall where it might.

"It should be taken as a proof of some clemency and patience on my part, I think, if, after what has passed between us, I consent to leave Estella in your care."

"From your point of view, yes; I am willing to admit that."

"Very well! And what, may I ask, is to be my relation to the household of which my daughter is a member?"

"As Estella's father, you will receive all respect from me that is due you."

He smiled sarcastically. Estella's father! His estate was reduced indeed; but since he believed an important concession had been made, he gave his consent to her wish, and the interview closed.

XXIII.

Two days after the departure of Mrs. Somers and Estella, the little stone cottage was closed, and the key placed in the hands of a real-estate agent, with instructions to sell; while Roger went westward to carry out the literary enterprise that had been assigned him. Mrs. Clarke and Nina left home for New York within the following week, the former telling her friends that they should remain away at least a year. Nina was to acquire the Parisian accent in her French, and to profit by other advantages of a foreign tour. Mr. Clarke shut up the house and took rooms in the hotel which he owned, down town; the neighborhood had a deserted look.

As Mrs. Somers had foreseen, Estella's life after her return to Monroe was varied with many contradictory moods. She kept a careful oversight of the girl, but not of a small, exacting order, letting her fall back on herself at times, striving to cultivate a healthy self-reliance, and to keep her mind occupied with rational objects outside itself.

Roger had made no attempt to settle the future relation of his two children, a matter concerning which he was not altogether indifferent, but which he felt unequal to. Mrs. Somers, sensible of a little compunction for the feelings she had cherished against young Watson, and her rather careless treatment of him, had written him from Garrison, giving an account of Eleanor's death, speaking of her own and Estella's speedy return, and counseling him to remain where he was. Since Estella had now full knowledge of things he meant to help preserve her in ignorance of, he did not himself see why he should upset all his plans and seriously hinder his work by leaving Monroe. He was glad Mrs. Somers's romantic demands had abated.

The first meeting between brother and sister was painful, but each felt the need of the other too much willingly to consent to lose sight of each other, or even to forego the help and happiness that were promised in an openly acknowledged relation.

Rather to Mrs. Somers's consternation, therefore, these two young people, equally serious and conscientious, inheriting, too, from their father, the courage that could meet and conquer a difficulty, resolved to let the relation between them be known. It was Estella whose wish in the matter was most anxious, though she was not the first to express it, keeping strict guard on it, instead; for she felt that hers was the position representing greatest guilt and reproach, that it was not for her to make advances. Her brother represented the side of the injured, and might well hesitate to ally himself, even thus indirectly, with the father who had forsaken him. To Estella this reunion with her brother stood in a measure for a degree of reconcilement with her father, for, remembering her mother's words, she would not have entered into any bond or agreement that excluded him. What Watson himself thought on this point he did not say. His father had written him just before leaving home, renewing his former offer, on the same conditions, which the son, in a brief but respectfully worded reply, had again declined. For Estella's sake, though she knew nothing of this affair, he would avoid a quarrel, but he could accept no help from such a source. Estella could not help but understand this feeling, which she felt much secret sympathy for, but nevertheless sometimes tried to overcome.

"He is our father," she said to him one day. "We have to remember that, and he has always been good to me. I — I can't think he is bad. I don't believe Mrs. Somers thinks so either, and she knows him so well, though they do not seem to be friends any more. People do such wrong things sometimes, when they are only trying to do the right thing," and she sighed.

She had been brought up in such a different atmosphere from her brother that they often failed to find a common point of view in the discussion of their problems. Though so much younger, he caught glimpses of mental expanse in her, the power to weigh and judge a question on its own merits, that excited both his admiration and alarm. His own mental processes seemed stiff and cramped beside hers, but he still distrusted a little those freer methods which inevitably tended, he thought, towards license. He listened to his sister's talk, at once so unrestrained and thoughtful, with grave and brooding face; a new ideal of character began slowly to rise before him, as unlike that which his aunt had striven to realize in him as it was opposed to that other, so different, his father had tried to embody. The mental currents were breaking from the icy fastnesses of social prejudice and distrust, gaining a warmth and elasticity never felt before. His step grew firmer and more buoyant. He was learning to hold his head erect, to like and trust his fellow-creatures.

In Estella, womanly tenderness, bereft of its chief objects in a mother dead and a father partially estranged, had found something new to caress and cling to. She still had her periods of melancholy introspection, of morbid complaint against fate. The old sense of injury would return, shame and a sudden distaste for everything, the revived memory of lost illusions and ideals. She would pass days in this dejected state of mind, but had the wisdom at such times to keep away from her brother, or at least to hide her feeling from him, knowing she would only do him harm. It was Mrs. Somers who was made the sharer of these downcast moods, not because they were selfishly imposed on her, — but because she had learned to read signs here, as well as those that prophesied the weather. Sometimes she let the mood spend itself, at others set herself to work to coax, laugh, or reason it out of existence.

One day when she and Estella were walking along the street, they met two women in black habits, each with a long swinging rosary by her side. They belonged to a cloistered institution on the outskirts of the town. Estella looked at them pensively.

"How pure and peaceful their faces are," she said to her companion.

"They are very weak and empty faces, I think," was the reply.

"How can you say that!" Estella rejoined, in a reproving tone. "I am sure they are very good."

"Oh, I dare say they are good enough," lightly. "But they don't look as if they ever had an idea."

"Ideas do not always bring happiness," the other said, with a touch of youthful wisdom.

"They do something better; they teach you how to get along without it," but the young have little use for heroic conclusions of this kind.

"Every one is on an equality with them," said Estella, pursuing the subject; "the poor with the rich, the unfortunate with the fortunate."

"I don't know about that. It is the business of some of the nuns out there at St. Mary's to scrub the floors, and of others to sit in the parlor and entertain visitors. Human nature is the same, whether you find it in a convent, or a dry goods store."

"They do not care if they do have to work,"

said Estella, "it is part of their religion. They go there because they have suffered, and wish to hide away from the world."

"They go there, more likely, because they were picked up on the streets when they were little homeless beggars, have been brought up there, and know no better." Estella was silent a few moments; she felt sure this was a very partial statement of the case.

"You dislike them, I suppose, because you do not believe as they do. You are a free-thinker, like papa." The words were spoken quietly, with no thought of giving offense, but Mrs. Somers winced and changed the subject.

The last days of the school year passed rapidly. When the term closed Charles Watson entered a law-office, for preparatory work during vacation in the profession he meant to enter. Mrs. Somers made her plans for a summer trip through New England, where she was to visit different points of interest, and describe the same in the correspondence column of one of the Chicago dailies. Estella obtained permission from her father to go with her, and was looking forward, with a young eagerness which no contradictory moods or dark memories could destroy, to her first long journey. They returned to Monroe in the fall, in time for Estella to enter the regular course in the university. Mrs. Somers will take a house, and thus provide a home for the brother and sister; the former will hold his position as assistant a year longer.

The relation between brother and sister was now well known, though it had been explained in its full details to no one, not even to Mrs. Black. There is still a little mystery attached to them in the popular mind, leading to romantic speculation in some quarters, wise shaking of the head in others, but to more indifference in all; for the popular mind, like the individual, is occupied with its own affairs, and disappoints alike our fears and our expectations by the measure of interest it takes in ours. The world went on much the same when it became known that Estella Hunt was Charles Watson's half-sister; and when Mrs. Somers saw that the university walls had not tumbled down, nor an earthquake opened to swallow the town, and hide its moral deformities, she breathed more freely, and said the right thing had been done.

The brother, as well as the sister, is coming to regard her as chief counselor and friend. Estella, loving her more each day, grows penitent from time to time, for the trouble and care she gives, the small repayment she seems able to make for the continued kindness she receives, while Watson deems his own case one of pure and unmitigated charity, so that Mrs. Somers, who has learned to be happy without entire self-justification, is more content than either. These other two, who have youth's exaltation of purpose, and who for many years to come will live in the shadow of another's misdoing, will be longer in learning this.

And Roger? The series of essays describing his excursion to the Pacific coast was more widely read than anything he had before written. The enterprise took him forward several paces in that literary reputation he is still working to win. Though he has not yet reached a very high round on fame's ladder, he has secured a firm foothold, with added strength for climbing. It is no small credit to him, in his own eyes, nor should it be in others', that his success, so far, has been won by no meretricious methods, that the claim to scholarship and a high standard of work, has been strengthened with every successive effort. He is no penny-a-liner, nor hack workman, who employs his talents to satisfy the modern greed for the sensational and the entertaining! He is of another species and cult than these poor worldlings! While naturally gratified at the recognition thus far received, had he not reached it, he would have found means to console himself in his disappointment. He would have remembered Milton and Keats, and possessed his soul in a proud patience. He is as able now as ever to stand alone; and by those who know him best he is permitted to do so. He often recalls, with pious gratitude, and an increased sense of desert, that twice within his late career he has been seriously menaced, but that in both cases he was able to avert the danger and teach his enemies a lesson. He is convinced that neither Mortimer Gray nor Kitty Somers is likely to interfere in his affairs again.

He thinks of the wife of his youth as a hardened creature, who deliberately planned his shame and ruin; of Eleanor as one for whom he sacrificed all, but who was able to give him in return almost nothing; of his two children, whose love for each other seems to place them in league against himself, with an increasing feeling of self-injury. His friends grow fewer as he grows older, but that only proves how hard it is to gain friends on terms of a high understanding. Mrs. Somers, when she saw him last, during a flying visit he paid Estella on his way to the East, repeated to the picture on the mantel what she had said before, that he did not change much. He never will.

Thomas Bailey Aldrich.

Novels and Poems. New *Uniform Edition.* Comprising Marjorie Daw, Prudence Palfrey, The Queen of Sheba, The Stillwater Tragedy, The Story of a Bad Boy, and Poems. *Household Edition.* 6 vols. 12mo, the set, $8.75 ; half calf, $16.00.

The Story of a Bad Boy. Illustrated. 12mo, $1.25.

Marjorie Daw and Other People. Short Stories. With Frontispiece. 12mo, $1.50.

Marjorie Daw and Other Stories. In Riverside Aldine Series. 16mo, $1.00.
These volumes are not identical in contents.

Prudence Palfrey. With Frontispiece. 12mo, $1.50 ; paper, 50 cents.

The Queen of Sheba. 12mo, $1.50 ; paper, 50 cents.

The Stillwater Tragedy. 12mo, $1.50.

Mary Hartwell Catherwood.

The Lady of Fort St. John. 16mo, $1.25.

Clara Erskine Clement.

Eleanor Maitland. 16mo, $1.25 ; paper, 50 cents.

Isaac Henderson.

Agatha Page. A Parable. With Frontispiece by Felix Moscheles. 12mo, $1.50 ; paper, 50 cents.

The Prelate. 12mo, $1.50 ; paper, 50 cents.

Mrs. S. J. Higginson.

A Princess of Java. 12mo, $1.50.

William W. Story.

Fiammetta : A Summer Idyl. 16mo, $1.25.

HOUGHTON, MIFFLIN & CO., Publishers.

Mary Clemmer.

His Two Wives. 12mo, $1.50; paper, 50 cents.

William Dean Howells.

Their Wedding Journey. Illustrated. New Edition, with additional chapter. 12mo, $1.50; 18mo, $1.00.

A Chance Acquaintance. Illustrated. 12mo, $1.50; 18mo, $1.00.

Suburban Sketches. Illustrated. 12mo, $1.50.

A Foregone Conclusion. 12mo, $1.50.

The Lady of the Aroostook. 12mo, $1.50; paper, 50 cents.

The Undiscovered Country. 12mo, $1.50.

A Day's Pleasure, etc. 32mo, 75 cents.

The Minister's Charge. 12mo, $1.50; paper, 50 cents.

Indian Summer. 12mo, $1.50; paper, 50 cents.

The Rise of Silas Lapham. 12mo, $1.50; paper, 50 cents.

A Fearful Responsibility, etc. 12mo, $1.50; paper, 50 cents.

A Modern Instance. 12mo, $1.50; paper, 50 cents.

A Woman's Reason. 12mo, $1.50; paper, 50 cents.

Dr. Breen's Practice. 12mo, $1.50; paper, 50 cents.

The Sleeping-Car, and other Farces. 12mo, $1.00.

The Elevator. 32mo, 50 cents.

The Sleeping Car. 32mo, 50 cents.

The Parlor Car. 32mo, 50 cents.

The Register. 32mo, 50 cents.

A Counterfeit Presentment. A Comedy. 18mo, $1.25.

Out of the Question. A Comedy. 18mo, $1.25.

A Sea Change; or, Love's Stowaway. A Lyricated Farce. 18mo, $1.00.

HOUGHTON, MIFFLIN & CO., Publishers.

Jane G. Austin.

A Nameless Nobleman. 16mo, $1.25; paper, 50 cents.

The Desmond Hundred. 16mo, $1.00; paper, 50 cents.

Standish of Standish. 16mo, $1.25.

Doctor LeBaron and His Daughters. 16mo, $1.25.

Betty Alden. 16mo, $1.25.

Edwin Lassetter Bynner.

Agnes Surriage. 12mo, $1.50 ; paper, 50 cents.

Penelope's Suitors. 24mo, boards, 50 cents.

Damen's Ghost. 16mo, $1.00 ; paper, 50 cents.

Helen Campbell.

Under Green Apple-Boughs. Illustrated 16mo, paper, 50 cents.

Harford Flemming.

A Carpet Knight. 16mo, $1.25.

Oliver Wendell Holmes.

Elsie Venner. New *Riverside Edition*. Crown 8vo, $1.50.

The Same. Crown 8vo, gilt top, $2.00; paper, 50 cents.

The Guardian Angel. New *Riverside Edition*. Crown 8vo, $1.00.

The Same. Crown 8vo, gilt top, $2.00; paper, 50 cents.

A Mortal Antipathy. First Opening of the New Portfolio. New *Riverside Edition.* Crown 8vo, gilt top, $1.50.

My Hunt after " The Captain," etc. Illustrated. 32mo, 75 cents.

HOUGHTON, MIFFLIN & CO., Publishers.

www.ingramcontent.com/pod-product-compliance
Lightning Source LLC
Chambersburg PA
CBHW021708110726
47902CB00005B/1109